Valerie could have sworn that Alex still loved her. But it had to be an illusion, something she wanted to believe. He had a fiancée. And for a moment he seemed to have forgotten that and lost control. Shed called what happened leftover lust, but was that really what it was? Her body still tingled from his arousing kisses and caresses. Shed been close to succumbing to the temptation to make love with him. God help her, she was still in love with this man.

CHERISH THE FLAME

BEVERLY CLARK

Genesis Press, Inc.

Indigo Love Stories

An imprint of Genesis Press, Inc.
Publishing Company

Genesis Press, Inc.
P.O. Box 101
Columbus, MS 39703

ISBN-13: 978-1-58571-221-2
ISBN-10: 1-58571-221-3
Manufactured in the United States of America

First Edition 2001
Second Edition 2007

Visit us at www.genesis-press.com or call at 1-888-Indigo-1

PROLOGUE

Detroit, Michigan

Alexander Price started thumbing through the mail his secretary had put on his desk. When he came to an envelope postmarked Quinneth Falls, Michigan, his heart began to pound hard and fast.

Surely it couldn't be from...

There was no return address on the front of the envelope, only a gold embossed waterfall. Alex flipped the envelope over. When he saw Quinneth Falls City Council printed on the sealing flap, his heart returned to a more normal rhythm. For one insane moment he had thought it was from Valerie Baker. But considering what she had done to him, the woman surely wouldn't have the gall to get in touch with him. Her betrayal still burned like acid inside of him. He had never forgotten or forgiven her, and never would.

Alex shook the painful memories of the past away and picked up the silver letter opener his fiancée had given him, slit the envelope and scanned the contents. The Quinneth Falls City Council had obviously learned that Price Industries was looking for a suitable place to build a new factory. They were practically begging him to consider their city since the mill, once the spine of the entire town, providing jobs for the majority of the people, had fallen into financial trouble. The council had listed and described in detail several promising sites with accessibility to water sources, which was a crucial factor in the operation of a metal processing plant. Alex read the letter again, then punched his personal assistant's com-line.

"Justin, would you come in here, please?"

"Is anything wrong? Your voice, you sound—"

"Nothing is wrong."

Seconds later Justin Forest strode into Alex's office.

"Justin, I want you to conduct a feasibility study in a town called Quinneth Falls, Michigan. If the place proves satisfactory for our needs, I might seriously consider building a Price Industries plant there. As usual, I want you to keep a low profile until the negotiations are completed. If it comes to that."

"I'll get right on it," he said, turning to leave.

"Oh, and Justin, I want you to hire an investigator to run a check on a woman named Valerie Baker."

He turned around. "Who is she?"

"A former employee." And lover, he silently added.

Justin frowned. "I've been here six years, and the name doesn't ring a bell."

"It wouldn't. She worked at Price Industries eight years ago."

"Why look her up after all this time? I don't understand?"

"You don't have to. Just hire the investigator, Justin. I'll fill you in later."

CHAPTER ONE

Quinneth Falls

"Tyler, you be careful on that scooter," Valerie Bishop instructed her son. "I will, Mama. Dang, you think I don't know how to ride it or somethin'."

"Tyler Bishop!"

"Yes, ma'am," he answered in a chastened voice as he walked his scooter out the front door.

Valerie shook her head. He was so like Alex, with his sherry-brown eyes, dark golden-bronze skin and unruly, black curly hair, it brought tears to her eyes. At seven Tyler was tall for his age. She was sure when he grew to manhood he would look just like his father.

As Valerie watched her son guide the scooter out the gate, a feeling of sadness swept over her because he would never know his real father.

"Where's Tyler, Valerie?" Kelly Harper asked her niece as she entered the living room.

"Out riding on the scooter you bought him. What else? You really shouldn't spoil him."

"But I like doing it, honey." Kelly smiled fondly. "I couldn't afford to when you were his age."

"I know, you were too busy working your fingers to the bone trying to keep a roof over our heads. I want you to know how much I appreciate everything you've done for me, Aunt Kelly."

"You and Tyler are all the family I have left. I wouldn't change those years I raised you for anything in the world."

"If it wasn't for me you would have gotten married and had kids of your own."

"If I'd really wanted to, I could have had it. You're all the family I need or will ever want, Valerie. Now, I don't want you to say any more on the subject, you hear?"

Valerie noticed the yards of white satin and frothy lace draped over her aunt's arm. Her aunt had turned the two-room garage apartment into a seamstress shop.

"Who does that dress belong to?"

"Candace Maynard. You know she and Edward Winston are getting married the first of September."

"Didn't you make her sister's wedding dress?"

"And her two cousins. They're the crème de la crème of Quinneth Falls society. If you ask me, they look like a pod of great white whales when they get together." She laughed.

"You're bad, Aunt Kelly. I thought you were going to leave more of the work to Grace and take time off for yourself."

"I was, but you know me. I like to keep busy."

"The point of getting an assistant is so you can take it easy."

"If you're suggesting putting me out to pasture, forget it."

"Now would I do that to you?"

"Yes, if it was what you thought was best for me. You remind me so much of your mother. Lydia was the real nurturer in the family. My sister was always worrying about other people, never herself." The last few words seemed to catch in her aunt's throat.

Valerie walked over to the couch and sat down next to her. "You two were closer than most sisters, weren't you?"

"Yes, we were. It's been almost thirty years since her death, and I still haven't gotten used to it. I don't think I ever will."

"I wish I could have known her and my father. But you've been both mother and father to me, Aunt Kelly, and I love you very much," she said, hugging the older woman tight.

"Talk about somebody delegating responsibility, you're the one who needs to practice what she preaches," Kelly pointed out. "I know Mary Ellen wouldn't mind taking on more responsibility, because she told me so. She said you've worked way too many hours at the plant since George died."

"Mary Ellen is a worrier. I enjoy my work, Aunt Kelly. When I'm in the lab, I can forget all my troubles and concentrate on helping to improve things. Right now I'm working on a formula that will strengthen building materials so they'll be able to withstand the stress in earthquakes or during other natural or unnatural disasters. You remember all the tragedies resulting from collapsing freeways."

"I do indeed." Kelly regarded her niece fondly. "You're so dedicated to your work."

"I'm glad George insisted I go for my science doctorate."

"Your husband was so proud of you, honey. Too bad Tyler's real father couldn't see what a treasure he had in you.

Valerie stiffened. "You don't know the circumstances, Aunt Kelly."

"No, I don't, because you refuse to tell me or anyone else the details."

"Let's not go there, okay? I don't want to talk about him," she said, rising to her feet. "I'm going to check on Tyler."

As she headed down the walk, Valerie scolded herself for being so short with her aunt. But she just couldn't talk about Alex. He was a part of her past. He was out of her life for good and there wasn't the slightest chance she would ever see him again.

The next day was Sunday, June 19th, the day of the town's annual picnic at Quinneth Falls Lake. Valerie had helped organize the event for the last five years. It seemed strange doing so without her husband. Next Friday would be a year to the day George had died in a chemical fire at his company, Resource Chemical.

George had been thirteen years older than she, and she had respected and admired him as far back as she could remember. The relationship between her and George had been a good one, but they'd never shared any of the hot, flaming passion she'd had with Alex. He'd spoiled her for other men. Still, George had been a good man. Although he'd known that Tyler wasn't his biological son, he'd loved him as if he were and had etched a special place for himself in Tyler's heart. Valerie knew how much her son still missed

George. Now, as she stood watching Tyler playing games with the other children, she realized that, like Alex, he was a natural athlete.

"It's about time you got out and started giving the men in this town some notice," Hattie Mae Atkins, her plant manager's wife said righteously as she walked up on Valerie. "It ain't natural, a young, pretty girl like you being all alone. I loved George like a son, but he's gone and you're still very much alive."

"Now, Hattie, don't start."

"You know I'm telling it like it is. My Howard's been crazy about you since you were in first grade and he was in the fifth."

Oh, no, not that again. Valerie sighed. Why was it when a woman was single everybody and their mothers with marriageable sons were intent on changing her status?

"I just don't understand you modern girls. Let me tell you back in the day when I was your age…"

Valerie tuned the rest out because she knew this particular story by heart. She'd heard it enough times that she could probably recite it in her sleep.

"Are you listening to me, child?"

"Yes, ma'am."

Just then Howard Atkins walked up. "Mama, Daddy is looking for you."

Hattie smiled. I'm glad you're here. Maybe you can make her see the light," she said, walking away.

"Mama giving you a rough time?"

"You guessed it."

"Take a walk with me down by the falls."

"All right. But I don't want you to get the wrong idea."

"I won't. If anything happens between us it has to be mutual. I know you're not interested in a relationship right now."

"You're right, I'm not. You're such a nice guy, Howard. Why haven't I fallen in love with you?"

"Because you're not ready, that's why."

"And you're so understanding."

He laughed. "Yeah, that's me, good old understanding Howard."

Valerie looked into his dark intelligent eyes. He was an attractive man with his rich mahogany skin coloring, but unfortunately, her only interest in him was as a friend. Taking a deep breath, and clearing her mind of him, Valerie concentrated on her surroundings as she and Howard strode down the path leading to the falls. She never got her fill of looking at the falls. It was summer in Michigan, and although having a short, humid growing season, this part of the state turned into a lush paradise between the months of June and August. Different varieties of evergreen plants, and fruit trees grew in abundance around the lake.

In the distance one could see rolling plains that had been formed by glaciers. During the Ice Age, sheets of ice had eroded the hill, and in some areas turned the land into flat, grassy fields. Many places throughout the upper and middle portions of Michigan had waterfalls similar to the one in Quinneth Falls, which produced nothing like the loud roar of Niagara Falls. Instead, she would describe its sound during the summer season as being soft and rushing, the result of a mild cascade spilling over rocks. Only in

early spring following the melt of heavy snowfalls did it
come anywhere close to a roar.

"I love coming here, don't you?" Howard commented.
"The falls are awesome."

"I agree. I don't know what made me decide to leave
here when this is obviously where I belong."

"Was it so bad in Detroit?"

"No, but it was nothing like Quinneth Falls, and could
never come close to taking its place."

They strolled over to the edge of the water and seated
themselves on a pair of flat rocks resembling small table-
tops.

"It's good to see you so relaxed, Valerie. My father says
you work too hard. According to him, you're at the plant
when he arrives in the morning and oftentimes still
working when he leaves to go home."

"Now you're not going to start nagging me, too, are
you?"

Howard quirked his lips into a wry smile. "No, it
wouldn't do any good. You'll do what you want to do
anyway. By the way, have you heard the rumor that the City
Council has been scouting around for a big company to
bring industry to Quinneth Falls?"

"No. Where did you hear that?"

"From Jake Spriewell. According to him, a big city man
has been sniffing around, checking us out, so to speak"

"Did he say who the man was? Or what company he
represented?" Jake was a man who managed to keep
everyone in town abreast of the latest news.

"No. I don't think he knows that yet, but Jake being Jake, it won't be long before he ferrets out every derail. I think a new industry in town could be a good thing if it ever comes to pass."

"If it does, I hope the company will take care not to destroy the natural beauty of Quinneth Falls in their quest for profit."

"So do I. Here comes Tyler. He sure is a fine looking boy, Valerie. George was so proud when he was born. He bought every cigar he could get his hands on and passed them out to the women as well as the men." He laughed.

"I remember," Valerie said softly.

"Mr. Atkins, you gonna join us in the tug of war contest? I want you on our team."

"Isn't it the team that won last year?"

"Yes, sir," Tyler said proudly. "Then, they only let me on at the tail end 'cause I was little. This year I got moved up since I got bigger and stronger. See, feel my arm," he said, flexing his biceps.

Valerie's lips twitched as Howard felt Tyler's arm. Her son didn't have an ounce of modesty in his lean little body.

"You go help lead Tyler's team to victory, Howard."

He gave her one last pleading look to rescue him as Tyler dragged him away.

Valerie had to laugh. She stood up and slapped the dirt off the back of her jeans and headed in the direction of the picnic tables. She caught the end portion of a conversation between Jessie and Stella Mason, the town's leading gossips.

"It ain't natural Kelly Harper staying single all these years, I tell you. You don't think she's funny, do you?"

"You mean— She could be. I remember when John Pearson kept company with her a few years back. The poor man finally gave up when she refused to marry him for the fifth time in a row."

"I wonder why she did a stupid thing like that, unless she really is funny?"

"I don't know, Stella."

"Believe me, I wouldn't have turned him down if he'd asked me."

"Me either. But then we're normal." Jessie cleared her throat when she saw Valerie and had the grace to guiltily look away as if she were a thief caught shoplifting.

"Is talking about other people all you two have time to do?"

"Now calm down, Valerie. We didn't mean any harm. You can't blame us for being curious."

"Curious, no, but you could at least be discreet if you're going to talk about somebody. You would have hurt my aunt's feelings if she'd heard what you said."

"We're sorry."

"You should be. I don't want to hear that you two were talking about her like that again." Then she stalked away. The nerve of those old busybodies, Valerie fumed. She could only imagine what her aunt had had to go through the last thirty years. But she'd never complained once.

Valerie glanced at her aunt, who stood in front of a picnic table stirring a large container of lemonade. Her aunt was generous to a fault. There was no one in the whole world Valerie admired and respected more. She wished she could spare her the pain of hurtful, gossiping tongues like the Mason sisters.

Valerie looked at the picnicking people and thought what it would mean economically for them to have a new industry in town. She hoped what Howard had heard was true and not just mere rumor. Valerie was curious to know what company had taken an interest in their little town. There were so many natural resources in Quinneth Falls just waiting to be tapped. She just hoped the company doing the tapping didn't exploit, then destroy, them.

CHAPTER TWO

Justin strode into the executive office suite at Price Industries. "Alex, I've completed the feasibility study you requested on the Quinneth Falls area. And I also received the investigator's report on Valerie Baker and looked it over. According to the information he gathered, you two were once involved."

"Yes, we were."

"Considering your past relationship with the woman, are you sure you want to build a plant in that town?"

"Very sure," he said, holding out a lean brown hand for the reports. "Besides, she probably doesn't live there anymore."

"According to the investigator's report she does. I think you suspected as much. It's why you had me hire an investigator. You just wanted your suspicions confirmed. And when I asked you before why the sudden interest in her after all this time, a strange gleam came into your eyes. Then you said you'd fill me in. But there's no need. I think I can guess. Valerie Baker's the real reason behind this whole thing, isn't she? It's incidental that the town is in desperate need of our business."

"Not at all. In their letter, the Quinneth Falls City Council presented a strong case for building a factory there."

"Yes, they did. And the feasibility study bears it out. It does seem an ideal location. But I think you're making a big mistake."

Alex's eyes locked with the sharp blue eyes of his personal assistant. "So you've said. I don't pay you to think for me."

"No. You pay me to follow orders, but in this case—"

"Don't sweat it, Justin. I know what I'm doing. I want you to set up a meeting with the City Council ASAP."

Justin shook his blond head. "It's out of revenge, pure and simple. Haven't you heard the old saying that if you dig a grave for someone out of revenge, hoping to bury them, you may as well dig a second one for yourself?"

"Yes, I've heard it, or words to that effect, but I'm not going to change my mind about this."

"All right." Justin shrugged. "I'll get on it."

Alex waited until his assistant left the room, then picked up the report on Valerie Baker. As he read it the anger he had harbored against her all these years bobbed to the surface. When he finished reading the report, he tossed it on the desk and let his thoughts drift back to the day they'd first met...

Alex had just returned from a wilderness camping trip in Canada. It was his first day back at Price Industries. And as he was hurrying to catch the elevator he collided with a woman. He caught her in his arms to keep her from falling. When she looked up at him, his heart dropped to his shoes. She had the most arresting face he'd ever seen. Her eyes were a dark, dark brown and she had shoulder-length, midnight-black hair.

"I'm sorry, Miss... Miss..."

"Valerie Baker."

"Do you work here?"

"Yes, I started three weeks ago. I'm the new apprentice chemist."

"Beauty and brains—what a dynamite combination." "What?" She laughed. "That's a line if I ever heard one."

"I must admit it's not original, but true nonetheless." He held open the elevator door for her to precede him inside. The woman had the sexiest lips imaginable. They were full and looked soft, inviting a man to taste and savor. He surveyed the rest of her and by the time he had finished his assessment, he was experiencing a hard-on the size of Texas.

"The lab is on the first floor. Where are you on your way?" Alex asked.

"To personnel. I have to fill out some insurance forms."

"Have lunch with me?" "Look, I don't even know your name." "It's Alexander Price."

"Not *the* Alexander Price." She gulped. "As in the owner's only son?"

"The very same. Do you have a problem with that?"

"I—ah—no, I guess not."

Alex grinned. "I think you do. But for the record I'm just a man like any other. When I see an attractive woman—"

"You come on to her. Right?" "Now wait a minute."

When she reached out to punch in the number of her floor, Alex pushed the stop button and drew her into his arms and kissed her soundly on the lips. He felt her body stiffen for a moment, then soften in surrender. Her lips opened and he slid his tongue inside. She tasted sweeter than he had ever thought a woman could and he didn't want the kiss to end. But the reality of where they were inserted itself and he reluctantly let her go. He smiled at the dazed look on Valerie's face.

"Do you welcome all the new female employees so...ah... enthusiastically?"

"Only the beautiful ones. Believe it or not, I've never done anything like this before. Are you some kind of a witch who just put a spell on me?"

"No, I'm just a lowly apprentice chemist."

"You can experiment on me any time, sweetheart. Meet me down in the lobby at, say, one?"

"I don't know."

"Come on and say yes. You know you want to."

"Oh, all right."

Alex released the stop button and seconds later the elevator stopped on Valerie's floor. He smiled as he watched her walk down the hall to personnel. Their relationship sprouted wings and took flight after that. They'd spent every spare moment together and he had loved her with all his heart...

Alex felt an unwanted tightening in his loins at the thought of her now. He shouldn't feel anything for her. But how could he not? He had once considered her his dream woman fantasy come true. He couldn't forget how she had responded to his lovemaking. Love. It had never been that on her part. To her, the end had justified the means, he ruminated bitterly.

Alex shot up from his chair behind the desk and strode over to the bank of windows overlooking the Detroit River. From the thirty-second floor, he had a perfect view of

Canada's lush greenery, but he hardly noticed. When he closed his eyes, the image of a girl with shoulder-length, jet-black hair, huge dark brown eyes and milk chocolate skin floated before his mind's eye and refused to go away. He recalled every detail of her beautiful body in all its naked glory including those long, sleek brown legs encircling his waist as his aroused sex plumbed the depths of her woman-hood.

He shook his head in an effort to fling the erotic picture from his mind. Why couldn't he forget? She'd played the role of Judas and betrayed him for the proverbial thirty pieces of silver. God, how it hurt knowing she had felt so little for him. When she had looked at him, all she'd seen were dollar signs.

He'd been so sure that she loved him because he had loved her so much. What a fool he'd been.

For the next five years he'd poured his energy into Price Industries, driving himself to the point of exhaustion. Then when his father retired two years afterward, Alex had taken over the complete running of the company. A year later Alex had gotten engaged to Althea Johnson, thinking he'd successfully exorcised Valerie Baker from his system. But a month ago, the letter from the Quinneth Falls City Council broaching the idea of building a plant there had changed everything.

Alex had known that Quinneth Falls was Valerie's hometown. Justin was right; it was the reason he'd had the investigation done. He'd wanted to know what she'd been up to all this time. The report said she'd returned to Quinneth Falls to live and had married George Bishop a few weeks later. When Alex learned Valerie had a son, pain streaked through him. The boy could have been theirs if…

He stopped the thought. It did no good to dwell on what might have been.

Alex walked back to the desk and picked up the feasibility folder and studied its contents. His resolve to open a plant in Quinneth Falls and oversee construction himself burned stronger than ever with each word he read. When the plant was finished, he would personally supervise the running of it and, in the process, find a way to even the score with Valerie Bishop.

Alex felt the tension start to build as he and Justin left Detroit a few days later, heading northwest to Quinneth Falls. As Justin drove, Alex watched the green, tranquil countryside slip past the window and tried to relax. But his thoughts shifted to the plans for the projected Quinneth Falls plant. If the area was half as promising as the feasibility study indicated, his company as well as the town would profit greatly from the venture.

Who are you trying to fool, Alex? a taunting voice whispered through his mind.

Building a plant in Quinneth Falls is a sound business investment.

That may be true, but your reason for doing this is for revenge. You can dress it up any way you like, but the bottom line isn't about profit or benevolence.

Revenge would be sweet, if he could find a way to exact it. Alex's jaw twitched with rage at the thought of how thoroughly Valerie had used him. He could still hear his father's words as if it were yesterday…

"I have the cancelled check for $1,000,000 right here, Alexander. You can't excuse away what that woman has done. It was the money she was after all along."

"I can't believe she came to you and demanded money after what we shared. She loved me. Damn it! I know she did."

"Women like her don't know the meaning of the word. It's best to stick with your own kind."

Tears stung Alex's eyelids. "I loved her so much, Dad. I wanted to marry her."

His father took him in his arms. "I know you did, son, and I'm sorry it turned out this way."

Blinking away the moisture from his eyes, Alex backed away from his father. "I don't understand how it came about."

"Well, when I heard the gossip about you two, I went to the source and asked her if the two of you were considering marriage and she laughed and said, 'Do you think I'd pass up a golden opportunity like this? Of course I'm going to marry him.' When she said that, I knew she was out for all she could get. In the next breath she said if I made it worth her while, she'd walk out of your life for good.

"I offered her $100,000, but it wasn't enough. She wanted ten times that amount. I couldn't let the unprincipled bitch ruin your life. I didn't care what I had to do or how much I had to pay to get her out of your life, so I wrote her a check for the outrageous amount she demanded."

Alex was in shock. "I don't understand how she could have done it, Dad," Alex cried.

In that moment Alex's whole world had come crashing in on him.

Valerie had married George Bishop within weeks of kicking Alex to the curb. She'd evidently been using him the entire time they were together. Her desire couldn't have been faked, though. Valerie was an extremely passionate woman. She'd gone up in flames whenever he'd touched her. But then he'd been her first lover.

Why hadn't she saved her virginity for Bishop? Money? That had to be the reason. In order to get the money for him, she'd used her virginity to fool Alex into believing how special she thought he was. Once Valerie had gotten her money, she hadn't wasted any rime giving it to Bishop to save his ailing chemical company from going bankrupt.

"If looks could kill," Justin quipped, jolting Alex out of his reverie.

"When you fall in love, I hope you fall hard, Justin. Only then will you have any understanding of where I'm coming from. Maybe you'll have better luck in your choice of a woman than I did."

"I didn't mean to bring up painful memories."

"I know. But the pain of her betrayal will always be with me, no matter how much I wish it would go away. After a while, you learn to live with it. Eventually the pain dulls, but never completely goes away."

"Just don't let it poison your soul, Alex. When you've worked this out of your system, Althea will be waiting."

"Probably."

"You don't sound that overjoyed at the prospect. If you don't love her—"

"We get on well together. We'll have a successful marriage."

"You make it sound more like a business deal than a marriage."

"I'll never let myself feel for any woman what I once felt for Valerie Baker. What I have with Althea is different. We're comfortable with each other. We're friends. We come from the same background. We like the same things."

"That's your father talking, not you, Alex. Everything is business with him.

"I don't want to get into a discussion about my father. Okay?"

"You're the boss."

As each member of the preservation committee and other interested citizens filed out of the conference room in the administration building, Howard passed out packets that contained the information Valerie had covered in her speech, along with the petitions to be circulated around town.

"I hope it does some good."

"I'm sure it will. You gave it your best shot," Howard said approvingly as he helped Valerie gather up her sketches and ideas for the lake area to put back in her portfolio case. "You did seem preoccupied near the end of the meeting."

"I was thinking about something else."

"Like the loan payment on Resource?" Howard commented as he took the portfolio case from Valerie as they made to exit the room.

"You're a mind reader." And a good friend, she thought. He was also a loan officer at the bank and had helped George obtain the loan to buy Resource Chemical. And since her husband's death he'd been a godsend. "We'll be able to make that payment only barely with the extension you convinced the bank to give us. I can't thank you enough for buying us that time."

Howard put his arm around her shoulder. "That's what friends are for. Besides, you should be getting the money from that government contract any day now, right?"

"I just hope it arrives in time."

Valerie veered to the right into the man standing beside the door.

"I'm sorry. I wasn't watching where…" When she looked up and saw who it was, her throat clogged with emotion and she whispered, "Alex!"

"Valerie Baker. It's been a long time."

For a heart-stopping moment no other sound left Valerie's lips. All she could do was stand and stare. Finally she managed to utter, "Yes, it has." She cleared her throat. "Howard Atkins, Alexander Price." Howard extended his hand.

"Mr. Atkins." Alex shook his hand, then cleared his throat and checked his watch. "If you'll excuse me. I have a meeting to attend," he said, opening the door and striding inside the conference room.

Valerie stumbled over to a bench against the wall and sank down heavily on it. Alex was actually here in Quinneth Falls!

"Are you feeling sick?" Howard asked, obviously concerned by the stricken look on Valerie's face.

"No, I'm all right." I'm in shock, not sick, she wanted to tell him. Sick didn't begin to describe how she felt at that moment. She recalled earlier hearing the door to the conference room close after her presentation, but by the time she had looked around it was too late. The door had closed, preventing her from knowing the identity of the person who had walked out of it. A strange, eerie feeling had quivered through her as if someone had walked over her grave. It had been Alex! How could fate be so cruel? She'd survived so far because she hadn't been near Alex, but now... My God, what was he doing in Quinneth Falls?

"I'm taking you home," Howard said, pulling her to her feet. "You don't look all right to me."

Valerie didn't argue, she just let Howard guide her out of the building to his car.

"Don't worry about your car, I'll have someone drive it out to your place later today. The important thing is to get you home."

CHAPTER THREE

Alex could barely keep his mind on the proceedings. He should have left the negotiations to Justin, but no, he'd had to do things his way. He hadn't known how he would feel once he'd seen Valerie, but he definitely hadn't expected to feel as though he'd gone fifteen rounds with Evander Holyfield.

"Which of the properties do you think best suits the plant's needs, Mr. Price?" Jackson Crawford, head of the City Council, inquired.

"It would seem the Indian Woods property adequately fits our needs. Then too, the environmental issues have to be considered. It's far enough away from drinking water facilities and yet close enough to a water source, so the projected new plant can safely utilize it."

Alex heard the relief hiss from Crawford's lips. What was it about the lake property that evoked such interest from Valerie and her preservation committee and now the head of the City Council?

"But then again the lake property sounds equally suitable," Alex added. "I'll have to give it more thought."

"How long do you think it'll be before you make a decision?" Crawford asked, his voice anxious.

"Soon. I know how important the prospect of bringing new industry to Quinneth Falls is. According to the study my personal assistant conducted, the population has grown from 60,000 to 100,000 in the last three years without any significant influx of businesses to the area to support the increase. I'll let you know within a reasonable length of time which one I've decided on."

Alex turned on his tape recorder and tried to keep his attention centered on the discussion about the projected plant. But his thoughts drifted to Valerie Bishop. When he and Justin had arrived at the administration building earlier and found the doors to the conference room closed, Justin had gone to the coffee shop in the lobby. Alex had walked over to the sheet posted on the wall by the conference room. The preservation committee was having a meeting. Curious to know the subject on the agenda of a small town like Quinneth Falls, he'd slipped inside and had taken a seat near the door.

He'd seen the back of a woman as she walked over to an easel displaying a drawing of the Quinneth Falls Lake area.

"The falls is one of the last historical monuments this city has. What we need to do is impress on the council the importance of preserving the area for future generations."

Alex's heart skipped a beat at the sound of the woman's voice. Then when she turned and he saw her face, his breath caught in his throat. He hadn't known how he'd react when he saw Valerie again, but surely not with this instant rush of desire jetting through his system after what she'd done to him.

But God help him, desire was exactly what he felt!

Almost immediately anger overpowered the desire, molding it into hard, bitter resentment. As he continued to listen to Valerie's impassioned spiel, an interesting thought entered his mind: How he could round out his revenge. But he needed time to think and plan. He got up from his seat and silently walked out of the room and waited outside for the meeting to conclude.

Valerie hadn't changed that much in the last eight years. But enough, he thought, recalling the feel of her firm, rounded breast against his arm when she'd inadvertently bumped into him while exiting the conference room. Why couldn't she have gained a hundred pounds and looked like a hag? Her body was perfect from what he could see. Before she'd been rail thin, but not anymore. She now had voluptuous curves and her body was more desirable, if that were possible.

He shook his head in an effort to clear it. Valerie appeared to be a pillar of the community, and he knew he shouldn't let himself forget the kind of woman he was dealing with, but try as he might, the crushing pain she'd dealt him came back to torture him anyway. Anger at himself and her for making him feel desire for her again shuddered through Alex.

He reached inside himself for the strength he needed to stay focused on his objective: Valerie's betrayal and the payback he intended for her. He wondered if the man with her was her lover. And had he been so before her husband's death? He wouldn't put anything past the deceitful bitch. She'd taken money from his father, a hell of a lot of money.

He recalled the conversation he'd overheard between Valerie and her companion. She was grateful to him for helping to get her loan extended. He obviously held an influential position at the bank. Like a cat, Valerie always managed to land on her feet. But not this time. He would see to that.

After the meeting with the City Council, Alex and Justin were taken on a tour of the two properties in the council limousine. Jake Spriewell had been appointed their official guide. A more talkative man Alex had never met. He had to laugh when he started telling them the history of Quinneth Falls and volunteering information about its leading citizens.

Alex ached to ask him about Valerie Bishop, but knew it would arouse his curiosity, and that Alex definitely didn't want to do. He'd find out all he could about her personal life on his own. He knew the basics from the investigator's report, but it scarcely touched on anything personal.

Jake took them to the Indian Woods property first. As the feasibility report stated, it did have an adequate water source less than a mile from the site and was fairly isolated, so it wouldn't interfere with the community. Price Industries had to think about possible environmental contamination since the company was chiefly an ore and metal processing plant.

The property near the falls impressed Alex on sight. He thought it was absolutely magnificent. It lay recessed from the lake to the west about a quarter of a mile. Alex thought it was much too fine for the site of a metal and ore processing plant. He'd never been so struck by a place. He could understand the preservation committee's concerns. The council must have offered the lake property as a lure to potential businesses and investors. He wondered how Valerie and her committee would react if Price Industries bought this particular property.

"So, are you thinking about building here?" Justin asked.

"You have to admit it is an ideal spot."

"Then you're gonna buy it?" Jake probed.

Alex could almost see the wheels turning in the man's head. He knew whatever he said would be broadcast all over town with the speed of sound.

"I'll take it under serious consideration, Mr. Spriewell."

"Call me Jake, everyone does."

Jake drove Alex and Justin to the Quinneth Falls Inn. They'd be heading back to Detroit in the morning. That night Alex stayed awake thinking over all he had learned, wondering what would happen if he went through with his revenge.

❧

"What's wrong?" Kelly asked Howard as he helped Valerie into her living room.

"She's not feeling well, but refuses to admit it. Maybe you can talk some sense into her. She keeps making noises about going in to work this afternoon."

"I'm not sick," Valerie insisted.

"You're obviously ill, Valerie. Don't argue with me," Kelly said, then looked to Howard. "Thank you for bringing her home. I'll take over from here."

"If she feels any worse you should take her to the doctor."

"I don't need a doctor. Would you both please stop fussing over me."

"You go on to the bank, Howard. I'll handle this."

Howard gave Valerie a concerned, sympathetic look before leaving.

"Now what happened?" Kelly asked.

"Less than half an hour ago, I saw Alex."

"What?"

"He was at the administration building waiting to attend a meeting following the preservation committee's."

"Do you have any idea what he's doing in Quinneth Falls?"

"No. The only thing I could think is—no, wait a minute. The council was scheduled to meet after us. Surely..."

"What?"

"I'm not sure. It couldn't be that."

"Couldn't be what? Valerie!" Kelly said, frustration lacing her words at her niece's vagueness.

"A few weeks ago Howard mentioned there was talk of an industrial company interested in building a plant in Quinneth Falls."

"I heard that rumor too."

"The company can't be Price Industries. No way. Alex knows Quinneth Falls is my hometown. Surely he wouldn't want to build here. I've got to find out why he's here."

"It's more than the shock of his being in town that's making you feel sick, isn't it?"

"What do you mean?"

"It's your innermost feelings. You're worried that you still might have them for this man. He is your son's natural father."

"As far as I'm concerned George is Tyler's father. And I loved him," she answered, her voice defensive.

"I'm not saying you didn't, but the feelings you had for him didn't come anywhere close to the ones you had and probably still have for Alexander Price."

"I'll admit what George and I shared wasn't the wild passion Alex and I—I mean…"

"I know what you mean, honey. You're going to have to reach deep inside yourself and sort out how you really feel about this man. We can sometimes fool ourselves into believing what we think we ought to feel. In the end we have to be true to ourselves. I think you should go lie down for a while. Stress has a way of draining the life from a person, even to the point of making one feel physically sick"

"Tyler will be home any minute from summer camp."

"And I'll look after him the same as always. Now you go lie down."

After her aunt left the room, Valerie dragged herself to her feet and headed down the hall to her bedroom, then collapsed on the bed. But she couldn't rest. How could she? Alex was in town. The look he'd given her… It was as if he'd never known her. And he'd known her better than anyone ever had, better than even her own husband. A feeling of shame washed over her at that admission. She'd never given herself completely to George. She'd always held back a part of herself. The only man she'd ever truly been one with was Alex. She'd loved him with her whole heart and soul. It had torn her apart to leave him.

Although Alex had turned thirty-five three months ago, he was still as fine as she remembered. The cold indifference she'd seen in his face and heard in his voice hurt. She wondered if he was married and had children. The last thought that pounded through her brain before she closed her eyes was that she had to stop thinking about him.

Valerie woke up at three-thirty. Her headache had dulled, but she felt groggy as she walked into the living room. Just then she heard two cars pull up and peered out the window. Jake Spriewell was driving her car and his son Ralph was behind him in his. Howard had evidently gotten Jake to deliver her car. She wondered what he knew about the council meeting.

"Thanks for dropping my car off, Jake."

"No problem. When Howard told me you'd suddenly taken sick, I volunteered to bring it to you. Did you know I was appointed official guide to the two big city men interested in bringing business to our town? It'll mean jobs for a lot of people, if the deal goes through."

"What deal, Jake?"

"You mean you don't know? Price Industries is the company that's gonna pull this town out of a hole. Mr. Alexander Price is considering buying the lake property, although the one at Indian Woods seems like a better choice. But if Mr. Price thinks the other one will—"

"We can't allow him to buy the lake property and build a metal processing plant on it! It's one of the last truly beautiful historical sites Quinneth Falls has left. Who— how did this—"

"Mr. Crawford and the council offered both properties. I guess they figured the lake property would draw more interest. It looks like they were right. I can't see Mrs. Crawford liking the idea, though. Old Jackson is likely to catch hell when she finds out, her being the president of the preservation committee and all."

Valerie wanted Jake gone so she could think. She smiled at him. "Thanks again for bringing my car home, Jake."

"My pleasure, Valerie."

Valerie watched until Ralph's car had disappeared down the street.

"Valerie, did Jake tell you what's going on with the council?" Kelly asked, walking up behind her niece.

"Oh, he told me all right. According to him, the council offered the lake property to Price Industries as well as the Indian Woods one. I can't believe Alex would consider building here, period. I wonder if he'll handle the negotiations personally. I'm sure Price Industries has any number of people qualified to do the job."

"That might very well be true. But one thing is sure: We'll find out when he's ready for us to."

Valerie stood staring out the window of her laboratory. She had been shell-shocked to find out all her suspicions about why Alex was in town had been confirmed. He was evidently serious about building a Price Industries plant in

Quinneth Falls. Was Michael Price, Alex's father, aware of what his son had in mind? She knew he wouldn't be over-joyed at the prospect. She remembered reading in a finan-cial magazine a few years back that Michael Price had turned the running of the company over to Alex. What would he do when he found out what Alex was up to? The thought of what it could mean to her personally sent shivers of fear and dread down Valerie's spine.

Despite your fear, it's not the only thing worrying you.

Had Alex somehow found out about Tyler?

No, he couldn't have. The council had approached Price Industries, not the other way around. Considering their past relationship and how it had ended and knowing Quinneth Falls was her hometown, she would have expected Alex to reject the proposition out of hand, but he hadn't.

That had to mean he was interested in building in Quinneth Falls for the sake of business. Which meant she was probably worrying for nothing. Alex's life was in Detroit. And to supervise construction himself would mean that he'd practically be living in Quinneth Falls. Now, knowing that she still lived here, surely he wouldn't want to do that.

You hope he wouldn't because you don't want him anywhere near Tyler. Or you.

Me?

Yes, you. You haven't forgotten what being in his arms felt like, no matter how you've tried to convince yourself of that over the years.

What happened between us happened a long time ago.

Not long enough apparently. A lifetime wouldn't be long enough. And you know it.

I don't still feel anything for him. I don't.

"Valerie. Are you all right?"

Valerie shook her head to clear it and glanced at her assistant. "I'm fine, Mary Ellen."

"Are you sure? The timer on the experiment went off ten minutes ago."

Valerie gasped and rushed over to the nearly empty beaker. Her experiment was ruined. The properties she'd been trying for had boiled away, altering the chemical balance, which meant she would have to repeat it. That made three tests she'd ruined today. She had to forget about Alex and concentrate on her work. But how was she going to do it?

"You're as tense as a rubber band stretched to the limit," Mary Ellen remarked. "What's going on with you?"

"I've just had a lot on my mind lately."

"I can take over for you. Why don't you go home? You've been working yourself into the ground. My daddy would say all work and no play makes Jill a dull girl—if she doesn't collapse first."

Valerie laughed. "Your daddy is something else. I remember when he owned Resource and let me work summers here when I was in high school. He said I had a scientific mind and encouraged me to pursue a career in science. I was surprised when he sold the company to George and he and your mother moved to Arizona."

Mary Ellen's fine grey eyes misted. "He'd just found out he had a serious lung condition. The doctors said if he quit smoking, the dry desert air could help him. Daddy had smoked most of his life and thumbed his nose at any far-reaching consequences. How he could be so wise in some things and so completely careless with his health…"

"I can sympathize with you. He did make provisions for you, his youngest child before he left. He didn't have to make it a condition of the sale that you work here at Resource while you got your science degree. I'm sure George would have suggested it himself."

"I think he would have too. George Bishop was a good man. I liked and respected him."

"He was a special person." Valerie cleared her throat. "Since I've ruined a whole day's work, I think I will go home."

"Say hi to your aunt and Tyler for me."

"Will do."

$$\sim\!\!\times\!\!\sim$$

When Valerie got home, she found her son talking animatedly with her aunt about the subject on every tongue in town: Price Industries' projected new plant.

"Danny Cranson said Price Industries is gonna change everything and give jobs to people that can't find one. Is it true, Mama?"

"I imagine it will mean more jobs. You aren't thinking of applying for one, are you?" she teased.

"Heck, no, I'm gonna work at Resource when I'm old enough and learn science stuff. I wanna be a scientist just like you. When will I be old enough, Mama?"

"You've got a few years to go, baby." Kelly smiled. "Why don't you get washed up for dinner? I cooked your favorite fried chicken and made a peach cobbler for dessert."

"Yes!" he exclaimed, scrambling out of the room.

"You've been thinking about his father, haven't you?" Kelly asked Valerie.

"What if I have? As far as I'm concerned, George was Tyler's father in all the ways that count."

Kelly frowned. "You keep saying that, but I've seen pictures of Alexander Price in the magazines. Tyler is his spitting image, Valerie. What are you going to do if he comes back to town? Once he sees the boy, he'll know Tyler is his son."

"He probably won't come back."

"What about Alex's father?"

"I doubt if he'll come here. Look, I don't want to talk about that man ever."

"I can understand why you wouldn't. He thought you weren't good enough for his son and told you so, but you've got to face reality. One or the other, or both, will in all likelihood be visiting the new plant from time to time."

"I'll just have to make sure they don't see Tyler."

"You can hope the visits are brief, few and far between. But what if they aren't, then what?"

"I'll deal with it if or when I have to."

CHAPTER FOUR

It had been a week since Alex and Justin had returned to Detroit. Alex had pored over the papers he'd brought back from Quinneth Falls several times. He would have to make a decision soon about which of the two properties he would buy. Once he decided, it meant making another trip to Quinneth Falls to discuss price and arrange negotiations for building the plant. He could and should let Justin handle it.

But you won't. Be honest, Alex. You want to do this. You can tell yourself it's about business and revenge, but those two things aren't the only ones preying on your mind. You desire Valerie Baker as much as you ever did. Seeing her and being near her has resurrected long dormant feelings, the triumphant voice of reason declared.

No, that can't be true. All I want is revenge.

Oh you want that all right, but it's not all you want. It is. Exacting my revenge will be enough for me. *Will it?*

One evening several days later, Alex and Justin went out for a drink at the Club LeRoux.

"I strongly suggest rethinking your plans for the Quinneth Falls project," Justin said to Alex as they sat at the bar.

"What is there to rethink?"

"Since you are so determined to go ahead with this, at least let me handle it for you from here on in."

"Justin, we've been all through this."

"What about you and Althea?"

"What about us?"

Justin looked curiously at Alex. "You're going to marry the woman, aren't you? You think she's going to understand why you'll be spending so much time in Quinneth Falls? Does she even know about Valerie Bishop?"

"No, she doesn't." Alex picked up a handful of peanuts and dropped a few into his mouth.

"Don't you think you should tell her?"

"Why? This has nothing to do with her."

"It has everything to do with her if you really plan to marry the woman. This affair you had with Valerie Bishop occurred before I came to work for Price Industries six years or so ago. Right? A long enough period of time has gone by. You should have gotten over her, but you haven't. She still has the power to affect you so strongly that you are going to these lengths to, as you said, 'exact your revenge.' Whatever it was between you two must have really been hot."

Alex took a sip of his drink. "It was more than that. Hot doesn't begin to describe how it was between me and Valerie Bishop, Justin. I once loved the deceitful bitch to distraction. I was completely besotted and she knew it. That part is over. If you don't mind, I'd rather not talk about her right now. We came here to relax and unwind."

"I think you need to talk about it. The bitterness is warping your thinking, Alex. Whether you realize it or not, she's still pushing your buttons. Maybe you should go see her and have it out and clear the air."

"You think it's the logical thing to do. But you don't know very much about love, do you?"

"No. I've never been in love."

"I didn't think you had. Neither simplicity nor logic enters into it. It's something that takes your mind and body by storm and completely encompasses your very soul. You can't turn those feelings off and on like a light switch. This one special person in the whole world can make your heart soar to the heavens, or plunge your soul into the deepest depths of hell. I had heaven. Then Valerie Baker turned it into a living hell. And she's going to pay for doing that to me. As far as I'm concerned we'll never be able to clear the air to my satisfaction."

"Why haven't you done anything about her before now?"

"Because I didn't trust myself to be anywhere near her without wanting to strangle her." His fingers tightened around his glass. "Besides, revenge is a dish best served cold."

"I feel sorry for the woman."

"Don't. She deserves whatever I do to her."

Monday morning Michael Price stormed past Alex's secretary into his son's office.

"I'm out of the country for a few weeks and you lose your damn mind. What's this I hear about you building a plant in Quinneth Falls? You know it's where that Baker woman lives. What are you, some kind of masochist? A glutton for punishment? What is this all about, Alexander? I don't understand you!"

"Please calm down, Dad. You're getting all worked up over nothing. I know what I'm doing."

"I don't think you do. Of all the towns in this state why pick Quinneth Falls?"

"I have my reasons."

"It's for only one reason and her name is Valerie Baker."

"Bishop actually. She's Valerie Bishop now."

Michael frowned. "You've gone to the trouble of finding this out? You really are out of your mind. You haven't signed any contracts with these people yet, have you?"

"No, but—"

"Then you can easily back out."

"I could, but I'm not going to. By the end of next year we'll have a fully operational Price Industries plant in Quinneth Falls. So, Dad, you might as well resign yourself to the inevitable."

"I won't let you do this," he blustered.

"You no longer run this company, I do. Nothing you say will change my mind."

"Alexander—"

"I mean it, Dad. It's settled. Now if you have nothing else to discuss, I have a lot of work to do and projects and responsibilities to delegate before I can make an extended trip to Quinneth Falls." Studying his father's face, Alex thought his father would expound on the subject, but he surprised him by leaving without uttering another word.

Alex knew he was less than pleased with his son's decision, but knew he had little choice but to accept it.

"I just saw your father leaving the building. If I don't miss my guess he was not a happy camper," Justin said upon entering Alex's office.

"You didn't and he isn't. I haven't seen him that angry and agitated in a long while. Not since he and my stepmother were going through their messy divorce."

"Is she the reason he's so bitter?"

"She took being a bitch to an entirely different level. You see, my mother died when I was seven and my father was totally lost without her. Then several years later he met Irene Bailey at a business convention. She lived in a neighboring town just outside of Houston and had come to the city to work. She was a maid at the convention hotel. Dad was lonely and vulnerable and she easily seduced him.

"Soon after their arrival in Detroit, she began making Dad's life a living hell. She spent his money as if there was no tomorrow. After six years, unable to take it anymore, he divorced her. He'd been so blinded by Irene, he hadn't got her to sign a prenuptial agreement. In the end he paid a fortune to be rid of my stepmother. To his way of thinking any relationship with a woman has its price, whether monetary or emotional."

"So when your involvement with Valerie Baker seemed headed down that same path, and history threatened to repeat itself, he approached her and found out she had about as much integrity as his ex-wife. Or so he thought. In his bitterness and disillusionment, he could have read the situation wrong."

"He didn't read it wrong. Valerie accepted money from Dad to get out of my life, Justin, to the tune of one million dollars."

"Whew, that much, huh?"

"Yes, so let's not talk about this anymore, okay?

"I'm telling you Price Industries is going to buy the lake property. I seen surveyors marking off the boundaries," Jake told Valerie and Howard as they sat at a table having lunch at LET'S DO LUNCH cafe.

"But that doesn't necessarily mean—" Howard began.

Jake cut him off. "I think it does. As I told Valerie last week, the council appointed me their official guide and welcoming representative. I showed Mr. Price and his assistant the two properties. When we came to the one by the falls, right off the bat Mr. Price was awed by the place. You mark my words, he's going to buy that one." Jake stood up. "I've got to be back at work in twenty minutes. When I saw you two sitting here, I knew you would want to know that piece of news, since the lake property was tops on the preservation committee's list of saves. And because both of you are among the committees strongest supporters."

"You're right, we are. I'm glad you told us, Jake," Valerie thanked him.

Jake smiled and then walked out of the cafe. "The Indian Woods property would be the better choice environmentally. Don't you think, Valerie?" Howard asked. "Surely this Alexander Price will see that for himself."

"But what if he doesn't? The area around the falls could be ruined."

"You don't know that for sure."

"You're right, I don't." Valerie glanced at her watch. "I have to get back to Resource." She stood up to leave.

"Are you all right, Valerie?"

"I'm fine."

"You sure? You seem kind of—I don't know—stressed for some reason. You've been on edge ever since we ran into Alexander Price at the administration building and just now when Jake mentioned the man's name. Considering that you're already acquainted with Mr. Price, you could go to him on behalf of the committee and persuade him to choose the Indian Woods property."

"What?" Valerie gulped. She didn't want Price Industries to build a plant in Quinneth Falls, period. She certainly didn't want to be the one to discuss it with him.

"You look as if I asked you to take on a saber-toothed tiger without a weapon to protect yourself. What we should do is call an emergency committee meeting to discuss the issue." Howard rose from his chair.

"That's the logical thing to do. I'll see to it."

Howard glanced at his watch. "I have an appointment at two so I'd better be going. I'll call you later."

Dazed, Valerie followed Howard out of the cafe. She didn't know whether to laugh or cry. Howard had no idea how close he'd come to the truth with his statement about taking on a saber-toothed tiger. She likened doing battle with Alex to that.

Valerie sat in her car for a few minutes after Howard had driven away.

Talk to Alex! He had to be crazy. Valerie's stomach knotted tight with tension and the lunch she'd eaten roiled around inside at the very idea, making her nauseous. Inasmuch as she didn't want Price Industries to build in Quinneth Falls, she knew the town desperately needed the business. And she was concerned that if they bought the lake property it might be destroyed. If they had to have a plant in Quinneth Falls, Price Industries should choose the Indian Woods property. She didn't relish the idea of going to Alex. But could she allow him to ruin a place that meant so much to her and Quinneth Falls when she could do something to prevent it? Was there really anything she could do? She was damned if she went to him and damned if she didn't.

Valerie was sure Alex hated her for walking away from him. And she couldn't blame him. But then he'd never known about the wrenchingly painful choice she had been forced to make eight years ago.

"You came just in time. There's a call for you, Valerie." Mary Ellen held out the receiver to her as she entered the lab.

Valerie put her purse down on the desk and asked, "Who is it?"

"Mr. Price."

Valerie swallowed hard and reached for the phone.

Was it Alex or Michael? Whichever one it was, she wouldn't be a coward. She took the receiver and signaled to Mary Ellen that she wanted to take the call in private.

After Mary Ellen left the lab, Valerie cleared her throat and said. "This is Valerie Bishop."

"I have just one thing to say to you. If you don't convince Alexander to change his mind about building a plant there, I'll make you sorry you were ever born."

"It wasn't my fault he picked Quinneth Falls. He's the one you should be talking to, not me."

"I don't care whose fault it was. All I know is that you'd better do something to stop it."

"Mr. Price, I might not be able to change his mind about that."

"You'd better at least convince him to put someone else in charge. I mean it. I don't want him anywhere near you. Now, if you don't get him to do one or the other, you know what I'll do."

Before she could respond, Valerie heard a loud click and slowly cradled the receiver. Fear leaped inside her at what Michael might do. She'd never forget the last time she'd seen him...

Valerie had received a message to attend an urgent meeting in the executive office suite. She was in the middle of testing an experiment in the lab when she got the summons, but knowing that Alex couldn't wait until that evening to see her sent quivers of excitement jetting through her system.

She turned the Bunsen burner off, slipped her hands into insulated gloves and moved the beaker onto the counter, then took off her lab coat and hung it up. She would have to redo the experiment when she got back. Her full lips eased into a smile. Any chance to be with Alex definitely took priority over any experiment.

For the first time in her life Valerie was in love, heart, body and soul-deep in love. She couldn't believe Alexander Price, heir to Price Industries, could love a small town girl from Quinneth Falls, Michigan. It was only eight months ago, fresh out of college, that she'd opted not to take a job at Resource Chemical to seek employment and a more exciting life in Detroit.

Despite having no on-the-job experience, she'd been hired as an apprentice chemist at Price Industries. She never imagined that along with an impressive job she'd meet the man of her dreams. But she had, and Alex was that man.

When she opened the door to the executive office suite, Valerie's mouth fell open. It wasn't Alex sitting behind the desk waiting for her: It was his father, Michael Price.

"Come in and close the door, Miss Baker. We have a lot of ground to cover," he said frostily, peering at her over the top of his gold-rimmed glasses. "Please, take a seat," he said, waving his hand for her to sit in the chair in front of the desk.

Apprehension skittered down her spine. "I don't understand. I thought Alex would—"

"My son won't be joining us," he said, clearing his throat. "What we have to discuss doesn't require his presence."

"Is this about my job performance?" "No, Miss Baker. You're a very promising chemist. It's your relationship with my son."

"What about my relationship with Alex?" "You see, I know you're sleeping with him. Frankly, I don't believe you're good enough for him other than to sow his wild oats. I have in mind a much more suitable match with a woman of breeding. I'm sorry to say you don't fall into that category."

"Now wait a minute, you can't—" "I can do and say whatever in the hell I damn well feel like when it concerns my son and all I've built. Now, how much will it cost me to get you out of his life?"

"You can't be serious. I happen to love Alex very much and he loves me." Valerie rose from her chair. "There's no point in discussing this with you."

"On the contrary. We've only scratched the surface. Sit down. I believe I have something of interest to share with you." Not waiting to see if his order would be obeyed, he pulled a file folder from the drawer and tossed it on top of the desk

"What is this about, Mr. Price?"

"Read for yourself," he said, shoving it in front of her. Valerie reluctantly picked up the folder and opened it. Her breath sucked in sharply as she read its contents.

"If you don't do as I say—well, you know what to expect," he said, letting his voice purposely trail away. "You can't mean to—surely you wouldn't use this?" "In a heart-beat. I'll do whatever I have to to get you out of my son's life."

"But my aunt has done nothing to hurt you or anyone. How could you threaten to destroy a person you don't even know?"

"Quite easily, Miss Baker."

"It's taken her years to build up her sewing business. She's sacrificed a lot to raise me."

"If you care anything about this aunt you claim to love, you'll do as I say. Now, how much will it take, Miss Baker?" he said, reaching inside his jacket pocket for his checkbook.

"Don't you care that your son is in love and happy?"

"He only thinks he's in love. Alexander is young, he'll get over you in time. How much, Miss Baker?"

"I told you. I don't want any of your money, Mr. Price. Weren't you listening to me? I happen to be in love with Alex. How many times do I have to say it? No amount of money you offer me could ever change that."

"I've got a lot of money. I can make it well worth your while."

"Don't you get it? My love can't be bought."

"You talk about love. How much do you really love your aunt? Enough to see that she's not hurt? I'm sure you wouldn't like for every member of your close-knit little town to know that she has slept with a certain married leading citizen."

Valerie gasped.

"I purposely whited out the name of this man. But make no mistake, I wouldn't hesitate to splash his and hers across the front of the town newspaper. I'll personally send each citizen a letter if you force me to. So what's it going to be?"

Valerie's head was spinning, her emotions in complete turmoil. What should she do? How could she make a decision like this? Tears rolled down her cheeks. Her heart ached unbearably. How could she give Alex up? But on the other hand, she couldn't allow Michael Price to destroy her aunt.

Valerie gulped, forcing down her misery. "I'll go, but I don't want any of your money."

"Be reasonable, Miss Baker. You deserve compensation."

"Not with your money, I don't."

"All right then. Have it your way. When you finish today, stop by personnel. Your regular pay, and the customary employee severance check, will be waiting for you. You've got three days to pack up your things and leave town. If you're not gone by then, I'll do exactly as I've said."

Exactly! Exactly! echoed through Valerie's mind.

She stopped the painful walk down memory lane. Reality said she had to protect her aunt and her son from that monster. The only way to insure it was to do as Michael said and somehow convince Alex not to go ahead with the plant. Or convince him to put someone else in charge because if she didn't, her aunt would be the one to suffer. The idea of doing anything Michael Price wanted

burned like acid. She didn't want to have any dealings with
Alex, but it seemed she had no choice. Damn you, Michael
Price. Damn you to hell.

Pain entered her heart like the thrust of a sharp knife.
Why did Alex have to pick Quinneth Falls? Why did he
have to totally disrupt her life?

CHAPTER FIVE

Detroit

Alex and Althea had gone to the theater to see a new version of the play *My Arms Are Too Short to Box with God.* Afterward, as he sat next to his fiancée in a nearby restaurant, Alex couldn't help comparing her to Valerie. Althea was beautiful in a sophisticated way with her expertly cut hair and couturier clothes, but she had none of the earthiness Valerie possessed in abundance. He hadn't really thought about the differences until he'd read that letter from the Quinneth Falls City Council which had resurrected the old feelings and the bitter pain of Valerie's betrayal.

"Alex, what's wrong? You hardly watched any of the play. And you've barely touched your dinner."

"I'm sorry to be such bad company this evening. I have a lot on my mind with the plans to build the new branch of Price Industries."

"Justin is your assistant. Can't he do that for you? It's what you pay him to do, isn't it? Or is there some other reason you're so preoccupied with this project?"

Alex smiled and took her hand in his. "I've been neglecting you lately, haven't I? When the negotiations for the plant are set, I'll make it up to you. I promise." He leaned over and kissed her lips. He saw Althea's closed eyes. The kiss was pleasant, but had none of the fire... He had to stop thinking these thoughts. Once he'd had his revenge and gotten Valerie out of his system he'd forget her and concentrate on Althea.

In your dreams, Alex, a little voice inside his mind taunted. *You'll never feel for any woman what you felt for Valerie Baker. And revenge isn't going to change that.*

"When are we going to set a date for our wedding?" Althea asked. "You've been putting it off for the last few months."

"It'll be soon. First, I want the plans for the new branch and the construction well underway. Maybe in September."

"You sound as if you're going to get personally involved in the running of this plant. If that's true you'll be spending most of your time there. What about us?"

Alex kissed her hand. "This really isn't the time or place to discuss this, Thea."

"Will a right time ever come, Alex? Am I also competing with another woman for your affection?"

"No. Where did you get an idea like that? I'm engaged to you."

"But do you love me?"

"I'm marrying you, Thea. In a few months you'll be my wife."

Althea didn't look at all impressed by his answer, Alex thought. He had to hurry his plans for revenge or he might lose Thea. Justin was right. It wasn't fair to keep her floating in limbo like this. It wasn't fair that he'd put their plans for the future on hold because of Valerie Bishop. But when he was through dealing with Valerie, then and only then would he be able to get his life back on track.

That night after taking Althea home, Alex drove around for a while thinking about all that Justin had said about telling Althea the truth. She did deserve better.

If you care about having a life with Althea, you should drop your quest for vengeance and let Justin handle the Quinneth Falls project. You know it's the right thing to do.

He did care about having a life with Althea. And he knew letting Justin handle things was the right thing to do, but he also knew that the desire for revenge was strong in him. He'd been entangled in his bitterness toward Valerie for too long to just give it up. But if he didn't, he could lose Althea. Did he really want to risk it?

Alex returned home. As he started up the stairs, he heard his father call out to him from the living room and he groaned. He wasn't up to a confrontation or a lecture from him.

"Have you come to your senses yet, Alexander?"

"Dad, I told you what I'm going to do. Nothing has happened to alter my decision about the plant. Now, if you would—"

"I thought after what Valerie Baker did to you, you'd wisely stay as far away from her as possible. Evidently I was wrong. I've done everything I can to keep you from being hurt."

"I realize that and I appreciate it. She doesn't have the power to hurt me any more. For the record, Quinneth Falls has splendid potential."

"So do several other towns I can think of."

"My mind is made up, Dad. End of discussion."

"At least leave the work to Justin and stay here where you belong. If you don't you're going to regret it, Alexander."

Alex didn't respond to his father's words. Instead, in a tired voice, he said, "I'm going up to bed."

Michael Price glanced up the stalls at his son's retreating figure. Valerie Bishop had to convince him to change his mind about the plant. He'd tried to without success.

He didn't know if she could do any better, but maybe she could at least convince him not to handle things himself.

Earlier that day when he had left Price Industries, Michael had felt a headache coming on. As he drove down Jefferson along Grosse Pointe Shore, his mind was desperately seeking to come up with a plan to stop his son from making the biggest mistake of his life.

Michael loved his son and felt he was headed for disaster if he went ahead with this project. Eight years ago he had managed to avert trouble, but would he be able to do it again? When Alexander had broken down and cried in his arms, it had torn his heart in two.

He'd tried over the years to keep his son busy. He'd even retired early to insure it. He'd encouraged a relationship with Althea Johnson. He didn't want his son anywhere near Valerie Baker.

When he had got home, Michael went straight to his study and unlocked his desk drawer and brought out a folder. If Valerie Bishop became a problem, he would be forced to use the information in the file. Maybe it wouldn't come to that, but whatever he had to do to protect his son, he would do.

Valerie tossed and turned, trying to find sleep, but knew she wouldn't. She'd decided to drive to Detroit in the morning, and she was dreading it. The thought of seeing Alex froze her insides. Considering his attitude the last time she'd seen him, he definitely wouldn't have any nice words to say to her. She hoped he wouldn't give her another one of his cold, indifferent stares. She didn't think she could handle that. She knew she couldn't handle that.

Valerie got out of bed and walked down the hall to her son's room to look in on him. She smiled. Tyler had left his flashlight on and a history book of Michigan Indians was draped across his lap. She took the flashlight and lifted the book off his lap and set them on his desk. She kissed her son's forehead and quietly left the room and went back to her own. If not for Michael Price, she and Alex and their son could have been together and happy. She knew that would never happen now. Thanks to him, she was going to see Alex and try to convince him to change his mind, which she knew she had little hope of accomplishing. Alex wasn't a man you could dictate to. And once he'd made up his mind he rarely changed it.

Oh, God, please help me get through this, she prayed.

"Mr. Price, a Mrs. Valerie Bishop is waiting to see you," Alex's secretary informed him on the phone.

Valerie was here to see him! Alex frowned, curious to know what she wanted. "Send her in, Cheryl."

After their last brief encounter Alex sensed that Valerie felt uncomfortable in his presence. More than uncomfortable, really. He'd have to say frightened was a better word to describe the look in her eyes. Good, he thought, waiting for her to be shown into his office. As soon as the door closed behind his secretary, Valerie spoke.

"Alex, I've come to convince you to—"

"Drop the plans for the new plant in Quinneth Falls. Right? Even though you know what it could mean to the town. You're still the same selfish bitch you were eight years ago, aren't you, Val?"

She flinched, wanting to deny it and tell him the truth. The realization that he felt such hatred for her hurt. "If it was up to me Price Industries wouldn't be my choice for new business in Quinneth Falls. But since it isn't up to me and the town does need your business, I won't try to change your mind about that."

"Good, because you couldn't anyway. Price Industries is going to build a plant in Quinneth Falls. If you didn't come here for that, then why are you here?"

"I came to persuade you to choose the Indian Woods property."

"What difference does it make which one I choose?"

"I know you were the one who sat in on our preservation committee meeting. And that you know how important the falls and grounds around the falls are to our town and to future generations as a historical landmark."

"And you think building a plant on the lake property would ruin it? You really believe I would allow such a thing to happen?"

"I don't know if you would or not."

Alex studied Valerie. Now she was this caring civic-minded person. She cared more for a piece of ground than she had about him eight years ago. She'd taken the money and run back to Quinneth Falls, straight into the arms of George Bishop. Alex rose from his chair and walked around his desk.

"You expect me to fall for this pillar-of-the-community act you're putting on?"

"It's not an act. It would be better for everyone if you chose the Indian Woods property."

"You're all business now, aren't you? You weren't always, though, were you, Val?" He came within inches of her. "I remember a time when you—"

She could smell his cologne and it was driving her crazy, causing her to embarrassingly betray her vulnerability to him. "Don't, Alex," she said, her voice barely above a whisper, as she inched away from him. "I only came to—"

"You want me to believe your motives are altruistic. What if I were to tell you that I'd also be personally supervising the project, whichever property is chosen?"

"But you won't be. Will you?"

"Does the prospect scare you?"

"Of course not."

He reached out and touched her face. "It should. And I think it does. Before you came here, I was considering letting Justin Forest, my personal assistant, handle the negotiations and supervise the building and running of the plant, but I've changed my mind."

"But why? You can't want to be around me after—"

"You trampled my heart beneath your feet? And then walked away from me as if I was of little or no account?"

Valerie bit back the words she wanted desperately to tell him: that it wasn't true and that she had really loved him with all her heart, but she couldn't.

"You don't have a comeback to that, do you? Your coming here was counter-productive."

"In what way? You mean you intended to buy the lake property all along? Is that what you're saying?" she accused.

"Whether I did or not it's my business. Know this. There will be a Price Industries plant built wherever I want it to be built, and I'm going to handle it personally. Every time you look around I'll be in your face. You might as well prepare yourself for that eventuality. Do you understand what I'm saying?"

Valerie turned to leave. He grasped her arm and swung her around to face him. Then his eyes probed hers, analyzing her reaction. "Do you understand?"

"Yes, I understand all right. You used to care about environmental concerns."

"So now you remember that about me."

"I don't want to believe you would destroy—"

"Why do you assume I would? I have to admit a lot has changed since you walked out on me. If you don't like the way I am you have only yourself to blame. I am what you made me."

For a moment Valerie thought to stay and reason with him, but realized it would be useless. Hadn't she told Michael as much? She stared at Alex for long, emotion-packed seconds before quietly leaving his office.

Alex stood watching as the door closed. What remorse he had momentarily felt was gone. Seeing Valerie had strengthened his resolve. He would proceed with his plans with a vengeance. He was going to see that Valerie paid some serious dues.

That night Alex tossed and turned before drifting into a dream-filled sleep...

Valerie was working on a metal erosion experiment when Alex entered the lab at Price Industries. As he stood watching her, he thought of the reasons why he loved her so much. She was fun to be with. She did crazy off-the-wall things like leaving notes on top of his desk, instructing him to turn to a certain page in the Yellow Pages where she had circled the place she wanted him to meet her for dinner. Like the song "You Light up my Life," Valerie did just that. But that was only a small part of it. Just being around her made him happy.

"I've been hearing good things about you, Miss Baker."

"Alex! What are you doing here?"

"I came to take you away from all this drudgery."

"I happen to like all this drudgery, I'll have you know. Besides, what would people say?"

"They'd say Alexander Price is crazy in love with Valerie Baker. And they'd be right."

"Do you really love me, Alex?"

"If you have to ask, I'm not doing my job properly."

"And what job is that?"

He took her lab coat off and started hustling her toward the door, barely giving her a chance to pick up her purse. "Let me take you home and show you."

"What about the experiment?"

"I told your supervisor you'd be going home early today."

"Did he ask why?"

"Yes."

"And what did you tell him?"

"I had a prior claim on your time today."

"No, you didn't."

"Yes, I did." Alex couldn't wait for them to get to her apartment. Every chance he got to be with Valerie, he took advantage of it. She was everything he'd ever wanted in a woman: warm, generous, sweet and loving. She was the woman he intended to marry. At the door of her apartment he had her close her eyes and let him lead her into the living room.

"You can open your eyes now." He delighted in the look on her face when she saw the stack of presents. It was like watching a child who'd never received any presents before.

"You're going to spoil me."

"Open this one first," he suggested, pointing to a long flat box.

She tore the ribbon off the box opened it and lifted out a heart-shaped diamond pendant on a gold chain.

"You shouldn't have."

"Yes, I should. Read the inscription."

"'To the most wonderful woman God ever created.' Oh, Alex, I love it and I'll treasure it forever. Oh, how I love you."

He fastened the chain around her neck. He smiled, thinking about the receipt inside his jacket pocket for the engagement ring that matched the necklace. He could picture the look on her face when he put the ring on her finger.

"You're all the woman I'll ever need or want, Valerie Baker. You own my heart. You're my soulmate. I love you, girl."

"You're my life. I can't stand being apart from you for even a day."

A sensuous light passed between them. Valerie gazed longingly at him and then buried her face in the corded muscles of his neck. His insides melted at the contact and he closed his eyes.

"What are you doing to me, Val?"

"All the right things, I hope."

When he kissed her soft, sweet lips the sensation sent him skyrocketing to the heavens. He lifted Valerie in his arms and carried her into the bedroom and undressed her slowly, worshipfully, then undressed himself. He paused before continuing, whispering his love for every part of her body. Then he laid Valerie on the bed. When her long slender fingers found him, all thought flew out of his head. The throbbing erect organ between his legs stretched and tightened painfully.

"Make love to me, Alex."

He made them one and started to move within her, stroking deep again and again. And as he felt the inner walls of her femininity quiver around him, his passion reached the explosion point. Then Valerie's body began to fade away.

"No," he cried out, "Val, don't go! Come back! You can't leave me. You can't leave me…"

Alex awoke with a start to find himself entangled in the sheets. He shook his head in disgust because he knew what the sticky wetness clinging to his body and the sheets meant. Nothing like this had happened to him since he was a teenager. Damn you, Valerie. Damn you for reducing me to this. He stripped the sheets from the bed and took a shower. He was going to make her pay. She wouldn't escape his wrath this time.

By the end of the week Alex was ready to make a return trip to Quinneth Falls.

CHAPTER SIX

Tears rolled down Valerie's cheeks on the long drive back to Quinneth Falls. Michael Price wouldn't be pleased that she'd been unable to change Alex's mind about building the plant in Quinneth Falls. But he would be overjoyed to know how much Alex hated her and wanted nothing to do with her.

Price Industries business would be a life-giving injection to Quinneth Falls' economy. And she couldn't in good conscience have disregarded that, no matter her personal feelings. Considering how Alex felt about her, she was surprised he'd want to supervise the construction and running of the plant himself. Revenge and bitterness had to be what was driving him. But she wouldn't be the only one to suffer if he went ahead with his plans.

When Valerie reached home, it was past Tyler's bed time and he was asleep. She went straight to her bedroom, stripped off her clothes and stepped into the shower, wishing she could wash away her problems and heartache so easily. After drying herself and putting on a nightshirt, she climbed into bed but didn't fall asleep. She was still too wired from her encounter with Alex.

The problem of what to do about Tyler squeezed her heart in a vice. She had to keep Alex away from him. She wondered how long it would take Price Industries to finalize the papers for the new plant. A week? Maybe two? Three at the most? Could she keep her son hidden from Alex until then? Even so, she was afraid it would be a stopgap measure since he intended to handle everything himself.

Her head started to throb and Valerie reached inside her nightstand for a pain killer. But no pain killer invented could take away the renewed agony of losing Alex. Her aunt was right. Not even the injection of Michael Price into the equation could alter the complex emotions raging through her after seeing Alex.

This thing with the lake property. Because he hated her, would Alex pick it instead of Indian Woods? She prayed he would choose the latter because the falls was sacred to her. She'd gone there countless times in the past when things became too much to bear. She couldn't, without a fight, let a metal processing plant destroy or mar the spot's beauty.

Maybe if she made one last plea to Alex... No, she couldn't go to him again, not now. When they talked earlier, she could tell he had no leftover good feelings for her.

He hasn't forgotten that you walked out on him. No man could ever forgive that and remain on friendly terms with the one who did the walking.

Valerie closed her eyes in an effort to block out his face, but it was no use. Her heartbeat quickened just remembering those sherry-brown eyes and how they used to blaze with fire and desire when he looked at her. She recalled the time they had been walking through the park and got caught in a downpour and had sought protection from the rain beneath the covering at a bus stop. How the combination of his lips and the rain had tasted.

Oh, God, if things were only different. But they weren't and never would be. She'd left Alex and come back to Quinneth Falls and married George Bishop. And had given birth to Alex's son. George had been an exemplary father and a faithful, loyal and loving husband, but now that he was dead, she had pangs of conscience. Was it fair for her to keep Tyler from knowing his natural father? Was it fair to continue keeping Alex from knowing he had a son?

What about Michael Price? Surely you haven't forgotten about him.

No. She definitely hadn't. Even the threat he held over her head couldn't sever her connection to Alex. All she had to do was look at Tyler. She recalled in vivid derail the night her son was conceived…

It was the evening after her confrontation with Michael, and Valerie waited for Alex to come to her apartment. She picked up his picture from the end table and eased her fingers across the full lips, dark-bronze face and short, unruly black curls. She lifted the heart pendant he'd given her from her chest and studied it. Alex was so sweet and dear to her. The thought of everything she'd be giving up threatened to crush the life out of her. Only by sheer force of will was she able to stave off her tears. This night with Alex would have to last the rest of her life. And she intended to make it as memorable as possible.

When she heard the key turn in the lock, Valerie let the pendant go and composed herself, then stepped over to the dining table and started lighting the candles.

"Whatever you've cooked sure smells good," Alex exclaimed with a grin as he entered the apartment. "So what's up with the candles? Is it a special occasion?"

"Every occasion with you is special. I've fixed your favorite roast veal for dinner."

He came up behind her and circled his arms around her waist and nuzzled her neck. "With your out-of-this-world dill mashed potatoes and peppered green beans?"

"Yes, everything is just the way you like it."

"Does that include my woman? You know, I'd rather have my dessert first," he said, kissing the side of her neck, then moving on to the sensitive area behind her ear. "Your skin is velvety smooth, like chocolate pudding."

"And you want to taste, right? You're a wicked man, Alexander Price."

"But you love me. In fact you're the one who encouraged me to be this way," he said, easing down the zipper of her dress.

"Oh, so it's all my fault."

"I don't care whose fault it is. I want to embed myself so deeply inside your beautiful body that we become one flaming entity."

"I want that more than anything." Tears stung her eyes. "Oh, Alex, I love you so much," she moaned as he caressed her breasts.

"Not nearly as much as I love you."

"That's impossible."

Alex melded his lips to hers and not breaking contact, lifted her in his arms and carried her into the bedroom.

What followed was a beautiful memory and she knew that no matter what happened she'd always have that. Four weeks later she realized she'd have more because she was carrying Alex's child beneath her heart.

Alex and Justin arrived in Quinneth Falls and went to the Quinneth Falls Inn, where Justin had reserved the presidential suite. It would be their temporary headquarters until the building they'd leased was available.

Alex loosened his tie and tossed it over the back of the brown velvet, overstuffed lounge chair, then headed for the well-stocked bar and poured himself and Justin a brandy.

"So have you decided on the lake property?" Justin asked, taking the drink and sitting on the couch.

"It is a fantastic piece of property."

"You sound as if you're more interested in it for personal use. Are you? I doubt if Althea will want to live in a town like Quinneth Falls. Or that you would even consider it when you know Valerie Bishop lives here."

"What better revenge than for Valerie to see the man she used at every turn and wonder and worry about what he has in mind to do to even the score?"

"Man, I know you were hurt, but to—"

"I want her to know the pain I felt. She used me to finance another man's dreams."

"That was a long time ago. You should have gotten over it and moved on. Things are different now, Alex. The woman is a widow with a child and is trying to run a business that is on shaky ground. I'd say she's had her share of suffering."

"Not as much as she's going to suffer by the time I'm through with her."

"Surely you're not going to—"

"Oh, I don't plan to physically harm her. You know me better than that. No, I intend a more subtle revenge. I won't interfere with her livelihood. Although I may alter it a little."

Justin frowned. "What exactly do you have in mind? I thought I knew. Now I'm clueless."

Alex smiled. "You'll know soon enough. Tomorrow, while I'm in with the city planning commission, I want you to pay a visit to Resource Chemical. According to Jake Spriewell, Valerie will be attending a preservation committee meeting. She has an assistant that might give you a better picture of Valerie and the company's future plans. Her name is Mary Ellen Spencer. I saw a picture of her. She's a real knockout. You like redheads, don't you?"

Scarlet color streaked across Justin's cheekbones. "You don't expect me to—to seduce the information out of her!"

"Use your charm, man. Whether things go beyond that point is up to you." Alex raised his glass in salute. "I have every confidence in you, Justin. Look, it's getting late. I'm going to bed. I want to be fresh for tomorrow's meeting.

Justin set his glass on the coffee table and rose to his feet. "Sometimes, Alex, the best laid plans of mice and men go awry."

"Another one of your philosophical platitudes."

"The thing about them is how true they are and how well they apply to everyday life. I hope one day you won't regret doing whatever it is you have in mind to do. I'll say good night."

Alex watched Justin as he went to his room. Regret was what he wanted to see in Valerie Bishops' eyes and hear spill from her lips. Then maybe he could let go of the past and begin a new life with Althea.

Justin returned to the inn late that next afternoon and found Alex in their suite sitting in a chair with his shirt sleeves rolled up, eating a sandwich as he pored over some papers.

Alex glanced at him. "So how did it go with Valerie's assistant?

Justin strode over to the tray of sandwiches on the table, picked up one, then put it back. "I feel like a rat."

"You were doing your job. Why should you feel that way?

Justin's blue eyes glittered. "I wasn't being completely honest with the woman, that's why. She's loyal, and very protective of her employer."

Alex put the papers on the coffee table, leaned back in his chair and observed Justin's tense features. "What exactly did you say to her?"

"I told her we were interested in the community and I wanted to get her opinion of Valerie Bishop and the company's position regarding Price Industries. She gave it to me, all right. For one thing, if God were a woman, her name would be Valerie Bishop. Two, Resource Chemical is the best place on earth to work. Three, she isn't sure how her boss feels about the projected new plant. And four, she confided that she is worried about Resource Chemical's financial situation because of the delays in payment of monies the government owes the company."

"Why would her telling you that make you feel like a rat?" Alex's eyes narrowed. "It's not what she said, is it? It's the woman herself."

"Yes, damn it," Justin growled.

"I see. You're quite taken with Mary Ellen Spencer, aren't you? By telling me all, you feel you're betraying her trust. You really aren't, Justin. You're just doing your job. She'll come to understand that."

"And what? Forgive me?"

"You haven't done anything for her to forgive."

"Not yet. If you go through with your plans for revenge it's exactly what'll happen."

"Justin, I'm not going to close down Valerie Bishop's company and put your lady friend out of a job."

Justin frowned skeptically. "You're not?"

"What I do or don't do with Valerie Bishop will only affect her personally."

"You've found out something about her, haven't you?"

"Yes, I have, and what you've told me confirms it. You won't be involved in this from here on out."

"But I work for you, Alex. And when something goes wrong with her boss Mary Ellen is sure to blame me."

"And tar you with the same brush, so to speak. Don't worry. If it's so important to you, I'll see that she learns the truth."

"I hope she'll accept your explanation."

"You're really hung up on this woman, aren't you? What she thinks really matters to you."

"I don't want to start off on the wrong foot with her."

"From now on you'll be dealing exclusively with Price Industry business."

"Thanks, Alex." Justin smiled and headed for his room.

Alex picked up the papers he'd abandoned earlier and made an attempt at studying them, but it was no use. He couldn't concentrate on the information. It looked like love at first sight for Justin. He hoped this Mary Ellen Spencer didn't break Justin's heart the way Valerie had broken his. He gritted his teeth. He had promised himself he wasn't going to go there. Why was it when he thought about Valerie the old pain threatened to escape from the abyss where he'd flung it to savage him?

Valerie Bishop was his past, his very painful past. But his past nevertheless and it had been over between them years ago.

Is it really over, Alex? Or are you just deluding yourself? It is over, damn it. Once I've exacted my revenge I'll forget Valerie Bishop ever existed and get on with my life.

If you buy that lake property it'll only be the beginning. Can't you see that?

Alex tossed the papers back on the coffee table and shot to his feet. Was his need for revenge that twisted? No, it wasn't. He was going ahead with his plans. He'd suffered for years after Valerie had walked out on him, and all the while she'd been happy with another man. She'd given the man a son that should have been his. Had given him a part of her life she should have shared only with Alex. That he could never forgive. If she'd needed the money for herself he could have understood that, but to prostitute herself for another man... Until now everything had gone her way. But the tide had definitely turned and she would learn what it felt like to be used and then carelessly tossed aside.

CHAPTER SEVEN

Alex drove out to the falls late that evening because he was restless and couldn't sleep. He got out of the car and walked over to the water's edge and just watched as the water leisurely flowed over the twenty-five foot high rocks. It's soft sluicing sound was soothing. He'd never heard anything quite like it. And he'd heard and seen the waters of Lake Michigan lap against the shore. Heard the rush of the Atlantic Ocean and the waves wash over Pacific beach sand, but none of them compared to the calming effect the falls had on him.

Valerie had lived here all her life. She had ultimately come back, married and had a child. He couldn't help wondering what would have happened if…

She dumped you, man. Can't you get that through your head? His stomach churned with anger and bitterness. Pain clawed through him like a savage beast, slashing his insides to pieces. No, he couldn't forget. He would never forget. And neither would Valerie, because he refused to let her.

❧

"A phone call for you Valerie. Mrs. Crawford on line two," Mary Ellen announced over the com line the following morning.

Valerie depressed the button. "Yes, Mrs. Crawford, how may I help you?"

"I just got a disturbing phone call from Jake Spriewell. He said that Alexander Price has bought the lake property as well as the Indian Woods one. Do you have any idea which of them he's going to build the new plant on?"

"No, I haven't got a clue." Valerie tried to keep the shock from her voice.

"Well, can you talk to him, dear? Convince him to choose the Indian Woods property. Please," she beseeched Valerie. "I know what the lake property means to you, as well as the rest of us. We all agreed that it should be preserved for future generations. Why the council made it available, I'll never understand. I suppose they never thought anyone would actually buy it. Or maybe they did. I told Jackson I wouldn't be pleased if Mr. Price chose the lake property. Getting back to what I called about. Will you talk to Mr. Price?"

"I do care about the lake property, Mrs. Crawford, but I can't guarantee that I'll be able to influence him one way or the other."

"You're a clever girl. I know you will. Thank you so much, Valerie. I'm going to tell the rest of the committee as soon as I hang up with you. You'll let us know how it turns out after you've talked to Mr. Price, won't you, dear? Bye now."

"Mrs. Crawford, wait I—" Valerie heard the phone click, then the hum of the dial tone. Her hand started shaking. She put the receiver back on its cradle, then got up and walked over to the windows and wrapped her arms around herself. Why did Alex have to buy that property? Why? Why? Why?

"What did Mrs. Crawford want?" Mary Ellen asked as she entered Valerie's office.

"She wants me to plead the committee's case with Mr. Price."

"You shouldn't have a problem if he's anything like his assistant." She smiled dreamily. "Justin Forest was very nice when he came here the other day. He seems genuinely interested in Quinneth Falls and its people."

One "people" in particular, Valerie thought, glancing at Mary Ellen. She could see how impressed she was by this Justin Forest. But since he worked for Price Industries she had to wonder if he had another motive besides his personal interest in her assistant.

"According to Jake, Mr. Price and his assistant are staying at the Quinneth Falls Inn. Could you get him on the phone?"

"Sure, right away." Mary Ellen stopped at the door. "You don't look like you really want to talk to Mr. Price. Why is that? Did you know him in the past and hate his guts?"

"Just get him on the phone, please."

Minutes later the phone buzzed. Valerie licked her lips and reached for the receiver, then depressed the button.

"Mr. Price? Alex?"

She heard the hesitation in his voice when he answered.

"Valerie?"

"Yes, it's me. I'd like to speak to you about the lake property."

"Can you come to my suite this afternoon at, say, one o'clock?"

At the hard sound in his voice, she swallowed past the lump in her throat and answered. "Yes."

"I'll see you then."

It took a moment for Valerie to calm her frazzled nerves. Why should she be nervous? She'd just seen him in Detroit a few days before.

Be honest, girl, you're aching to see him again. And not because of the lake property. You want to see the man that you still love.

I don't love him anymore. I don't. I can't possibly love someone who—"

Who what?

He sounded so cold. His tone was so businesslike, not a trace of emotion in it. He would probably deal with her in like manner.

You can always hope he won't. You walked out on the man, even though your motives were selfless.

The hands on the clock seemed to sprout wings. Before Valerie realized it it was a quarter to one. She'd worn a simple skirt and blouse to work, never imagining she'd be going to face Alex. It probably wouldn't matter what she wore. She sighed. She'd better get a move on or she'd be late.

You can call and cancel. But you won't, will you?

Alex ordered lunch from the best restaurant in town, which luckily was only a few doors down the street. He'd chosen all of Valerie's favorites. He remembered how much she loved seafood.

And how enthusiastically she made love.

He wouldn't think about that. He had to stay focused on his objective.

He heard a knock at the door and went to answer it.

Alex smiled. "You're right on time. Come in." He waved his hand and moved back from the door.

Valerie followed him into the living room.

"I'd like to get down to business," she said coolly.

"I ordered some of your favorites for lunch. Why don't you sit over here and enjoy them while we talk." He indicated a chair set before a table in the center of the room.

"I'm really not hungry."

"Have you eaten lunch?"

"No, but—"

"Then I insist," he said, pulling the chair out from the table.

It was too late to change her mind and run, so she sat down.

"I took the liberty of ordering white wine to go with our lunch. I remember how much you enjoyed it with your seafood."

"Alex, about the lake property."

He filled her glass. "Taste this and see how you like it."

Valerie reached for the glass. When her fingers accidently touched his, she gasped and nearly spilled her wine.

"I'd say you need to relax. Take a sip to calm your nerves."

"I'm not suffering from an attack of nerves."

"If not nerves, then you must be in need of nourishment." He took up his fork and started to eat.

She felt so frustrated. All she wanted to do was get this over with and leave. And here he was acting as if this was a social call.

Didn't you say you were going to be honest about why you came?

She was being honest. She was.

As she ate her thyme-seasoned, sautéed shrimp, she had to admit that it tasted wonderful. She hadn't eaten shrimp cooked this way since—since before they broke up.

Alex watched Valerie as she made short work of her meal. He recalled how he liked seeing her eat. Although she'd been reed slim, she could really put the food away. That much hadn't changed. She now wore her hair in a loose chignon at the nape of her neck. And he noticed that she still wore only lipstick, no other makeup. She'd filled out exquisitely in all the right places. In his mind's eye, he could still picture her naked. He remembered that she had a mole just above her left hip.

When Valerie looked up, she saw the expression on his face and knew lunch and the lake property were the farthest thing from his mind. His sherry-brown eyes had darkened and he wet his full bottom lip with his top one. Oh, God, this couldn't be happening. She hadn't come here to rekindle past desires.

Oh, didn't you? Could have fooled me.

"Alex, I think we should talk about the lake property. Is that where you're going to build your plant?"

He wiped his mouth with a napkin, then rose from his chair. "Let's go over to the couch where we can be more comfortable. Then we'll talk."

Valerie let out a sigh of relief now that they were finally going to discuss the lake property. She left the table and followed Alex over to the couch.

She began, "Our preservation committee is concerned that you, that your company will—"

He scooted closer to her. "I haven't made up my mind which of the two properties I want to build on."

"When will you know?" She inched toward the arm of the couch.

He inched closer to her. "Maybe in a few days or a week or even longer. I just don't know. A lot of things need to be considered."

"Why buy both properties when you can only build on one?"

Alex was almost thigh to thigh with Valerie. When he put his hand on hers, she jumped and made to get up. He aborted her flight and pulled her into his arms.

"Alex."

"Yes," he whispered, his mouth only inches from hers.

"Let me go."

"And if I don't want to?"

"You have to." She gasped when he flicked his tongue across her lower lip.

"Do I? Who's going to make me?"

Valerie tried to avoid the contact of his lips on hers, but he wouldn't allow it. They found their target and he slanted them over hers. Her body trembled, shocked by the intensity of his sensuous kiss. Instead of continuing to fight him off, she stilled her struggles, returning his kiss with ardor. He slipped his hand under her blouse and rubbed his thumb across her nipple. She felt it tighten inside her bra and almost immediately she felt her panties dampen. She had to get away from him or...

Alex kissed her again and her mind went hazy. Before she realized it, his other hand was beneath her skirt and at the juncture of her thighs.

"You're wet. And so hot you could rival the steam building in a pressure cooker. Tell me, Val, are you about ready to blow? Isn't your lover taking proper care of you?" he said in a husky, taunting voice.

Valerie stiffened at the significance of his words and struggled to free herself.

Alex released her and grinned. "And here I thought you were willing to do anything to get what you want. It worked for you in the past. So why abandon a good thing?"

"You rotten son of—"

"Watch what you say. When I make a decision about the lake property you'll know about it when everyone else does. Now, if you want to sweeten the kitty, I'll be more than happy to oblige you."

Valerie scrambled to her feet, straightened her skirt, then stumbled to the door. When she reached it, she turned. "It'll be a cold day in hell before I ever—"

He chuckled. "Never say *ever.*"

Gritting her teeth, Valerie walked out, leaving the door standing open.

Justin came in moments later.

"Wasn't that Valerie Bishop I passed in the hall?"

"The very same."

"She sure was disheveled and in a rage. What did you do to her?"

"No more than what she wanted me to do. And it's only the beginning of what I plan to do to her and with her." The fact that she was by no means immune to him would work to his advantage. It would make revenge all the more sweet when he took it. She was as passionate as he remembered. For some reason that bothered him. Had she displayed that kind of wild passion with her husband or her present lover? He would find out the answer very soon.

CHAPTER EIGHT

Valerie drove out to her sanctuary, the falls, and got out of the car and ambled over to her favorite spot by the water's edge. She couldn't go back to work until she had pulled herself together. How could she have let Alex couch her like that?

Because you wanted him to, that's way.

How could she have responded to him like that?

Girl, please.

She couldn't go anywhere near him ever again. Alex was no longer the same fun-loving, wonderful man she had known eight years ago. Had what she'd done changed him so completely? His father had said at the time he'd forget her and get on with his life. That obviously hadn't happened. Alex hadn't forgotten anything, and definitely hadn't gotten over her. He wanted revenge, and she now had no doubts as to the method he would employ to reach his goal. She knew she was particularly vulnerable when she was around him. There had been more between them than sexual attraction, even if he chose to forget it. For eight wonderful months, they had shared a life together in Detroit.

The Alex she loved, the father of her son, was gone, replaced by this ruthless, vengeful stranger. Knowing this, she could never let him near Tyler.

You'd better hope he never sees him.

Valerie sat down on a rock and watched the water flow over the rocks into the lake. The familiar sound of soft rushing waters had always calmed her in the past, but not today.

Alex actually seemed to hate her! She'd said the words before, but now after finding out it was true, she couldn't get used to the idea.

Did you expect him to welcome you with open arms?

No, but she hadn't expected this all-consuming hatred.

If what he felt was hatred, what was your response all about?

She refused to analyze that question.

Valerie looked across the lake at the property that now belonged to Price Industries and thought about the Indian Woods property. Why would Alex buy both? He could only build on one. Did he plan to use the other in some way to get back at her for what she'd done to him? Surely he couldn't be that vindictive.

Couldn't he? Who says a woman is the only one capable of feeling scorned and then acting upon it?

Oh, Alex, what have your father and I done to you?

Valerie glanced at the falls one last time before leaving, hoping in vain it would give her the knowledge and the wisdom to handle the situation she'd been thrust into.

"Well, how did it go with Mr. Price?" Mary Ellen asked as Valerie walked through the door of the lab.

"He didn't relieve my mind, if that's what you mean."

"He didn't tell you which of the properties he intends building on?"

"No. For some reason he's holding off on his decision. As to why, I haven't been able to figure that out."

"How long do you think he'll keep us in suspense? I've never known Mrs. Crawford to be so anxious about anything. I wonder what she'll do when she finds out?"

"Probably call or pay me a little visit. I'll worry about that later. In any case, I have work to finish before I go home. By the way, I've decided to let you handle the jewelry alloy project."

"You really mean it?"

"The formula you stumbled onto needs to be tested. Think you can handle it?"

"Oh, yes." Mary Ellen's gray eyes glittered and her voice rang with excitement and gratitude. "Thank you. I won't let you down."

Valerie smiled. "I know you won't."

The phone rang as Valerie pulled on her lab coat.

"I'll answer it," Mary Ellen said, reaching for the receiver. "Right here, Mrs. Crawford." She hunched her shoulders and smiled, then handed Valerie the phone.

"Valerie dear, what did Mr. Price say?"

"He hasn't made a decision, but it shouldn't be long."

"That's not very reassuring. Didn't you explain to him how historically important the area is to the community, the state even?"

"Yes, I did."

"But he still didn't give you any idea when he might make a decision? Or what that decision might be?"

"No."

"Maybe Jackson can shed some light on the subject."

"It's possible."

"If I find out anything more, I'll give you a call."

"Please do." Valerie hung up the phone and let out a soul-weary breath.

"Mrs. Crawford is like a dog with a bone; she won't stop gnawing until she's satisfied her hunger," Mary Ellen said sagely.

"It's what she'll do if she doesn't that I wonder about," Valerie laughed.

Valerie got her answer a several days later when she received an invitation to a get-acquainted party Mrs. Crawford was throwing for Alexander Price. Valerie wondered how long Alex was going to stretch this thing out. She'd heard from Jake that people were out at both properties surveying the areas. Price Industries couldn't build a plant on them both. So what was really going on?

When Valerie walked into the lab, Mary Ellen was talking on the phone.

"Oh, *yes,* I'd love to go to the party with you, Justin. We'll talk when I see you later this evening. Listen, I've got to go."

"You got your invitation, I take it," Valerie said wryly.

"Everyone in town who is anybody did. You know how Mrs. Crawford is. She loves giving parties. Any excuse will suffice."

"I know, but I think this time she's hoping to entice the head of Price Industries into committing himself, whether he's ready to or not."

"You're probably right. I'm going with Justin. You going with Howard Atkins?"

"He hasn't asked me."

"Oh, he will. He's crazy about you. Everyone in town knows that."

Valerie didn't dispute her assumption; she just started on the day's project.

"When are you going to let the council know what you've decided?" Justin asked Alex.

"Tonight. This party is the perfect vehicle to set my plan into motion. Valerie will no doubt attend."

"And just what are you planning to do? I'm your assistant and you haven't even told me which property you've decided on."

"You said you didn't want to be involved in any part of my plans for revenge, didn't you?"

"I don't, but, Alex—"

"When your Mary Ellen sees that you're as surprised as everyone else, she'll have no reason to blame you."

"Blame me for what?"

"Just wait and see, Justin."

He gave Alex a frustrated look before leaving the suite to go pick up Mary Ellen.

Alex walked into his bedroom, retrieved one of the two blueprint cylinders leaning against the wall and smiled, patting it before putting it back down and leaving the suite.

Valerie wanted nothing better than to not have to go to the party, but she knew nothing short of death would be remotely acceptable. Mrs. Eugenia Crawford would never let her hear the end of it if she didn't come. And as a prominent member of the preservation committee it was her duty to attend.

She couldn't use Tyler as an excuse since he was spending the night at Danny Cranson's house. Although the Cransons were going to the party, too, they had twin teenage daughters to babysit the boys.

"Howard should be here any minute to pick us up. You about ready to go?" Kelly asked as she stood in the doorway of Valerie's bedroom. "As ready as I'll ever be."

"Don't sound so down. Chances are nothing out of the ordinary will happen this evening."

"Come on, Aunt Kelly. You don't believe that anymore than I do. Tyler's father is going to be at this party. He's the guest of honor. And you call that nothing?"

"Something happened when you went to see him the other day, didn't it?"

"You're wrong. Nothing happened. I just don't want to be anywhere near Alex for any reason."

"I think you protest too much. There's more to this party than welcoming Alexander Price to town. Eugenia Crawford might have her own reason, but what about his for agreeing? Has he brought up the past?" "Yes, in a way. Why do you ask?" "If he was as hurt by what happened as you seem to think, he might use this party as a way of exacting his revenge."

When Valerie thought about the scene in Alex's suite, it sent a quiver of fear up her spine. If revenge was what he was after, she was sure he had more of the same in store for her. This party would only be the beginning. Just simply settling for humiliating her the way he had in his suite wouldn't be nearly enough.

After all this time he should have moved on with his life and forgotten about her. But if what her aunt believed was true and he hadn't... She hadn't wanted to believe he could be that vengeful because she'd been in denial. Alex was a powerful man and probably angry enough to go after what he wanted without remorse.

Valerie got up from her vanity and put on her dress. She didn't know how she was going to get through the evening, but go to the party she would.

Alex stood by the windows at the Quinneth Falls Entertainment Hall watching Justin dance with Mary Ellen. Judging from the look in his assistant's eyes, he was most definitely smitten. It was as though he and Mary Ellen were the only ones there.

While waiting for Valerie to show up, Alex took in the ambience of the room. It had been tastefully decorated, using a summer theme. He saw a beverage fountain resembling the falls. Flower garland streamers made from flowers he'd seen growing in profusion near the Indian Woods property were cleverly laced about the huge room. He had to hand it to his hostess; she didn't miss a trick.

Finally Valerie and the man Alex had seen her with at the administration building and an older woman arrived. Noting the resemblance between the two women, he figured that the other woman was Valerie's aunt. He recalled how Valerie used to talk about her as though she were some kind of saint. He wondered if she had been a party to Valerie's scheme to bilk money from his father.

"Mr. Price, here you are!" Eugenia Crawford exclaimed, squeezing the arm of the man beside her. "You've met my husband, Jackson. He's head of the council."

"Yes, I have. Jackson." Alex extended his hand. "You didn't bring your wife?" Eugenia asked. "I'm not married, Mrs. Crawford." "Oh, you're not." She smiled as if to say not for long. "Please, call me Eugenia."

"Have you, ah, made a decision about which of the two properties you're going to build the plant on?" Jackson anxiously asked Alex.

"Yes, I have. I'll be making the announcement later this evening. If you'll both please excuse me, I see someone I must talk to."

Valerie was alone, but as he started to walk over to her, but the man she'd arrived with returned carrying two cups of punch. Damn, he growled. His frown soon changed into a smile when moments later an elderly woman gained the man's attention and practically dragged him away.

"You're looking lovely tonight, Val," Alex said in an appreciative tone of voice. And she was, too, he had to admit as his eyes roved her slim figure dressed in an aqua summer dress. The color complemented her milk chocolate skin and coal black hair. And those dark, dark eyes.

Valerie's hand shook and she barely missed spilling punch down the front of her dress. "Ah, thank you."

"I've thought about what you said concerning the lake property and I've decided not to build the plant there."

Valerie's eyes widened and she smiled. "You have? That's wonderful. I, Mrs. Crawford and the rest of the committee can't thank you enough. Tell me, what are you going to do with the lake property now that you've made your decision?"

The corners of Alex's lips turned up. "I've decided to transform it into a residential estate,"

Her smile faded. "A residential estate? I don't understand."

"I intend to make my home here in Quinneth Falls."

"What?"

"I like this part of Michigan. The lake property is exactly what I've been looking for. Quinneth Falls seems the perfect place to raise a family. You must have thought so too or you wouldn't have come back here to live and start a family after—well, after you left Detroit." "But you can't…"

"Oh, but I can, and I fully intend to." "Mr. Price—Alex, I have several friends I'd like you to meet," trilled Eugenia Crawford. She wrapped her arm around Alex's, pulling him in the direction where two ladies stood.

Valerie was in shock. Oh, God, tell me it's not true! Alex can't be planning to move to Quinneth Falls!

"I'm sorry Mama broke into our conversation, Valerie," Howard apologized as he walked up. He frowned. "What's the matter?"

"N—nothing." She headed for one of the window seat benches and sank down on it. Howard sat down beside her.

"I saw you talking to Alexander Price just now. What did he say to upset you?"

"He's going to make his home in Quinneth Falls. It's the reason he bought both properties."

"What's so bad about that? At least he's not going to ruin the area if he intends to make it his place of residence. I wonder what made him decide to settle here. Is he married? If not, then maybe he's engaged."

Valerie hadn't considered that possibility until Alex mentioned raising a family. She glanced across the room and saw Alex smiling and talking with several ladies Eugenia had introduced him to. If he wasn't married or engaged, Eugenia Crawford would see that he was very soon. Or at least that he didn't become bored for lack of female company.

"He said it was the perfect place to raise a family, so if he isn't married, or engaged, he may already have someone in mind."

Howard's eyes narrowed. "You lived in Detroit, didn't you? The way you acted when you saw him at the administration building... Were you and he involved? Is that why the idea of his settling here has you so freaked?" Valerie looked away. "I guess I have my answer. You still hung up on the guy?

"No. What happened between us was over a long time ago. I married George and got on with my life."

"If that's true then why—"

"Let's drop it, okay? Here comes Aunt Kelly."

"Do you mind if I steal this handsome young man and dance with him?"

"No, of course not." Valerie forced a smile to her lips and watched as her aunt and Howard glided out on the dance floor. She tensed when she saw Alex striding toward her.

"From the look your lover just gave me, he's found out what we once meant to each other. It must have come as quite a shock. Why hadn't you told him before this?"

She ignored the dig and answered, "Because you're a part of my past, Alex," she said simply.

"The past has a way of echoing to the present."

"What do you really want here in Quinneth Falls?"

"Why to make it my home," he said, taking her hand, urging her out on the dance floor.

"I don't want to dance with you," she hissed, trying to pull her hand out of his grasp.

"We don't always get what we want all the time. Eight years ago I wanted you. I had a ring made for you. I was going to ask you to be my wife, but that was never a part of your scam, was it?"

"Alex, I—"

"Your Mrs. Crawford is watching, so smile, sweetheart." He angled his head in her direction.

Valerie glanced where he indicated and seeing that he was right, she pasted a smile on her face.

"What was he like? Your husband, I mean."

"Why would you want to know that?"

"I'm curious to know what he had that I obviously lacked."

"We shouldn't be talking about this. What happened between us is over."

"Is it? I wonder."

"What do you mean?" A glitch of fear lurched through her. Did he—could he know about Tyler?

Alex's enigmatic smile widened. "The music has stopped." He then led Valerie over to the windows.

She put her hand on his arm. "Alex, what did you mean?" she persisted.

"Since I've decided to make Quinneth Falls my home, we'll have plenty of time to talk. If you'll excuse me…"

Valerie stood dry mouthed and thoughtful as Alex made his way over to Clive Turner, a prominent member of the city planning commission. A few minutes later he announced his intentions for the plant and the town's excited citizenry immediately surrounded him. Valerie knew the people of Quinneth Falls needed the business and couldn't begrudge them that. But what about Tyler? Having Alex move here might very well destroy life as she knew it.

CHAPTER NINE

A week later found Valerie still trying to figure out why Alex had made such a point of telling her about his personal plans for the lake property. He had a reason, but what was it exactly? Damn him for being so mysterious. Maybe his aim was to punish her by keeping her off balance and wondering. The thought of seeing him with a wife or fiancée disturbed her.

Why should it if he doesn't mean anything to you anymore?
He doesn't.

He was your first love and you never wanted to part from him. And you had his child.

She smiled. Yes, she did. Evidently nothing had changed her feelings for Alex, not time nor the intervention of Michael Price. Only she and God knew how hard the man had tried. The thought of Michael Price made her insides churn in fear and revulsion. She wondered if he knew about Alex's plans to make Quinneth Falls his home? Probably not or she'd have had a call or a visit from him. It wasn't too late; that could still happen.

Valerie left Resource Chemical with the intention of heading straight home, but she made a detour by the falls. As she drove up to the lake property Alex had bought, she saw the men clearing away ground. Alex wasn't wasting any time constructing his house. Jake Spriewell's son Ralph saw her and waved, then walked over to her car.

"Mrs. Bishop, how have you been?"

"I'm doing good, Ralph." She greeted him with a smile as she got out of the car.

"Me and my brother was hired to clear away the land and help build Mr. Price's house. He's one hell of a nice fellow, that Mr. Price. He sure is anxious to finish the house. House? Hell, it's more like a mansion from what I've seen of the blueprints. He showed them to me personally," Ralph said, pride shining in his eyes because Alex had singled him out for such an honor. "Here he comes now."

The muscles in Valerie's stomach jerked as she saw Alex striding toward her with a roll of blueprints under his arm. It had been a long time since she'd seen him in jeans and a T-shirt. Back then he'd been leaner, but now he had heavier, well-defined muscles. She could tell that he worked out.

Alex said to Valerie, "I see you're curious about the house I plan to build." He smiled at Ralph. "You want to go help Stan?"

"Sure thing, Mr. Price." And he walked away.

Still smiling, Alex inched closer to Valerie. "Want to take a look at the plans?" Not waiting for her to answer, he unrolled the blueprints.

Fresh air, the sun's heat and the closeness of this man assailed Valerie's senses and set her heart racing as he pointed out where the living room was going to be. She swallowed hard because they had once discussed moving into a house with a similar set-up. Oh God, why was he showing this to her now? Why was he making her remember? Why was he torturing her so?

He frowned innocently. "Don't you like my house? I remember a time when you were oh so eager to move into one with me."

"Yes, well," she cleared her throat, "I need to be getting home."

"Why the rush? You just got here. You were curious to know if my tastes had changed, weren't you? Well, they have and they haven't. My taste as far as women are concerned certainly has." He looked pointedly at Valerie.

Like the sharp point of an arrow, his words pierced her heart. When he said *women* and gave her that distasteful look, she knew he was referring to her.

Alex continued. "My desire for a house and to raise a family remains intact, though. You see, I'm building this house for my fiancée."

Valerie gulped. "Congratulations, then. I'm, *ah,* happy for you. Look, I really do have to go home."

"That's right; you have a son. What's his name?"

She didn't want to tell him, but seeing no way out of it, she reluctantly answered. "Tyler."

"Tyler," he said testing the name. "Tyler Bishop."

Alex could tell by her expression that Valerie didn't want to discuss her son with him, but he wasn't letting her off the hook so easily. "Tyler would have been ours if you'd been the kind of woman—why did you do it, Valerie? Why did you walk away from me?"

"My reasons no longer matter. We've both moved on and really shouldn't be talking about the past. You have your life and I have mine."

"And never the twain shall meet. Is that what you think? Well, they will meet and often, Val, because I'll be right here in Quinneth Falls to insure that they do." He rolled up the blueprints.

"I'll be around and I'll learn all there is to know about you, your son and your life. Knowing that, I wonder how you're going to handle it," he said and walked away.

Valerie's legs wobbled as she made her way back to her car. Her aunt was right. Alex evidently did have long range plans for revenge. Nothing she could think of would come close to derailing those plans or the man. Oh, God, what was she going to do?

"We've been here going on a month, Alex. How is Althea taking your prolonged absence?" Justin asked as they pored over the papers for the plant in their new accomodations. For two weeks now they'd been in the building Price Industries had leased. The back half had been converted into two suites for their personal use.

"Althea understands that business comes first."

"But it isn't all about business, is it? When are you going to clue her in on your other plans?"

"I don't know why you're so bothered about my private life, Justin. You're off the hook." He arched a curious brow. "How are things progressing with Mary Ellen Spencer?"

Justin's frown eased into a smile. "Great. She's really something special."

Envy streaked through Alex. He'd once felt that way about Valerie. He'd loved her above all else. Her betrayal had ripped his heart to shreds. She'd damaged a part of him that would never heal. Or maybe it would when he was through exacting his revenge.

"Getting back to the subject of Althea—" Justin plunged on.

"Give it a rest, Justin."

"She's a nice woman and doesn't deserve to be used."

"I'm not using her," Alex answered, indignant.

"Aren't you? Admit it, Alex, you're so hung up on getting revenge against Valerie Bishop you can't think straight."

"I'm not, as you say, 'hung up on the woman,'" he said in a defensive tone. "I just want to make her pay for what she did to me."

"Revenge can be a double-edged sword."

"Deliver me from another one of your platitudes. I'll handle my life my way, so back off, Justin."

"All right, I will. Just remember that I cared enough to offer advice."

Alex hated being at odds with Justin, but the younger man didn't understand the pain or damage Valerie's betrayal had caused.

He doesn't have to understand to know what your desire for revenge is doing to you.

"Look, Justin, I know you're only trying to be a friend."

"But you want me to butt out. Right? You got it. I won't say another word."

Alex laughed. "Yeah, right. Until the next episode. By next week you'll be back to gnawing on the same bone."

Justin smiled but didn't say anything else on the subject.

The phone rang and Alex picked it up.

"Alexander? Why haven't you come back to Detroit?" Michael Price demanded.

"I've been kind of busy, Dad."

"Busy doing what? You've got Justin and a whole slew of lawyers and construction engineers at your disposal to do all the mundane work. I don't see why you have to physically be there to supervise this project. Let the people do what they're paid to do and come back to Detroit where you belong."

"Dad, this is my project and I intend to see it through to the end. Justin and the others have their hands full with what I've assigned them to do."

"It's the Bishop woman, isn't it? She's the real reason you're spending all your time in that little hick town."

"I'm not involved with her. Anything else I plan to do is my business."

"What about Althea? Doesn't she deserve some of your time and attention? She is, after all, your fiancée."

"I haven't forgotten that, Dad."

"It looks like you have to me. I took her out to dinner the other day. She didn't say anything, but I know your neglect is hurting her."

Alex sighed. "All right, Dad. I'll be home this weekend. Is there anything else?"

"No."

"I'll see you then." He hung up the phone.

"It seems I'm not the only one concerned about your fiancée."

"Don't go there, Justin."

"Okay." Justin smiled, shrugging his shoulders.

Valerie sat in an easy chair in her living room reading a science journal. She looked up from the magazine and glanced at her son sprawled on the floor playing with his Playstation game. A mental image of Alex slipped into her head. She imagined that Tyler looked very much like his father must have at that age. Her heart ached with a longing she'd thought was dead and buried until Alex came to town.

Alex was building a house for the woman he now loved. That fact hurt more than she ever thought it could. She was sure Alex sensed her feelings and was enjoying her misery. His revenge would be complete the day he and his fiancee moved into their new house. It would be an in-your-face victory dance. She now realized why he'd made such a point of going into detail about his plans. Well, it had accomplished his purpose. It was one thing for him to seek revenge against her, but what about Tyler? He could get hurt in the fallout. If Alex found out he had a son, what would happen then?

Kelly came into the living room with a bowl of popcorn and handed it down to Tyler.

"Thanks, Aunt Kelly, I was gettin' kinda hungry."

"How could you be after all the food you ate at dinner, Tyler?" his mother exclaimed incredulously.

Kelly laughed. "He's a growing boy. As I recall, when you were his age, you had an appetite that rivals your son's."

She was right, Valerie thought. Alex used to tease her about having such a big appetite, saying she had a hole in the bottom of her stomach that went somewhere other than the rest of her body. Nothing she ate ever ended up where it was supposed to go and, because of that, she had been rail thin. That all changed after she had Tyler.

Kelly came over to the chair and sat on the arm. "You never did tell me what made you so late getting home. But then you didn't need to, I can guess."

"Ever since Alex informed me he was going to build a house near the lake, I wanted to see it for myself."

"Wanted to? Or couldn't help yourself?"

Valerie glanced down at her son. And even though he seemed totally into playing his game, she felt uneasy discussing it around him.

"I don't really want to talk about this right now, Aunt Kelly."

"When will you want to? You're going to have to face up to your feelings sometime."

Valerie knew her aunt was right, but she didn't want to face them. But it seemed it wasn't up to her because Alex intended to make her face them whether she was ready to or not.

Valerie checked through her mail the following morning, expecting to see a check from the government for the work she'd done for them, but it wasn't there. She wondered what the hold up was. It was nearing the deadline for her loan payment. The bank had been patient so far, but she didn't want to press her luck. Maybe the check would come in the next day or so. But if it didn't, she would have to make inquiries, she thought as she walked into the kitchen.

"Are you ready to talk about things now?" Kelly asked as she entered the kitchen behind her niece.

Valerie nodded. The bus had come a half an hour ago to pick Tyler up and take him to camp.

"There's really nothing to talk about."

"You can't keep Alexander Price from seeing Tyler forever, Valerie. Maybe it would be best if you just went to him and told him the truth."

"I can't do that!"

"I don't see where you have much choice. He's bound to see the boy sooner or later. It's an established fact that he's moving to Quinneth Falls."

Valerie saw the wisdom in what her aunt said, but she couldn't quite bring herself to do as she suggested, at least not yet.

When will you be able to, girl?

That was the million dollar question and she knew she wouldn't be afforded the time she needed to come up with a satisfactory answer. Her son had to be protected, but how was she supposed to do that?

CHAPTER TEN

Detroit

Alex observed the house as it came into view when he drove through the gates of the Price estate. His stomach started churning at the thought of a confrontation with his father. He definitely wasn't looking forward to it. He knew the kind of reception he was likely to receive when he walked in. And he wasn't disappointed.

"It's about time you came home and took care of your responsibilities," Michael scolded his son.

"Dad, I'm tired from the drive. Don't start with me, okay?"

"Someone has to. The way you've been treating Althea is inexcusable."

Alex sighed, gritting his teeth and silently repeating "God give me strength" several times. "I haven't been treating her any way, Dad. Althea understands that business comes first."

"Business yes, but not—"

"Don't say it. I already know your opinion on the subject of Valerie Bishop and the plant I'm building in Quinneth Falls."

"And you don't give a damn, do you?"

Alex walked over to the bar and poured himself a drink. "You want one?"

"No, I want to—"

"I know what you want, and it'll have to wait. When I finish this I'm going up to my room to take a bath and then go to bed."

"This is important, Alexander."

Alex didn't finish his drink. He put it down on the coffee table and left the room, heading for the stairs.

"You can't just walk away from this."

"Good night, Dad. I'll talk to you in the morning."

Michael sank down heavily on the couch. His son was getting involved with the one person he shouldn't: Valerie Baker-Bishop. He rose and walked over to the bar. He needed that drink after all.

Over the years he'd tried to forget about what he'd done. He'd been so sure he was right. What he'd done to Alexander was cruel, but sometimes a parent had to be cruel to be kind. In his opinion Valerie Baker hadn't been, and still wasn't, good enough for his son.

Michael's ex-wife Irene had shown him how deceitful women could be. If only Alexander could find a woman like his mother. Allege had been the epitome of woman-hood. His lips eased into a fond smile. She had been beautiful inside and out. She'd had a funny sense of humor. And above all she loved him, Michael Price, for himself, not for what he could give her.

Michael's smile faded into a frown. He had thought he'd found another special woman in Irene, but he'd been wrong. Oh, how wrong he'd been.

He'd been afraid that if Valerie Baker married his son, she'd destroy him. He knew that all women weren't like Irene. His late wife and his sister-in-law, Joyce, were the exceptions. But when it came to his only son, Michael hadn't been willing to take any chances with his future. Althea Johnson was a safe choice. Michael had known her all her life. She and Alexander had grown up together. He was sure she'd be perfect for him.

Michael had tried everything he could to keep Valerie Baker away from Alexander. Some of the things he had done he wasn't proud of. Right now he was at a loss as to what to do since Alexander had completed the negotiations for the new plant and would be around her all the time. All he knew to do was to try again to convince Alexander of the wisdom of letting Justin take over for him. As to whether he would succeed…

Alexander was all he had left. He knew he hadn't always shown him how much he loved him but he had tried to protect him, keep him from suffering as he had at the hands of a devious woman.

You didn't actually know for sure Valerie Baker was really that kind of woman, did you?

When he'd had the investigation done and found out what her aunt had done, he had assumed that… This aunt of hers had raised Valerie and she was no doubt as bad as Irene. Or worse. The man Kelly Harper had been involved with had been married. What kind of example could the woman have possibly been for her niece? No, he hadn't been willing to risk it. He still wasn't. He would somehow convince his son to leave things in Justin's capable hands and come back to Detroit where he belonged.

When Alex came down to breakfast, he found his father sitting at the table. He had expected him to be primed and ready to pick up the conversation where it left off the night before, but for some reason he seemed strangely subdued. Well, no matter, Alex knew he couldn't put it off; he would have to tell his father about his latest plan before someone else did.

"I have something to tell you and you're not going to like it."

"Tell me you're not involved with—"

"I told you the last time we talked that I wasn't involved with Valerie."

"Then what is it?"

"I've found the perfect place to build my future home."

"Where?" Michael's eyes widened with interest. "You've decided to buy the Delefield property. I'm glad you've…

"I didn't buy the Delefield property"

"Then where? Surely you didn't choose one in Quinneth Falls! Have you completely lost your mind, Alexander?"

"I've already bought the property and had plans drawn up for the house and have even broken ground. As for my reasons, they are my own business. Look at it this way. After Althea and I are married I'll be around to oversee the new branch of Price Industries."

"What about the head office here?"

"You can take a more active interest in the business. Or let Uncle Steve or one of my cousins help you. I always thought you retired way too early. You're only fifty-seven, hardly old enough to have been retired for three years. Who knows? You might even remarry one day."

"I seriously doubt that," Michael said bitterly.

"All women aren't like Irene, Dad."

"I don't want to discuss it. My private life is not the issue; Valerie Bishop is. You're doing this to be near her."

"Actually you're right about that, but not for the reason you think."

"What other reason can you have?"

"Did you think I wouldn't make her pay for what she did to me?"

"I don't think you should go ahead with this. She's the past, and a life with Althea is your future. Forget about Valerie Bishop and any scheme you have for exacting revenge."

Alex was stunned my his father's attitude. Of all people, he would have thought he'd empathize with him.

"I don't understand you, Dad. I've seen you deal with your enemies and exact unholy revenge. I can't believe you wouldn't want me to do the same."

"What you have in mind has nothing to do with business. Don't you see that? If you do this you're going to end up losing the one person you don't want to lose."

"I'm not going to lose Althea."

"If you don't stop this nonsense right now you just might. I guarantee it. How do you think she's going to feel once she finds out why you're building a house in Quinneth Falls, where your ex-lover just happens to live? How are you going to explain that to her?"

"Dad, Althea doesn't ever have to know about that. Valerie is certainly not going to tell her."

"How do you know she won't?"

"Because she'll have enough problems of her own. If you'd seen her you'd know that she doesn't want to have anything to do with me."

"Who are you trying to fool with this? Certainly not me. You still want her, don't you? You've never really gotten her out of your system. Go ahead and sleep with her, but don't make the mistake of moving to Quinneth Falls."

"My mind is made up. I'm moving on with the building of my house. It'll be finished in a few months. I've got men working around the clock to hasten its completion."

"I'll tell you right now Althea won't move to that little nothing town, away from her family, friends and her way of life."

"I think you're wrong, but time will tell. I was going to call her later and take her out to dinner and explain."

"It so happens she's visiting friends at Martha's Vineyard this weekend. You should have called her before you came home."

"Once you knew I was coming to Detroit, I was sure you would do the honors." For some reason Alex felt relieved to hear that he wouldn't have to see Althea. What his father and Justin said about her bothered his conscience. He knew Althea was a social butterfly through and through. Moving to a town like Quinneth Falls would be a drastic change for her. He wasn't sure she'd be willing to live there with him. Was he being selfish and unfair to expect it of her?

If you love her, then maybe. But do you really love her?

He was fond of her. They had a lot in common. They were comfortable together.

But you don't feel for Althea a tenth of the passion you felt for Valerie Bishop. Is it fair to involve her in your scheme for revenge? You could end up seriously hurting her.

"What are you going to do about Althea?" Michael asked, interrupting his reverie.

"I'm going back to Quinneth Falls Sunday."

"Burying your head in the sand won't solve your problem."

"I don't have a problem."

"Not yet, but mark my words you're headed for trouble if you move *to* that town. Sell the property and leave Justin to run the new plant and come back to Detroit where you belong."

"I can't do that. I'll deal with Althea when the time comes."

"You're a fool, Alexander."

Maybe his father was right. In any event, he had some serious soul-searching to do. He recalled Justin saying that revenge could be a double-edged sword.

Michael glanced out the window as his son drove away, then turned, and walked over to the picture on the wall and looked into his first wife's beautiful face. He had failed. First, he'd failed to convince his son not to build the plant in Quinneth Falls. And just a few minutes ago he'd failed to convince him to put Justin in charge and not to move to Quinneth Falls.

"Arlene, I promised you that I'd take care of our son. I thought I had accomplished it by getting Valerie Baker out of the picture. But her hold on him is evidently stronger than I ever realized it could be. After all these years Alexander is still drawn to her like a moth to a flame. He's said that he wants revenge. Is that really all he wants?"

What was it about Valerie Baker that fascinated his son so? Michael wondered if he could have been wrong about her. Could she have genuinely been in love with Alexander as she had claimed? No, he had been right to do what he did.

Are you sure about that? Would Alexander agree if he knew the lengths loud gone to to get Valerie Baker out of his life? Michael frowned. What if he *had* been wrong about her? He wasn't sure his son would ever forgive him if that proved to be true.

As Valerie and her aunt sat eating lunch at Lucy's restaurant, the Crawfords walked in. Kelly put down her fork in seeming agitation. Valerie had noticed that she always seemed to get that way whenever the Crawfords were around. It had crossed her mind that Jackson might have been the leading citizen her aunt had been involved with all those years ago. But surely not Jackson Crawford. Still, she recalled how her aunt managed to never be where Jackson Crawford and Eugenia Crawford were if she could help it.

"What's wrong, Aunt Kelly? Are you feeling all right? You look a little peaked."

"I find that I'm not as hungry as I thought. Tyler will be home in another hour. I had better be going." She wiped her mouth with a napkin and reached inside her purse for her credit card.

"It's my treat. You have plenty of time. Why don't you stay and—"

"No!" Kelly stood up abruptly, nearly knocking over the tea that remained in her cup. "I'll see you when you get home."

Valerie watched as her aunt hurried out to her car parked out front.

Eugenia Crawford came over to the table. "Is Kelly all right? Jackson and I were concerned. She didn't seem like she was feeling well."

"She's fine. Just in a hurry to get home before Tyler does."

Jackson joined them. Valerie observed the look of concern as he watched Kelly's car disappear.

"That nice Alexander Price is coming this way," Eugenia trilled.

Valerie followed her line of vision and caught a glimpse of Alex just before he entered the restaurant. When he saw her, he headed for her table. Valerie's pulse started racing.

"Valerie, Jackson, Eugenia." Alex smiled at Valerie. "It's nice seeing you again. I was hoping to get a chance to talk with you. Since you pleaded your committee's case so eloquently, I wanted to discuss ideas for improving the lake area. Now that I've bought the property I need some advice on how to properly care for it. I found out from your assistant, Mary Ellen Spencer, it's a place that is close to your heart in a personal way."

"You're right, Alex," Eugenia supplied. "It is. I could have told you that."

"I'm not an expert on landscaping," Valerie answered. "Terence Sanders is an excellent landscaper. He'll probably be of more help to you."

"I don't think so. You see I'm looking for a more personalized touch, a feminine touch. Since you're a woman and you care, you're more likely to know what another woman likes. When I bring my fiancée here, you'll be able to help and offer advice."

Emotion suddenly clogged Valerie's throat. She couldn't be around the woman he loved, or him. She wanted to kick Alex in the shin for tormenting her like this. He had to have his pound of flesh. Damn him.

"I really won't have any time. You see, I'm working on a new state project. Terence's wife is also a landscaper. You might try approaching her."

"Valerie is right," Jackson answered. "In fact I have one of their cards." He took out his wallet and searched through it and drew out a Sanders Landscaping business card and handed it to Alex.

Valerie saw the momentary flash of anger Alex directed her way before he covered it with a charming smile. She could tell he was seething at being thwarted, and a feeling of sheer satisfaction pulsed through her.

"When your fiancée arrives, I'll have to throw you both a special dinner party," Eugenia interjected into the lull of the conversation.

"You don't have to go to all that trouble, Eugenia," Alex said quickly.

"Nonsense. It would be my pleasure. You'll be sure to let me know the moment she arrives, won't you?"

The only polite thing he could do was agree.

"Jackson and I must be going. It was so nice seeing you again, Alex, and you too, Valerie," Eugenia said as she and her husband left the restaurant.

Valerie took out her credit card and was about to signal the waitress when Alex put a hand over hers and eased it down on the table. His touch scorched her skin and she drew her hand away.

"That attraction is still alive and well, isn't it, Val?" He dropped his voice to a husky timber.

"I don't know what you're talking about. I really have to get back to work."

"Not just yet."

"You have a fiancée and plenty of work to do, I'm sure.

"I'll ask you again. Why did you walk out on me, Val? You never did answer me."

"Because I obviously don't want to talk about it."

"Don't you think you owe me a proper explanation?"

"Like I said before, whatever my reasons, it doesn't matter anymore."

"It damn well matters to me." Could there have been another explanation besides the money? Maybe if he could get her to tell him what it was, he could find it in his heart to understand and forgive her.

"I knew it wasn't going to work out between us, and I hate good-byes."

Rage boiled inside Alex. He knew the truth. So why did he keep on asking? What did he hope to wring from her? A confession?

"Is that all you have to say?" he said tightly.

"What do you want me to say, Alex? It's been over for years."

"It's not over, Val, I promise you. In the next few months you're going to come to realize it."

"Leave Quinneth Falls now before you destroy both our lives."

"You destroyed mine eight years ago. I intend to return the favor." He stood and, giving her an acid look, stalked out of the restaurant.

Valerie was shaking as she watched him stride out to his silver Durango. Alex was so bitter. She knew he'd been expecting an explanation, but she couldn't give him one, not with the threat from Michael Price hanging over her head. Why did Alex have to come to Quinneth Falls? Why did she still love him as much as she had eight years ago?

The rest of the day was misery for Valerie. She couldn't keep her mind on her work. Things didn't improve when she got home that evening. Her aunt was in a subdued mood. Only Tyler was oblivious to the tension. After he'd gone to bed, she went to her aunt's room.

"Was Jackson Crawford the man you were in love with thirty years ago?"

Kelly didn't pretend to misunderstand. "Yes," she answered simply and signalled Valerie to sit on the end of her bed. "I'd loved him since grammar school. In high school we dated, but it was Eugenia Reed he was interested

in, and married after graduation. Their marriage was shaky
and after only a year Jack turned to me. Our affair lasted a
few brief months. When Eugenia became pregnant, we
broke it off.

"A few weeks later she lost the baby. Eugenia slipped
into a deep depression when she was told she could never
have any more children. It put a strain on their marriage.
Out of loneliness Jack turned to me for comfort and again,
like the lovesick fool I was, I took him into my arms and
my bed. When his wife's health began to improve, he broke
it off. I left Quinneth Falls and moved to Chicago. I was
determined not to let him use me again."

"You told me that my mother was worried about you
and had my father drive her to Chicago to be with you."

"Yes."

"You still care for Jackson Crawford, don't you?"

"I guess a part of me always will."

"That's why you avoid being in his company or his
wife's."

"The only reason I came back to Quinneth Falls was to
bury my sister and her husband and settle their affairs."

"You said my mother went into labor in Chicago."

"Yes. They had an accident as they started back to
Quinneth Falls. Brian died instantly, but Lydia survived
long enough to give birth. I loved you the moment I saw
you and knew I wanted to raise you myself. I knew Chicago
wasn't the place to do it. The house your mother and father
lived in was left to me and Lydia in our parent's will. So it
came to me upon her death. I decided to move back here
and live. It was hard going at first being anywhere near

Jack, but I was determined to conquer my renegade urges for him and make a life for myself," she said, hugging Valerie tight. "And I think I did that."

"Yes, you did. It's a shame you never married, though. You're so pretty, Aunt Kelly. I don't understand why—"

"I had offers, but I never got over Jack. It wouldn't have been fair to marry another man feeling the way I did, so I never did."

"I wish things could have been different for you, Aunt Kelly."

She smiled. "I don't regret keeping you, Valerie. You and George and later Tyler became all the family I needed and wanted. Then, too, I had my sewing business."

As Valerie hugged her aunt, she wondered how long that would last if Michael Price decided to make trouble. She had enough on her mind without that. Her check still hadn't come, and Alex seemed more determined than ever to make her pay for walking out on him. If he continued with it, no telling what would happen next.

CHAPTER ELEVEN

Valerie's check was now over two weeks late. When she called to find out why, she was told by a government clerk that some kind of bureaucratic mix up was responsible and it would probably be another six weeks before she received it. She knew the bank wouldn't be any happier than she was about this latest development. Only because of Howard's influence had they waited this long. Fortunately, she had enough money in the reserve account to pay the utilities and the workers for another two or three more weeks. Past that...

Valerie was pacing back and forth before the bank of windows in her office, wracking her brain trying to figure out how she was going to solve her dilemma, when Howard called.

"You don't sound like yourself." "My check is going to come later than I expected. I mean really later. Like another six weeks later."

"Oh." Howard was silent for a moment. "Maybe I can——"

"No, I won't let you jeopardize your position at the bank. You've already gone to bat for me twice. And believe me, I appreciate everything you've done."

"Valerie, I—"

"No. I'll talk to Mr. Gaines and explain my dilemma and hopefully he'll be understanding and accept my explanation and wait." Lester Gaines was the President of the Quinneth Falls Bank, chairman of the board and also Howard's boss. She and her aunt had known him for years. Maybe that would hold sway with him.

"I wish I could do more." But you can't.

"What'll you do if the bank chooses not to understand?"

"I'll deal with that if and when it happens. Look, I've got to go. Talk to you later."

Valerie cradled the phone, then closed her eyes and massaged her temples. By the time her check finally did come she'd be behind in some of her own personal bills. And on top of that she'd also owe another two months' payments on her loan. It was a good thing the house was paid for. She had money coming from several of her other projects, but this delay would use that up in no time.

Valerie had a throbbing headache by the time she got home that evening and went straight to her room to lie down. She'd just managed to doze off when she heard a knock on her bedroom door.

"Are you all right, Valerie?" Kelly asked.

"I'm fine. Come on in, Aunt Kelly." Valerie raised up to a sitting position on the bed, then eased back against the headboard.

"What's the matter?" Kelly came into the room and sat on the edge of the bed.

"The check I've been expecting from the government is going to be late because of a bureaucratic foul-up. Unfortunately our bills won't wait. The bank has already given me several extensions on the loan."

"How much money do you need? I'd be more than happy to loan it to you."

"Thanks, Aunt Kelly, but even if you cleaned out your savings and cashed in your insurance policies it wouldn't be enough. I appreciate the thought, but I'll have to figure out another way to deal with this."

"But how, Valerie?"

"I don't know, but I'll think of something," she said with a confidence she was far from feeling.

"Mary Ellen is worried about her boss. Evidently, Resource is still having a hard time financially. The big government check they were expecting to pay the loan note and other bills has been delayed," Justin confided in Alex as they ate a late dinner at Lucy's.

"Surely the bank will be understanding and give her an extension."

"According to Mary Ellen, they've already extended her as much time as they can." "What is she going to do?"

"Mary Ellen doesn't know." Justin's brows arched suspiciously. "You don't sound very surprised or sympathetic. Alex, you're not going to—"

"What? What can I possibly do?" "I can think of several things off the top of my head. You wouldn't do anything to make things any harder for the woman, would you?" Alex shrugged. "You can't—"

"I haven't done anything, Justin," Alex said, annoyed. "I know you, man. You're being much too cool about this. What do you plan to do? And don't jerk me around. I want the truth."

"Calm down. I promised you I wouldn't ruin Valerie Bishop's business."

"As I recall, you said you might alter it." "So I did." Alex glanced at his watch. "Look, I have a round of early appointments in the morning. It's time I got back to the office. I have a few last minute things I need to do before I turn in."

"Alex—"

"Leave it, Justin."

"Damn it, Alex."

Alex smiled. "You worry too much." He signaled the waitress to bring the check. "Are you coming?"

Justin snorted irritably and rose from his chair.

Later in his office after finishing the day's paperwork, Alex thought about Valerie Bishop's plight. She had heavy responsibilities weighing down her slender shoulders. It couldn't have been easy taking over the reins of her late husband's company. And despite his feelings of anger and bitterness toward her, Alex had to admire her courage.

What was he saying? She'd used the money she'd extorted from his father to give to another man. If the company went under, it would be a kind of poetic justice. Wouldn't it?

Alex stacked the papers on the desk, rose from his chair and stretched his campy muscles before heading for his suite to shower. Minutes later he climbed into bed and tried to find sleep, but it wouldn't come right away. He punched his pillow. For some reason he couldn't get Valerie off his mind. He no longer cared about her, so why this niggling concern for her welfare?

Valerie tensed as she sat on the edge of her chair in Lester Gaine's office. He gave her a sympathetic look and said, "I'm sorry, but we can't extend you any more time on your loan."

Valerie looked to Howard, who was sitting in the chair next to hers. She was grateful for his presence. "I've spoken to the government and they've assured me that I should receive my check in a few weeks."

"Les, you know she's good for the money," Howard argued.

"You think I like this situation any better than you do? I've known Valerie and her aunt for years, not to mention admiring and respecting George." With a heavy sigh Lester tapped his pencil on the top of the desk. "You can't borrow on the house. The company is mortgaged to the hilt. I don't know what to suggest you do. Two more weeks is all you have left on the last extension we've given you."

Valerie stood up and put out her hand. "Thanks, Lester. Maybe I can come up with something."

Howard escorted Valerie out to her car.

"Damn it, Valerie, I wish I could do more to help you."

"You've done all you can."

"What you need is someone who will take over your loan, then wait until you get the money."

"They would also have to wait for the money for the next month's payment. I don't know anyone who has that kind of money."

"That's not quite true."

Valerie frowned. "Don't even—"

"Considering your past relationship with Alexander Price, he seems a logical choice. I'm sure he would—" "No," she cut him off, "I can't ask him to do that." "You never did tell me what happened between you two."

"And I'm not going to. I can't go to Alex, and that's final."

Valerie flung herself behind the wheel of her car and quickly headed back to Resource Chemical, leaving Howard staring after her.

Minutes later Valerie pulled into her parking place at Resource Chemical. She sat in the car and studied the building and grounds. Her husband had poured his heart and soul into this company. She couldn't let all his hard work go down the drain. But what could she do to save it? Her pride wouldn't allow her to go to Alex for help. After what she'd done to him, he'd probably laugh in her face. She had to think of another way.

Mary Ellen was waiting for Valerie when she walked into the lab.

"We received a check from the state project we did on wildlife water sources."

"I'm glad, we're going to need it. Still no check from the government?"

"I'm afraid not."

Valerie sighed. "The bank isn't going to wait much longer for their money."

"It's all so unfair. The check is in the mail, so to speak."

"Whoever said life was fair? How is the alloy project progressing?"

"I'm pleased with the test results so far. What are you going to do, Valerie?"

"I don't know, but I'll come up with something."

"Justin says his boss would—"

"You've been discussing company business with him!"

"Justin is very sympathetic, Valerie. I'm sure if I asked him he would put in a good word for you with Mr. Price. He seems like such a nice man."

"I don't want you to tell Justin Forest anything else about our situation. Do you understand?"

"But Valerie—"

"I mean it, Mary Ellen." She hated being so sharp with her assistant and felt a pang of guilt when she saw the hurt look in her eyes, but she'd never go crawling to Alex for help.

Valerie sat on the couch in her living room staring out the window, but her mind wasn't taking in the beauty of the moonlight silvering the lawn and hedges. She was deep in a turmoil that tumbled heavily through her mind like a load of wet clothes in a dryer.

"Chicken and dumplings are your favorite and you hardly touched any of it," Kelly said, sitting next to Valerie on the couch.

"I just wasn't hungry, Aunt Kelly."

"I wish I could do something."

"I know you do, but you can't."

"You could—"

"If another person suggests that I go to Alex, I'll scream."

"If you told him the circumstances surely he would—"

Valerie shot to her feet. "Like I told Howard and Mary Ellen and now you, I'm not going to go begging to Alex."

"You can't survive on stubbornness and pride," Kelly said sagely.

Valerie wrapped her arms around her midriff, walked over to the fireplace and then turned to face her aunt. "You don't understand."

"Oh, I think I do. Alexander Price is Tyler's father. If he knew he had a son—"

"But he doesn't and he's not going to find out if I can help it."

"You may not be able to, dear. You're living in a fool's paradise if you think he won't find out sooner or later."

"I walked out on Alex, Aunt Kelly. The man's never forgiven me for that and probably never will. I can't go to him."

"Why exactly did you leave him?"

"I don't want to talk about this."

"I know you said that his father thought you weren't good enough and he forced you to resign from your job, but you never told me exactly what his father held over your head to make you leave Detroit."

"Why are we rehashing the past? It won't change anything right now. I don't want to talk about Michael Price or his son any more."

Kelly rose from the couch and walked over to her niece and squeezed her shoulders. "One of these days I'm going to find out what you've been hiding."

Valerie watched her aunt leave the room and a frisson of fear twisted through her. Suppose her aunt decided to go to Michael Price for the answers. It would be nothing short of a disaster. Michael Price wouldn't be kind. Valerie was sure he'd have no compunction about spilling the entire story to her aunt. In fact, he'd probably relish doing so. No, she couldn't let her aunt find out the truth that way, it would kill her. But what could she say to steer her away from the subject?

If only Alex hadn't come to Quinneth Falls and decided to make it his home. She couldn't, wouldn't go to him. The best thing all around would be for her to avoid Alex. But how was she going to do that now since he intended to stay in Quinneth Falls permanently?

Valerie felt as though she were standing in quicksand and sinking fast. She had to protect the people she loved, but how? Damn you, Michael Price, for causing all this! Damn you to hell!

The next day Howard called Valerie to invite her out to dinner at the Tulip Room.

"You didn't have to do this, Howard," she said as he seated her in the chair across from his.

"I know I didn't. I wanted to."

"It's because you feel sorry for me. Right?"

"No, it isn't. I thought you needed a friend."

Valerie smiled. He was right; she did. "You're the best one I have right now."

"I'd like there to be more, but— Look, Valerie, when I suggested that you go to Alexander Price, I was only trying to help."

"I know that."

"I'm glad you do. My mother has been pressuring me to declare myself where you're concerned. I told her that you didn't feel the same way about me as I did about you. And you don't, do you? There can never be a you and me in a romantic sense. Right? You don't have to say anything, I thought as much. Friends is all we'll ever be, isn't it?"

"Look, Howard, I don't want to hurt—"

"You won't be hurting my feelings. At least not much." He laughed.

Valerie put her hand over his. "Are you sure, my very good friend? I never want to hurt you."

"I know you don't. Look, I can try hooking you up with a loan at another lending organization since you're determined not to go to Alexander Price. I have several friends I can contact that might be able to help."

"Thanks, I'd appreciate it. It won't make you beholden to them, will it? I wouldn't want to ruin your reputation in the banking world."

"You wouldn't be doing that. It would be all business. The only thing is that we don't have much time to do it. I'll get on it first thing in the morning. Frankly, when I mentioned going to Alexander Price, I didn't really think you would go for the idea. You're a proud, independent woman."

"Unfortunately, pride won't pay the bills."

"Then maybe you should reconsider approaching— never mind. I see that's the wrong thing to say. What are you going to order?"

"I'll let you order for both of us."

Alex was having dinner with Cole Turner, a member of the city planning commission, and his wife Louise several tables away from Valerie and Howard's. When he saw Valerie put a hand over Howard Atkins' and smile at the man, he saw red. What exactly did he mean to her? Had he managed to help her get another loan and they were celebrating? Was that look one of gratitude or something more? He would find out what was going on tomorrow. He was in a position to take advantage of Valerie's desperate situation. He wouldn't let her lover, or anyone else, keep him from exacting his revenge.

Alex smiled when he realized that Valerie had seen him. He saluted her with his wine glass. His smile faded when he saw Howard Atkins bend across the table and kiss her on the lips. His hand closed tightly around the stem of the glass, threatening to shatter the delicate crystal. Then Alex regained control and returned his attention to his dinner companions.

How dare he salute her and look at her like that? Valerie bristled.

"You've got it bad, haven't you?" Howard asked, looking from Valerie to Alex, then back to Valerie. "A little jealousy never hurt. I can help the situation." Before she could guess his intention, Howard bent forward and kissed her lingeringly on the lips.

When she could catch her breath after the kiss she said, "I don't need that kind of help. For one thing he's hardly jealous. And for another, I don't intend to have anything to do with him."

"I think you're wrong about the jealousy. He's going to have objections to your game plan."

"I don't have a game plan," she said, irritated by his attitude. "It doesn't matter if he does or not. There can never be anything between us."

"Why not?"

"I don't want to discuss it. It's a personal thing between us. Things were done that can never be reversed or forgiven."

For the next few minutes, they listened to the jazz singer's soulful rendition of "You Give Me Fever." Alex used to definitely give her the fever. She recalled the first time they'd made love. He'd taken her across the Detroit River to Windsor, Canada, to a convention one of Price Industries' affiliates was having at the Cleary Auditorium and Convention Hall to discuss their joint mining venture.

The convention concluded Friday night. Early Saturday afternoon they'd gone to the Art Gallery of Windsor, then on to Hiram Walker Historical Museum. After taking a stroll through Dieppe Gardens and Coventry Gardens, they were so tired by the time they got back to the hotel, they could barely make it to their rooms without collapsing into a deep sleep where they stood. Valerie remembered waking to the feel of warm fingers stroking her lips. She slowly opened her eyes and saw Alex sitting on the side of her bed, leaning over her, smiling.

"How did you get in my room?" she asked, her mind groggy from sleep.

"I have my ways," he grinned, taking her in his arms and raining kisses on her face and neck.

Minutes later he shed his clothes and climbed into bed with her. He gently lifted her gown from her and just looked at her for long moments before caressing her nipples into aching, aroused peaks.

"I'm going to make love to you. If you don't want this, say so right now and I'll put my clothes on and go back to my room."

"I don't want you to go," she said, joying in the feel of his lean naked body against her bare skin.

He slowly aroused her body to passion and when she quivered with desire he initiated her virgin flesh into the ways of love. His possession was the most exciting thing that had ever happened to Valerie. She hadn't known that making love would feel like this. She'd overheard some of the new friends she'd made since moving to Detroit talking about it, but they seemed to think it wasn't a big deal. They must not have had a man like Alex make love to them. She and Alex had spent the morning and afternoon making love. It was like an addiction they couldn't control. And they soon fell into a satiated, but exhausted sleep. Later that evening they woke up and made love again.

"I don't think I'll ever get enough of you, sweet woman," Alex said as they lay resting an hour after making love. He pulled her on top of him, and with a low growl embedded his swollen manhood deep within her. He groaned his pleasure when she began to move over him.

"You're learning fast, my little virgin girl. If you learn any faster you're going to kill me."

She kissed him. "But what a lovely way to die."

"If you're referring to the little death, I've died and come back quite a few times this weekend," he teased.

"Are you ready to experience it one last time before we go back to Detroit?"

Before he could say anything, she moved against him, rocking her body forward and backward over him. His breaths came in choppy pants. He groaned. She felt giant tremors of pleasure lurch through his lower body, then moments later he climaxed and his eyes closed and he went limp. She smiled, watching the pleasurable curve of his lips while he was lost in momentary euphoria. When he opened his eyes again, they were glazed a smoldering amber color from spent passion.

"I meant to take you with me," he said in a breathless gasp.

"You'll be able to do that in the future." She eased off him and lay on her stomach. Alex rose over her and raised her hips.

"I can't wait that long," he said, quickly entering her and moving sensuously against her. His thrusts seemed to go on and on forever and she didn't want them to stop. Then his breathing quickened as did hers. Pleasure tossed them both into a rapturous vortex as they reached for the moon together...

Valerie returned to the present with a jolt. Howard was staring at her. She glanced away, embarrassed, knowing he'd realized when her mind had drifted away to more pleasurable times.

"Are you ready to leave?" he asked.

"Yes, I'm ready." She stood up and straightened her dress and as they made to walk past Alex's table, she stumbled and he reached out to steady her. Valerie smiled and said hi to him and the Turners, then let Howard escort her out to the car.

Alex watched them leave. He'd seen the dreamy look on Valerie's face a few moments before she and Howard got up to leave. She used to pour that particular look all over him after they'd made love. It made him angry to know she could have that look on her face when she was with another man. He had to stop thinking about her in a sexual way or else the memories would devour him.

CHAPTER TWELVE

The grace period the bank had given Valerie had ended a week ago. And still her check hadn't come. Any time now she expected someone from the bank to serve her with foreclosure papers. When it didn't happen she grew anxious. She'd been waiting for Howard to call or come by, but he hadn't. Nor had Jake Spriewell, the town crier, spread any bad news about her around town. She knew she was being too hard on the man; he wasn't malicious, just a busybody.

Another week went by and still nothing had happened, so Valerie made an appointment to see Lester Gaines. He came out of his office to meet her and waved for her to precede him inside.

"How may I help you?"

Valerie stared curiously at him. Why was he acting like this? He knew the reason she was here. "About the loan payment, I—"

Lester put his arm around her shoulders and guided her into his office. "It has all been taken care of, my dear. Mr. Alexander Price now holds the notes on Resource Chemical. He came to us and explained that you two were longtime friends and he was glad to do this for you. I'm sure he was just waiting for the opportunity to inform you about it. He assured me that he'd work out the details with you regarding future payments.

"You see, the bank couldn't afford to keep your account any longer. And since we knew you probably wouldn't be able to come up with the money in the two weeks you had left—well, when Mr. Price approached us we gladly sold the mortgage to him."

Valerie couldn't believe this. Alex now technically owned her company! If he wanted to, he could foreclose and she could do nothing to prevent it. She wondered if Alex could be as ruthless as his father.

"Let me explain. Mr. Price reassured me that you had no need to worry because he intended to work with you, Valerie. I had no idea you knew each other that well. I had assumed you'd only met him since his arrival in Quinneth Falls. Then I remembered that you had lived in Detroit for a time after you finished college. Mr. Price said you worked for his company and that's how you two had met. It's a small world, isn't it?"

"It most certainly is. Thank you for seeing me, Lester."

"It's a pleasure, my dear. With a man like Alexander Price helping you, everything will turn out all right. I guarantee it."

Valerie was in a state of shock when she left Lester's office and walked out into the lobby. This had to be part of Alex's revenge. What would he do next?

"Val." Alex rose from his seat and strode over to her. "Just the person I've been waiting to see. I called you at Resource and your assistant told me where you'd gone." Alex smiled. "Why did you do it?"

"Do what?"

"Don't play games with me, Alex. You know damn well what."

Alex continued to smile. "Have lunch with me and we'll iron out the details of our...ah, business."

"I don't want to talk about anything with you."

"You really have no choice if you want your company to stay afloat. I've taken the liberty of making reservations at the Chandelier for one o'clock. You can leave your car; I'll drive you back to pick it up after we're through."

Valerie wanted to walk away from Alex, but knew she couldn't afford to do that. "All right."

"Don't look as though I've invited you to your own execution. I've saved your company and you from filing bankruptcy. You should be grateful."

"Of all the—you son—"

"I wouldn't advise finishing that sentence." He cupped Valerie's elbow and guided her over to his Durango. "Just get in, Val."

Going to lunch with him was the last thing she wanted to do, but go she would. As he'd said, she had no choice if she wanted to save her company.

She recalled the conversation she'd had with Alex's father when he'd forced her to break it off with Alex and leave Detroit. He'd thought his money could buy anything or anybody. Alex had evidently embraced the same philosophy. A feeling of deep disappointment and guilt knifed into her. Alex hadn't been like that eight years ago. Had what she'd done changed him so much?

As he drove, Alex glanced out the corner of his eye at Valerie's expressive features. He'd thought to see resignation, gratitude even, but judging from the proud tilt of her chin all he'd see was defiance. Didn't she realize that he held her future in his hands? Knowing how much she cared about her company and its employees, he had expected her to come to him for help, but she hadn't. She was stubborn and very proud. And right about now that pride had to be smarting.

None of this was making any sense. In the past she'd been a calculating bitch. But now... Something was wrong with the picture she now presented. Until he knew what that something was, he couldn't proceed with his plans.

Alex pulled into the restaurant parking lot located at the side of the building. As he and Valerie walked around to the front entrance, Alex noticed that the siding of the building was hewn from giant, weathered logs, giving it a warm, old worldly flavor. With its huge, cross-patterned picture windows the restaurant resembled a French Colonial inn/trading post dating back to the late 1700s.

When they entered the restaurant through the wide double doors at the front of the building, the scent of lemon and beeswax floated out to greet them. A hostess, clothed in a colonial costume complete with mobcap, smiled and guided them to the table Alex had reserved.

Valerie had always liked this place, but she hadn't been here since her husband's death. Her eyes misted as she recalled the last time. George had teased her about all work and no play. She'd just completed an eight-week project on soil erosion. Coming here was his treat. He'd been a thoughtful considerate husband. And she felt so guilty about not having loved him the way he deserved. Valerie gazed at Alex. Her lingering obsession with this man was the reason.

"You're so quiet. What are you thinking?" Alex asked.

"You may have a hold on my company, but that doesn't entitle you to know my private thoughts."

"I wonder about that." Alex picked up the menu and glanced through it. "The mackerel in white wine sounds good."

Valerie answered without thinking. "It is, George used to say…" Her voice faded.

Alex's lips tightened. Just then a waitress came to take their order.

A brief feeling of triumph flowed through Valerie when she saw Alex's expression. The subject of her late husband definitely wasn't one he wanted to expound on. After making her own menu selection, she remained silent. When they were halfway through their meal, Alex spoke.

"I had decided to let Justin work with you on Resource's payment arrangements, but I've changed my mind or, should I say, you've changed it for me." "What do you mean?"

"You're treating me like an enemy you want nothing to do with. Why is that when you were the one who ran out on me?"

"I left a note."

"Damn the note. You didn't have the guts to face me. You never loved me. I was just a—forget it. If you're finished, I think we should go to my office and discuss business."

What had he started to say? Valerie wondered. It was as though he were accusing her of something in addition to walking away from him. How could he think she'd never really loved him? They'd shared something rare and precious. She could understand his being angry, even hating her for what she'd done, but she somehow knew it was more than that. Did he suspect—no, he couldn't know about Tyler. If that wasn't it, then what else could have made him this bitter?

Alex's jaw tightened as he watched Valerie get into the car. He had wanted her at his mercy, but he hadn't expected to feel this overwhelming jealousy and desire whenever he looked at her. Valerie's husband was dead, for heaven's sake. What she'd done happened a long time ago. The pain of her betrayal shouldn't feel this raw, yet it did. Maybe Justin was right and he should forget about revenge and go back to Detroit and marry Althea.

Would you be satisfied with that?

The answer was hell no. He wanted her to feel his pain. And until she did he knew he would never be satisfied. He wouldn't leave, damn it. No way.

Valerie smiled when she entered the new Price Industries branch office and saw her friend Gina Amos sitting behind the secretary's desk. Already the injection of Price Industries into the area was making a difference in Quinneth Falls. The company was providing jobs for so many people. It didn't matter how she felt about Alex's being here.

"How long have you been working here?" Valerie asked Gina.

"Two weeks."

Alex cleared his throat. "Any messages?"

"No, sir."

"Mrs. Bishop and I have business to discuss. I don't want to be disturbed. Take messages and hold all calls until we've concluded our business." Alex waved for Valerie to precede him into the office.

Valerie's heart beat a loud tattoo at the thought of being alone with Alex after what had happened the last time in his suite at the Quinneth Falls Inn. When he looked at her and smiled that slightly wicked smile, she knew he remembered and was reveling in the memory.

"Have a seat, Val." He signaled her to take the seat in front of his desk.

Valerie glanced around the room. His office was almost identical to the one in Detroit.

Alex cleared his throat. "Something has to be done to make Resource Chemical a more viable company. I have a few ideas, if you care to listen to them." "If it'll preserve the company." "Anything for the company. Right?" "I have my son's future to consider. Look, if you—if we can't—"

"As a way of paying off the loan, there are several projects the new plant will need scientific documentation and experimentation on. You're familiar with the workings of Price Industries, and since Resource Chemical has handled similar projects, it seems a logical choice. And there will be other assignments as well. That way you won't have to worry about future payments if your checks from other corporations are late."

"Why would you want my help, feeling the way you do about me?"

"It isn't Resource Chemical's fault or your son's. I couldn't in good conscience let a quality company like yours go under because of my personal feelings. Whatever happens between us, I won't let it affect business."

"What do you mean when you say 'whatever happens between us?' What are you planning where I'm concerned?"

Alex smiled. "I'm not at liberty to say. You'll have to wait and see."

"Alex, I—"

Alex rose from his seat and circling the desk, he grasped her arms and pulled her to her feet, then looked into her eyes.

His sherry-brown eyes suddenly changed to a heated honey color and blazed hot with desire. Valerie gulped and tried to wriggle out of his hold, but he wouldn't let her go. His lips descended and instead of punishing, they were gentle. She thought she would melt when he deepened the kiss, and his tongue erotically stroked hers. God, how she'd missed this. She moaned and kissed him back with surprising ardor. When he finally moved his mouth away, she was trembling.

"I was right, your lover has been seriously neglecting you."

Valerie was so caught up in the momentary sensual haze, it took a moment for his words to penetrate. Oh God, how could she have allowed this to happen? She'd promised herself after the last time she'd never be put in this position again.

Alex took her mouth again. And this time the kiss rocked her world. What was wrong with her? She pulled away and touched her kiss-swollen lips.

When she saw Alex's expression, she realized she wasn't the only one in shock.

"I have a suite at the rear of the building. We can—" he rasped hoarsely.

"No, we couldn't. This can never happen again."

"You must be joking. You want me and I damn sure want you."

"It's only leftover lust, nothing more."

"Are you sure that's all it is?"

"Don't do this to me, Alex."

"What am I doing to you, Val?"

"You're making me a relationship wrecker. You're engaged to marry another woman. I can understand your desire for revenge. Maybe I deserve it, but she doesn't deserve to be betrayed in this way."

Alex gritted his teeth, and by sheer force of will, tamped down his desire. Valerie was right. He had to think of Althea.

"I'd better take you back to your car. I'll drop by Resource Chemical in a couple of days to discuss details. I'll bring Justin along and you can have your assistant present."

"Maybe you should let Justin—"

"Don't push it, Val. It's only a temporary reprieve. I'm not through with you. You haven't begun to pay for what you did?"

"Alex, forget about me and revenge. Go back to Detroit."

"I'm sorry, I can't. I have to see this through."

"What through?"

"Are you ready to go?"

Valerie wanted to say more, but she could see that it wouldn't do any good. Alex was determined to make her pay. He had no idea that it wasn't necessary. She'd lived in hell for a long time without his love to sustain her. She'd loved her husband, but she'd loved this man more.

CHAPTER THIRTEEN

After driving Valerie back to pick up her car, Alex sat in his Durango taking deep breaths to regain his composure. It was a while before the ache in his loins subsided, and he could drive back to his office. Valerie had called what happened between them leftover lust. Maybe that was true, but what they once shared transcended mere animal lust. It was the reason he'd had such a hard time accepting that she had taken money from his father as payment for services rendered. But the cancelled check was proof of what she'd done.

It was all in the past. He had Althea and the promise of a good life with her. Until Valerie had brought up Althea's name, he hadn't considered what he was doing to her. Justin had tried to make him see that, but he'd had tunnel vision where Valerie Bishop was concerned. He wanted her to pay for the pain she'd inflicted. He had to laugh. If that was really true, then taking over the loan on her company could help him do it. So why hadn't he moved to take advantage of the situation?

"I saw you and Valerie Bishop leave earlier. What's going on, Alex?" Justin asked as he entered the room.

"I bought the note on her company, and we were discussing means of paying the money owed on the loan, but we got sidetracked."

"Sidetracked?"

"I want you to sit in on the meeting at Resource Chemical."

"You said you wouldn't involve me in your—"

"And I'm not. Mary Ellen Spencer will be present at the meeting. I've decided to let you two handle the arrangements."

"Why? You were so adamant to handle it yourself. What happened to make you change your mind?"

Hell, he didn't even know. He was so damned confused. Nothing having to do with Valerie was going according to plan. When he'd tasted her lips and breathed in her scent, his brain had short-circuited and he had lost control. What had Valerie called it? Leftover lust? He didn't know if that was what he'd call it.

"She's getting to you, isn't she?"

"What do mean?"

"I hate to say I told you so, but you're becoming entangled in your own web."

"You're wrong."

"Am I? I don't think so. Trash your plans for revenge. Sell the lake property and go back to Detroit and Althea, and get on with your life."

"I can't. I've already started construction on the house."

"I'm going to ask Mary Ellen to marry me. Maybe we can work something out about that."

"The problem is I love that piece of land. I want to finish the house and live there."

"You've discussed it with Althea?"

"No, I haven't."

"Don't you think it's about time you did."

"I don't know what I think anymore."

"You're a decent man, Alex. I think you know the right thing to do. I know you were hurt, but it's time to put that all behind you before anyone else suffers."

Alex knew Justin was right, but could he do it? The pain in his heart cried out for retribution and wouldn't be so easily silenced.

Valerie could have sworn that Alex still loved her. But it had to be an illusion, something she wanted to believe. He had a fiancée. And for a moment he seemed to have forgotten that and lost control. She'd called what happened leftover lust, but was that really what it was? Her body still tingled from his arousing kisses and caresses. She'd been close to succumbing to the temptation to make love with him. God help her, she was still in love with this man.

What about Tyler? She'd decided during the drive home to tell Alex he had a son. They both deserved to know about each other. What Alex would think of her afterward she didn't know, but tell him she would. How was she going to tell her son so he would understand? Was he even old enough to understand? He really needed a father during this formative period of his life. The thing that frightened her most was Michael Price's reaction. Telling Alex he had a son didn't necessarily mean that she— that they'd—get back together. That wouldn't be reason enough for Michael to retaliate by hurting her aunt. Would it?

Tyler was riding his scooter when Valerie drove up. When he saw her he jumped off and ran to meet her.

"You're home early," he chirped delightedly.

"I wanted to spend some quality time with my big boy," she said, hugging him tight. She and George had wanted to have children of their own, but they'd found out he was sterile.

"I'm surprised you're not at Danny Cranson's."

"He's spending the week with his grandparents. I wish I had grandparents I could visit."

Valerie gulped. An image of Michael Price floated before her mind's eye. As much as she hated that man, he was her son's grandfather. George's parents and her own were dead. By not telling Alex about his son she'd deprived Tyler of knowing his grandfather. Maybe Michael Price would have wanted to know he had a grandson. But she hadn't been willing to take that chance. Valerie watched her son walk over to his scooter, pick it up and then glide down the street. Tears stung her eyelids. If only things could have been different. She and Alex would be together raising their son. As she started up the walk, she saw her aunt sitting on the porch swing, working on Candace Maynard's wedding dress.

"What happened? You look poleaxed. Is it that bad?" "We won't have to worry about the bank anymore." Kelly put the dress in her sewing basket and met Valerie on the steps. "No? Why not?"

"I think we should go in the house and talk about this," Valerie said in a tired voice.

Once inside Valerie explained all that had happened, leaving out the encounter in Alex's office, of course. "You know what you have to do?" "Yes, I do, Aunt Kelly. I should have done it when Alex first came to town. He's so bitter about the past I don't know how he's going to take it. He'll probably see it as another betrayal."

"Maybe he won't. Maybe he'll understand and—"

"What? Forgive me? I don't think so. He's missed the first seven years of his child's life. We once talked about having children. He wanted a houseful. And it would have all happened if his father hadn't interfered. Oh, Aunt Kelly," Valerie burst into tears.

Kelly took her niece in her arms and held her until she stopped crying.

"I'd like to give Michael Price a piece of my mind."

"Don't, Aunt Kelly. It'll only make things worse."

"I don't see how it can."

Her aunt just didn't know how dangerous it was to cross a man like Michael Price.

Alex observed Valerie at the meeting at Resource Chemical a few days later. She seemed nervous and distracted for some reason. When his eyes locked with hers, he saw an emotion that looked like fear, but before he could determine that, she covered it with a blank stare. Why the look? What did it mean?

"The construction on the plant is progressing on schedule," Justin informed Valerie and Mary Ellen. "It should be operational by the first of the year. Before it does we'll need to start on the intensive environmental studies, the water supply, mineral content and so forth that can affect the safe clean operation of the company. Alex suggested, and I agree with him, that your company should take on the job. With the fees from that you'll be able to meet your payments on Resource Chemical."

"It's very generous of you," Valerie remarked.

"We want to do everything possible to help the town and its residents." Alex smiled. "Now that we've solved your immediate problem, we can let Justin and Mary Ellen work out the details. I've outlined a system that should work."

"Thank you," Valerie said, twisting her ring around. "I have something I need to talk to you about."

Just then Alex's cell phone rang. "Excuse me. Hello. All right. I'll be there in fifteen minutes." Alex looked apologetically at Valerie. "I'm sorry, but something's come up and I'm going to have to leave."

"Maybe I can take care of it for you," Justin offered, "then you and Valerie can—"

"I wish you could, but I have to handle this myself."

Valerie waved her hands. "Don't worry about it. We can talk later."

"I'll call you or come by your house after I've concluded my business."

It had taken all her courage to work up the nerve to talk to Alex. She'd waited this long; she guessed she could wait a while longer to make her revelation. She knew it was cowardly to feel so relieved, but relief was exactly what she felt. Why? It was only putting off the inevitable. Whether it was later that day or tomorrow, she would tell Alex he had a son.

"Althea!" Alex exclaimed in stunned surprise when he opened the door of his office. Gina had said his father was waiting for him, but not that he had someone else with him. Alex could feel his father's manipulative hand in this. When Althea slipped her arms around Alex's waist, his automatically went around her shoulders. And when she looked up at him and offered her lips, he kissed her.

Michael smiled. "We thought to surprise you."

"I'd say you've definitely done that." Alex understood what his father was up to, and he was pissed. But now wasn't the time to vent his spleen. He'd deal with his father in private later.

Althea smiled at Alex. "We came to take you back to Detroit with us. You've been working much too hard the last month and a half. You need some R and R. Although this town is quaint, it probably doesn't have much to recommend it."

"I wouldn't say that. The scenery is beautiful. You should see the falls and the property surrounding it. It's like a paradise."

"If you're into scenery we can fly to Quebec or Montreal. They have spectacular falls. It's beautiful there this time of year. What we need is to get away together."

"I still have a lot of work to do on the new plant before I can take off for something like that."

"Work is exactly what I want to talk to you about. How long are you going to be in this little—here?"

"I don't know."

"Why don't you and Althea go on a holiday? I can take over for you," Michael volunteered.

"You aren't up on what's going on, Dad."

"Justin can clue me in."

"Dad," Alex warned and then turned to Althea. "I'm sorry, but I can't get away right now. Maybe in a few months—"

Alex saw anger flare to life in her dark brown eyes. "What's the real attraction? Have you found a diversion?"

"No. I've decided to make Quinneth Falls our home. In fact I've already started construction on the house."

"What? I can't believe you would do something like this without discussing it with me first."

"I, all, meant to tell you, but—"

"No, you didn't. You assumed I'd go along with anything you wanted. What about what I want?"

"Yes, Alex, what about that?" his father goaded.

Alex gritted his teeth. "Dad, Althea and I need to discuss this alone. I have a suite in this building. It's down the hall. The last door on the right." He tossed him the key.

Alex could tell that his father didn't want to do as he suggested, but finally, shrugging his shoulders, he walked out of the room.

When the door closed, Alex returned his attention to Althea. "I was going to tell you about the house when I came to Detroit a few weeks ago, but you were away visiting friends."

"Don't use that as an excuse. You've had plenty of time to tell me since then. There are such things as telephones. That's not even the point. You'd already decided to do exactly as you please. My input would have been inconsequential. What you planned to do was present me with a *fait accompli.*"

"The spot is really beautiful, Thea. Don't dismiss the idea without looking into it first. I know you'll love the place I've chosen."

Althea looked skeptical. "I'll look, but it doesn't mean I'll agree with you. I don't see myself living in a dull little nothing town like this. Maybe we could use it as a summer place."

How was he going to make her understand that he wanted it to be their primary residence? His father had warned him this would happen, and so had Justin, and again he hadn't listened. If *he* wanted it, it was all that was important. He realized what a selfish bastard he'd been to assume Althea would go along with everything he said. What if she out and out refused? What then?

Alex carefully monitored Althea's reaction as they drove out to the falls. He could see she wasn't all that impressed; in fact she looked bored. How could such beauty bore anyone? he thought. He circled the falls and headed for his property. After parking the Durango, he reached in back for the blueprint cylinder, and then unrolled the plans.

"It's quite impressive, I'll admit. But what I don't understand it why you want to build a house this magnificent in an insignificant town like Quinneth Falls?"

"I fell in love with this place the moment I saw it. I knew it was the perfect spot to live and raise a family."

"But it's so far away from everything," she complained.

"You can always drive to Detroit. And you have a pilot's license. You could fly there whenever you felt the urge to go shopping or be with your friends or relatives."

"You keep saying what *I* can do not what *we* can do together. It takes two to make a marriage work, Alex. That means compromise. If I read the situation right, I'm the one who is expected to do it all."

"I admit I was wrong not to tell you about this before."

"That's something, I guess."

Alex cupped Althea's elbow and took her on a tour of the house, pointing to the living room and study, which were already partitioned off. She didn't say anything for a few minutes, just stood taking it all in.

"If you agree to make this our summer home, I won't object to spending a couple of weeks a year here, but I want Detroit to be our permanent residence. The Delefield property seems a perfect choice."

Alex recognized an ultimatum when he heard one. He thought about what she'd said, but it went against the grain to even consider her conditions. He and Althea had come from the same background and had known each other all their lives, but he knew they would never agree on this issue. Was he willing and did he love her enough to compromise? He had some serious soul searching to do.

"I'll take you back to town."

"All right." She smiled. "I won't push you. I can see you need time to digest what I've said. Darling, I know you'll come to realize that I'm right. Our families, our friends and our way of life are in Detroit."

Michael paced back and forth in his son's suite, waiting for him to come back. Althea had been his last hope of getting Alexander to change his mind. And he gleaned from the conversation that that hope had a raindrop's chance of surviving in a blazing hot desert. That was no chance at all. His son was obsessed with Valerie Baker. And Michael realized it was his fault. By his actions he had unintentionally perpetrated bitterness and desire for revenge in his son. Whatever was between Alexander and Valerie was stronger than he ever imagined it could be. If it was that strong he had to face the possibility that he could have been wrong to separate them.

He hadn't really known what kind of person Valerie Baker had been. He had assumed that the aunt who had raised her was like Irene, and that Valerie had to be just like them: totally lacking in integrity. Had he done her a disservice? Had he let his own bitter experience color his judgement?

No, that couldn't be true.

But what if it was?

A half an hour later Alex dropped his father and Althea off at the Quinneth Falls Inn. He'd noticed that when he'd gone back to get his father, he had seemed preoccupied, not at all like himself, so he had decided to put off his confrontation with him until tomorrow. And instead of returning to his suite, Alex drove back out to the lake property to think about what Althea had said.

A year ago he would have agreed wholeheartedly with her about their lifestyle, but coming to Quinneth Falls and being around these down-to-earth people and becoming enchanted with the lake property had changed all that. It was as though the place had seeped into his blood and raced to his heart, irrevocably ensnaring his soul for all time.

Valerie's being here didn't have anything to do with it, right? Your desire for revenge didn't have anything to do with it either.

He had to admit that both Valerie and revenge had to some extent, but it was more than that. When he looked at the trees and the falls in the near distance, he knew it was love at first sight. No place had ever affected him like this; and he knew no other would again. The smell of the earth, the plants and the comforting sound of the water spilling over the rocks completely exhilarated him. For some reason he felt his roots were here. Why he should feel that way he couldn't explain, but all he knew was that it was how he felt.

CHAPTER FOURTEEN

Valerie sat on the couch in her living room, waiting for the phone to ring, willing it to ring. And when it didn't, she grew frustrated and pulled back the curtain and glanced out the window, expecting to see Alex's Durango drive up. She was anxious to get this all over with. Why didn't he call? Why didn't he come? What was so urgent that Justin couldn't have handled it for him? What could possibly be delaying him?

"I take it you didn't get around to telling Alex the truth?" Kelly asked.

"No, I didn't. He got a phone call and had to leave. He said he'd call or come by, but so far he's done neither." "He will. You never did tell me what happened about Resource."

"Alex is being unbelievably generous."

"You sound surprised. If you fell in love with him, he had to be a good person. Maybe he hasn't changed into the hardened, bitter man you believe him to be. Or even what he believes himself to be."

"I don't know what to think any more, Aunt Kelly. The man has managed to totally confound me. I have no idea where he's coming from. If it was his plan to throw me off balance, he's certainly succeeded."

They heard a knock at the door. Kelly went to answer it.

"Mr. Price." Kelly smiled. "Come on in. I'm Valerie's aunt, Kelly Harper."

Alex returned the smile and extended his hand. "Pleased to meet you."

Valerie shot abruptly off the couch at the sound of Alex's voice. Seconds later he followed Kelly into the living room. At that moment Tyler chose to come running into the room. Alex stood as if nailed to the floor. His eyes widened in shock when he got a good look at the boy.

"Alex, I—" Valerie's voice faded.

Alex eyed the younger version of himself for a moment longer, then stumbled over to a nearby lounge chair and dropped into it.

The room was held in ghostly silence; the adults temporarily incapable of speech, but not Tyler.

"I'm Tyler Bishop. What's your name?" he asked Alex.

"Alex—Alexander Price."

"All right! You're the man who's gonna give a lot of people jobs."

"I hope to, yes." Alex shifted his attention to Valerie's taut face, then he glanced back at Tyler. "How old are you, son?

"Seven, but I'll be eight next month," he said with pride.

Kelly cleared her throat. "Tyler, your mother has business to discuss with Mr. Price. Why don't you and I go out to the kitchen and sample some of the cookies I baked?"

"All right!" he said and followed Kelly out of the room.

Valerie noticed that sweat had suddenly dampened Alex's forehead. And he looked to be in a state of shock. She'd waited too late to tell him he had a son. She hadn't intended for him to find out like this. What was he thinking? How was he feeling?

"Alex, I—"

"Not a damn word. I can't believe you did this to me."
As if he were an old man, Alex slowly rose to his feet.
"What kind of woman are you? I thought I knew eight
years ago, but I was wrong."

"Alex, please let me—"

"What? Explain why all these years you neglected to tell
me I had a son?" He realized now why she'd reacted the way
she had when he first came to Quinneth Falls. He had to be
her worst nightmare come true. Earlier she'd been nervous
and distracted, almost fearful. Well, she damned well had
reason. The full impact of her betrayal hit him like a punch
in the gut. She'd not only walked out on him, and taken
money from his father, and then given it to another man,
to top it all off she'd kept Tyler a secret from him and
allowed another man to raise his child. Her list of sins was
endless.

"I didn't know I was pregnant when I left Detroit."

"Would it have made any difference? What about later
when you found out? Why didn't you tell me?"

"I had reasons."

"I'm sure you did," he said, his voice bitter. "The truth
is, you never had any intention of telling me I had a son. If
I hadn't come here I'd never have found out."

Valerie flinched at the pain and fury she saw on his face
and heard spewing from his lips. She'd never wanted to hurt
him like that. Damn you, Michael Price. Damn you to hell.

Alex's eyes were wells of pain as he went on. "I loved
you so much. What a first class fool I was."

"Don't say that! You were never that."

"I beg to differ with you."

"You don't understand, and I can't explain it to you."

"You're right. You can't because I'll never understand. As far as I'm concerned there can be no possible explanation I'll ever accept, so don't even try to offer one. I had practically put you on a pedestal, woman."

"Alex—"

"I've got to get out of here or else I won't be responsible for my actions." Fists clenched at his sides, he headed for the door.

"Alex, you can't leave like this."

"Believe me, I can't stay. I don't dare stay," he spat at her.

"We need to talk."

"You're wrong. We don't need to do anything right now."

"When you've calmed down, then—" Valerie saw the shimmer of emotion swimming in his eyes before he stormed out of the house.

Valerie clamped her hands over her face. Oh God, what have I done to him? The image of Michael Price and the pain she'd felt when he forced her to leave Alex came back in a rush. What would Alex do now that he knew about Tyler?

Kelly came back into the room. "How did he take it?"

"Oh, Aunt Kelly, I've never seen such a hurt, destroyed look in anyone's eyes. It was like watching a severely injured animal drag itself away to lick its wounds. If he didn't hate me before, he certainly has reason to now."

"Once he calms down and—"

"I don't think he'll ever forgive me, and I can't blame him."

"Valerie, you've got to tell him what his father made you do and why."

"I can't, Aunt Kelly."

"Well, I certainly can. I'll go see Michael Price."

"No! Please don't do that."

"Valerie—"

"I mean it, Aunt Kelly. This is my life and my problem. I'll handle it."

Tyler brought a plate of cookies into the living room. Looking around he asked, "Where did Mr. Price go?"

"He had to leave, baby," Valerie told her son. "Come over here and give your mother a hug and one of those delicious cookies." Kelly shook her head and went back into the kitchen.

❧

Valerie stood in the doorway of her son's bedroom that night and watched him sleep. She thought about Alex and what he'd missed out on. A pain the intensity of which she'd never felt before, even after she'd left Alex, gripped her heart. She'd deeply hurt the man she loved. All these years she'd enjoyed their son and hadn't given a thought to how he'd feel if or when he found out. She in fact had blocked it out. She should have told Alex she was pregnant and dared Michael Price to do his worst.

But knowing the man as she did, Valerie knew he wouldn't have hesitated to do as he had threatened. She hated to think what his revelation would have done to her aunt. Valerie could never have lived with herself

Nobody should have to make a decision like the one she'd been forced to make. But it was all water over the falls now. The damage was done and it did no good to dwell on it. It wouldn't change anything. It wouldn't take back the pain she'd inflicted on Alex or wipe out the misery she herself had suffered. It definitely wouldn't ease the agony Alex was feeling at this very moment.

Valerie made her way down the hall to her bedroom, undressed, showered, then got into bed. God, how was she going to get through this? After a few minutes, she climbed out of bed and walked over to the window and looked out. There was no way she'd be able to embrace sleep tonight. She stepped over to her dresser, took out clean underwear, then headed to her closet and pulled out a sundress with shoestring-straps. Minutes later she slid her feet into her sandals and grabbing up her purse and keys, left the house.

Alex drove out to the lake, got out of the Durango and with the slow, dragging gait of a man suffering from traumatic shock, made his way to a large, flat boulder near the water's edge and sank down on it. He absently looked out at the gently cascading waters of the falls, barely aware of how beautiful it was with the moonlight silvering it.

His mind in disorienting turmoil, Alex had been unable to face going back to his suite so he'd come here seeking a balm for his tortured emotions. The peace the falls usually gave him was non-existent now. It had been supplanted by a deep heart-rending sadness. Not even this wonderful place could stave off the pain or stop the agony that was ripping apart his very soul.

How could Valerie have done this to him? All he'd ever done was love her. At the thought of how thoroughly she'd betrayed him, he covered his face with his hands.

He had a son! He'd always wanted children. Along with that joyful revelation came a bitter, fathomless anger. He'd missed so much of his child's life. He'd never gotten to see Tyler's first tooth, see him take his first step, hear him speak his first words. Or gotten to hear his son call him daddy. God, it hurt so much. Tears fell from his eyes.

Another man had experienced all these things with his son. That man had raised his son, not him.

"Alex."

He froze at the sound of Valerie's voice. He hadn't seen her car drive up or heard her make her way toward him. When she put a hand on his shoulder, he jerked away from her touch and shot to his feet, then swung around to face her.

"What do you want?" he gritted out. "Haven't you done enough?"

"I never wanted to hurt you."

"Never wanted to hurt me! God, woman, I could…" His voice trailed away, becoming lost in the soft rushing sound of the falls.

"You have to believe me; I'm speaking the truth."

"I'll never believe another word that comes out of your mouth. As for the truth… The truth is you're a selfish, cold-hearted bitch. You'd better go, because at this moment I'm aching to do something I've never done in my life, hit a woman. So just go! Get the hell away from me!"

Tears slid down Valerie's face. "I can't leave you."

"You did it before," he said dully.

"Oh, Alex." When she reached up and touched his cheek, a tear fell on her hand.

His hand shot up to bat hers away, but at the contact he groaned. Valerie went up on tiptoes and kissed his lips. A helpless growl left his throat and he pulled her into his arms.

He knew he should push her away, but he couldn't bring himself to do it. Instead, he found himself drawing her closer until he was practically crushing her in his embrace. The scent of her enveloped his senses and the feel of her soft skin was wearing down his resistance to her. And against his will he succumbed to temptation.

He brushed the thin straps of her dress off her shoulders. His breath sucked in at the sight of her breasts. In the moonlight her bared nipples looked like dark, red grapes swollen with juice, near to bursting.

"God, Val," he groaned, caressing the tips of her breasts with his thumbs.

Since seeing her at the administration building when he first came to Quinneth Falls, he'd dreamed about doing this and more, despite what she'd done to him. Did that make him some kind of masochist?

When he heard her gasp of pleasure at his touch, it almost caused him to have an instant orgasm. He dropped his hands and backed away from her. Valerie moved forward and pulled his head down and kissed him. His arms went up around her waist as if by a will of their own, and he instinctively drew her body closer. This time the contact was so electric, currents of sensation melded their bodies together like two pieces of hot metal.

When he drew her legs up around his hips and rocked the cradle of her femininity against his hardened male flesh, Valerie shuddered in response to his expert stimulation of this sensitive, desire-laden part of her body, and she moaned. And moments later whimpers of ecstasy tripped off her tongue.

Her passionate cries accelerated his heartbeat and at the same time caused a throbbing ache in his groin that spread, reverberating through his entire body. He didn't understand how she was able to make him feel like this. His body didn't care about the hows or whys; it was responding to a primitive need deep within him, and he couldn't ignore its pull.

Alex kissed her lips and moved his mouth lower, placing nipping kisses on her chin, then her throat, lingering to feather more kisses on the rapid pulse beating at its base. He lowered her legs until she was standing before him, then pushed her dress down her body, sending her panties with it, forming a pool at her feet.

"Your body is unbelievably more beautiful than it used to be," he rasped.

Valerie unbuttoned his shirt and eased her fingers across his chest, brushing the tips against his nipple. She smiled when an involuntary hiss of arousal escape his control.

"So is yours."

"Men aren't beautiful."

"They may not be, but you are to me."

"Val, we have to stop."

"We can't. It's too late and you know it." She undid the button on his pants and delved her hand inside the waistband of his briefs, circling her fingers around his turgid male organ.

A shudder raced through his loins with the speed of lightning, and he cried out as sensation after sensation overtook him and he became a creature of aching need. As if in a trance, he wrenched off his shoes and socks. Then moments later he pushed his pants and briefs down his muscular legs, and after kicking them aside, stood as naked as the woman before him.

Alex drew her closer and bringing her legs up around his hips again, he wasted no time with preliminaries and just buried his pulsing manhood in her hot, desire-moistened heat. He heard her cry out in rapture as he built the hungry need inside by moving her body against his. The hot friction-building slide of her tight velvety flesh against his again and again and yet again almost pushed him over the edge.

When her mouth found his lips, she delved her tongue inside, transforming it into an instrument of pleasure as she sensuously stroked the walls and roof of his mouth. The double assault on his body obliterated all thought, and he reacted on pure instinct. Without breaking contact he lowered them both to the grass.

The feel of the cool damp grass on Valerie's hot skin caused rational thought to seep inside her brain. What was she doing?

Something you've secretly wanted to do for eight years. You might as well admit it to yourself.

She couldn't deny it now if she wanted to. And right now she didn't want to.

"Alex—"

"Don't talk now, Val. I'm incapable of comprehending your words."

She arched her body into his and heard his mindless growl of pleasure. Tongues of fire flicked through her core, rapture caused the heat to rise higher, and with each frenzied movement of their bodies, each arousing caress drew them closer to a blazing consummation.

"I need you so much, Val, I can't seem to make myself stop," he muttered feverishly.

"Neither can I," she gasped.

As Alex moved strongly between Valerie's thighs, she arched her body upward in an answering rejoinder that pushed them both over the precipice of passion. When he felt her inner feminine muscles tense, then start to spasm around his sex, Alex climaxed, propelling his seed deep inside her womb.

Alex collapsed over her body. As he struggled to get his breathing back to a normal rhythm, sanity and reality returned. He'd just made love to the woman who had so cruelly betrayed him. How could he have done that? Evidently what had passed between them went beyond his resentment, and was stronger than his anger and desire for revenge. He slowly eased his body off Valerie's.

"How did you know I'd be here?" he asked, striving to put a measure of distance between them.

"I went to your suite. Justin said he hadn't seen you since the meeting earlier. I remembered how much you seemed to love the falls and took a chance you'd come here. I often come here myself when life is too much to bear."

"I can't believe what we just did."

"You needed comfort, and I was the only one who could give it to you."

"What you mean is, you did it to assuage your guilt."

"That too," she confessed. "I know I've hurt you."

"You have no concept of how much, and never will. I can't believe I exhibited so little self-control." Alex grabbed his clothes and started dressing.

"Alex, self-control played no part in what we just shared. What are you going to do?" she asked, reaching for her own clothing, suddenly feeling exposed and vulnerable.

"I don't know. It's hard to take this all in. I have a son," he said in an awed voice.

"Yes, you do. We have to talk about Tyler."

"I can't right now. I have to go."

Valerie didn't try to stop him; she merely watched as he strode over to the Durango. Her heart felt heavy. She knew she'd hurt him deeply. What she'd given to him wasn't nearly enough to make up for it. What would he want to do about their son? Surely he wouldn't try to take him from her! If only she'd been the one to tell him about Tyler.

It wouldn't have made any difference how he found out or who told him, the result would have been the same. You kept him from knowing about his child. In his eyes, it's the most unforgivable of all sins, next to your walking out on him.

Valerie dressed and sat on the same boulder where she'd found him, and peered out at the falls. When she'd seen his solitary figure hunched over in obvious emotional distress, it had broken her heart. She knew she had to do something to ease his suffering. Not for the first time, she sensed that there was more to his derisive attitude than her walking out on him. As to what it could be, she had no idea, but she knew it existed. Could she get him to tell her what it was? She doubted he'd give her the chance in his present state of mind. She would have to wait until he was ready.

CHAPTER FIFTEEN

Alex let himself into his suite and walked over to the bar, poured himself a stiff drink and was about to take it out on the patio when he heard a knock. It could only be Justin. He must have heard him come in. Alex put the drink on the coffee table and went to answer the door.

"Valerie Bishop came here earlier looking for you. Is anything wrong?"

"You might as well join me for a drink." "I don't want a drink. Alex, what happened?" Justin asked, concern evident in his tone.

"I found out something that blew my world apart: I learned that Valerie's son is also my son." "What?" "You heard me."

"You mean she's kept it from you all this time?"

"That's exactly what I'm telling you."

"But how could she do something so—"

"Despicable? Cruel? The woman took a million dollars from my father. Do you need to know more?"

"No, I don't. I can't begin to absorb all this."

"If you can't, how do you think I feel?"

"Oh, man, I'm sorry."

"So am I," he said, picking up his glass and taking a healthy swallow of Scotch.

"Did she tell you why she'd kept it from you?"

"She wanted to talk, but I wasn't in any mood to listen."

"You're going to have to get in the mood."

Alex sighed. "I know, but I can't handle it right now." He started to pace back and forth before the sliding glass patio door. "I feel so numb."

"I imagine you do. Your father called."

Alex groaned. He was the last person he wanted to talk to right now, next to Althea. The thought of what he had to do struck his mind like a blow from a hammer. He could never have any kind of a life with Althea now. He had to face the fact that he didn't love her the way she deserved to be loved. If he'd never seen Valerie again, maybe he could have fooled himself into believing it. But now that he knew he and Valerie had a son, he was as irrevocably bound to them as he was to Quinneth Falls.

"Alex?" Althea smiled. "I didn't expect you to come by so early," she said, moving back from the door of her suite to let him in the next morning. Her hair was sleep-tousled and she was in her nightgown and robe.

"Have you come to realize that what I said is the only way for us?"

"I've come to realize a lot of things, but I didn't come here to talk about them."

Her smiled faded. "You didn't? Then why have you come here?"

"To tell you that we—that I can't marry you."

"Alex! You can't mean what you're saying. Is it because I refuse to make my home in this god-awful little town?"

"I don't love you the way a man should love the woman he intends to marry."

"What do you mean, you don't love me?"

"I do love you, but—" He paused to compose his words carefully. "I thought we could have a good life together, but it's impossible now."

"You've found someone else?"

"You might say that."

"I told your father the reason you wanted to move here was because you'd met and become involved with one of the local women."

"It's not what you think."

"But it is. Don't you see, if you leave this town you'll eventually forget about this woman."

"I'll never be able to do that. You think I like this situation? I didn't want things to end like this."

"What we have doesn't have to end."

"Yes, it does."

A pained look came into her eyes. She twisted the ring off her finger and handed it to him.

"I want you to keep it."

"I can't." She closed his fingers around the ring. "I think you'd better go."

"Althea, I—"

"Just go, please. I can't take any more."

"I never wanted to hurt you."

"But you have."

Alex started to say more, but changed his mind and headed for the door. When he opened it, his father was standing there about to knock.

"Alexander?" his father said in surprise. "Have you decided to come back to Detroit with me and Thea?"

"Dad, I—"

"No, he hasn't, Michael. He just broke our engagement," she cried, launching herself at him. Michael enclosed her in his arms.

"Why did you do it?" Michael demanded.

"Because it's not going to work out between us, Dad."

"He's found another woman," Althea said, her voice tight with pain.

"I have a pretty good idea who she is." Michael fixed is attention on his son. "You're a damn fool, Alexander." He walked Althea over to the bed and gently eased her down on it. "I'm going to drive Althea back to Detroit. You go on to that…that woman."

"Dad, you don't understand."

"And I don't want to. How you can choose someone like Valerie Bishop over a wonderful woman like Althea is beyond my comprehension. Althea is worth two of her."

"Dad, it's not what you think."

"Oh, I believe it is. And after what she did. I'm disappointed in you, Alexander."

Alex gritted his teeth. "I don't want to get into this with you right now. You go ahead and drive Althea home. We'll talk later."

"You're damned right we will. You've got some serious explaining to do. Mark my words, you're going to be even sorrier this time around," Michael said grimly.

Alex ignored his father's warning and fixed his eyes on Althea. "I'm sorry for hurting you, Thea. I guess this is good-bye," Alex said and left the suite.

Alex went back to his office and tried to get some work done, but it was no use. His concentration was shot to hell. He should have told his father he had a grandson, but he hadn't wanted to discuss it in front of Althea. He felt like such a bastard for hurting her like that, but it couldn't be helped. He just couldn't marry her.

Justin walked in. "We need to iron out the terms of payment for Resource Chemical's loan."

"Not now, Justin."

"But we need to have this settled as soon as possible."

"Forget about that. I intend to absorb the cost myself." "I can't see Valerie Bishop agreeing to let you do that." "She doesn't have a choice." "What are you going to do about your son?" "I don't know. I need time to think so I'm going away for a while."

"But what about the house? And Valerie Bishop?" Alex handed Justin a folder. "Here are detailed instructions. And papers that I want you to have her sign concerning Resource Chemical. As for the house, the construction engineer, the workers and the architect know what I expect of them."

"Are you sure you're all right?"

"No, but I'll live. Don't worry about me."

After getting Tyler off to camp, Valerie called Mary Ellen to tell her she'd be in later. Mary Ellen informed her that Justin had set up a meeting to discuss Resource Chemical that afternoon. At least Alex hadn't changed his mind about helping her with the company. That wasn't a concern, but Tyler's welfare was. What was Alex going to do regarding their son?

Valerie walked into the office several hours later and found Justin waiting for her. Judging from the look on his face, she wasn't going to like what he had to say.

Justin didn't waste time. He took a set of papers out of his briefcase and handed them to Valerie. He'd always been friendly and respectful to her before, but now his manner was wary, watchful and most definitely hostile.

After a few minutes Valerie looked up from the papers. "He can't be serious about this?"

"Oh, believe me, he is," Justin replied.

Valerie could tell by Justin's expression he knew about the situation between her and Alex and wasn't too pleased with that knowledge. Even so, there seemed to be more to his attitude. What was it with him and Alex?

"I don't know what Alex is up to, but—"

"He's not up to anything." Justin's look said he believed that she was however. "Alex is concerned about his son's welfare and yours since you're the mother of his child."

"I get the picture." She reached for the phone.

"You won't catch him in. Alex has gone away to think."

"Did he say when he'd be back?"

"No, but I'm sure you'll be the first to know."

"You don't like me very much, do you, Justin? I have reasons for what I did. I don't think you should judge me without knowing all the facts."

"I'm not judging you, Mrs. Bishop."

"Aren't you? This is between me and Alex. It's up to us to work it out."

"You're right, I'm sorry. It's just that I care about Alex as a friend as well as an employer."

Valerie called Mary Ellen in and as they went over the documents, she caught her assistant eying Justin as though he were some cold, unfeeling stranger. Valerie returned her attention to the papers. It was a carefully worded contract. It in essence gave Alex power of attorney over her business during the loan period. She didn't want to agree to any of it, but she had little choice but to accede to Alex's wishes. Agreeing to his terms left a bitter taste in her mouth. Was Alex doing this because of Tyler or for revenge? She would find out which when he got back.

Howard called Valerie right after Justin left.

"I know what went down about the mortgage on Resource Chemical. I'm sure everything will turn out for the best." He hesitated before going on. "Tyler waved to me from the camp bus this morning. I realized his face was a miniature of his father's. Tyler is Alexander Price's son, isn't he?"

Valerie sighed and reluctantly answered, "Yes."

"Does he know?"

"Yes, he found out when he came to my house last night."

"I would ask how he took it, but I can tell by the sound of your voice things didn't go well. What do you think he'll do?"

"I haven't got a clue, and that's what worries me."

"Did George know Tyler wasn't his son?"

"Yes. It's the reason we got married so soon after I came back to Quinneth Falls. He wanted people to think he was."

"I don't know what to say, Valerie."

"There's nothing you can say."

"I want you to know that I'll be here for you, no matter what happens."

"Thanks, Howard. You're a true friend."

Several days after Alex had left Quinneth Falls, Valerie stopped at The Pizza Parlor. She had promised Tyler that on her way home from work she'd pick up pizza for him and his friend Danny. As luck would have it, Jake Spriewell was there and started talking about Alex.

"I haven't seen Mr. Alexander for a few days. Not since his father and Mr. Alexander's fiancée left town."

"What? You mean Michael Price was here in Quinneth Falls!"

"Sure was. He and Mr. Alexander's fiancée left the day after they got here. Seems more than passing strange to me. When they left she was crying. The older Mr. Price helped her into his car. He drives a right smart-looking Rolls-Royce."

"You say the woman was crying?"

"Yes, and Mr. Price was comforting her. I wonder if she and Mr. Alexander done split up?"

"Jake!"

"I was just curious is all. My pizza's ready. See you around, Valerie. Take care of that boy of yours."

Michael Price had been here in Quinneth Falls. Valerie just couldn't get over it. And he hadn't tried to contact her. But that didn't mean that he wouldn't in the future. She wondered if Alex had told him about Tyler. If he had, he would surely have gotten in touch with her.

And what about Alex's fiancée? Why had she been crying? Was it possible that Alex had broken off their engagement? What did it all mean? She was going to go crazy while she waited for Alex to get back.

After spending a week roughing it in the wilds of the Superior Uplands region of Michigan, Alex was ready to go to Detroit and face his father. The trip up north had helped clear his mind as it had when he'd gone there after Valerie had walked out on him. When he arrived in Detroit it was to learn that Althea had left for New York. And of course, his father wasn't about to let him forget the reason for her flight.

"You've just lost the best thing that's ever happened you, Alexander," Michael said the moment Alex walked into the living room at the Price mansion.

"There are reasons other than Valerie Bishop for my breaking my engagement to Althea."

"So you've said. I believe she's the foremost reason. Wasn't what she did to you enough for you?"

"I found out her son is my son, Dad."

Michael looked stunned. Recovering he asked, "How do you know he's yours? Didn't you tell me the woman got married right after she returned to Quinneth Falls?"

"If you saw Tyler you'd know he was mine."

"Why hasn't she said anything before now?"

"I don't know, but I intend to find out."

Michael cleared his throat. "I don't understand why that would make you break it off with Althea."

"I have different priorities now, Dad. I want to get to know my son. That means living in Quinneth Falls. Althea would never agree to that. My house is half-finished, and when it's completed, I intend to make a home for Tyler."

"I still don't understand."

"You will when I'm finished with all the arrangements."

"What arrangements? What are you talking about?"

Alex didn't answer, just smiled and turned on his heel and bounded up the stairs.

Michael stumbled over to the couch and dropped down on it. He covered his face with his hands. What had he done? He'd been responsible for keeping Alexander from knowing he had son. And himself from knowing he had a grandson. While he was busy manipulating the situation to his satisfaction, it never occurred to him that Valerie Baker might be carrying Alexander's child.

Valerie could have come to him and asked for the money he'd tried to bribe her with when she found out she was pregnant. But she hadn't. She could have taken the money and aborted Alexander's child. But she hadn't. She would have done both of those things if she had been that kind woman. But Valerie Baker had obviously been nothing like his ex-wife or her aunt. She'd married George Bishop to give her child a father.

Because you had denied you own grandson his rightful father. What do you tell yourself now to justify what you did?

What could he say? He'd been wrong.

Are you going to rectify the situation?

How could he do that and keep his son's respect and love? Alexander would never forgive him once he knew the truth.

You've wronged an innocent woman and in so doing deprived your own son of being with the woman he loved; deprived him of knowing and raising his son. You even deprived yourself of a grandson. Your list of crimes is endless. How are you going to live with yourself?

The conscience he had thought he no longer possessed was now pricking Michael mightily. And he had never felt more miserable in his entire life.

CHAPTER SIXTEEN

When he returned to Quinneth Falls, Alex found out from Jake Spriewell the location of Tyler's summer camp. And the next morning when Tyler got off the bus, Alex was waiting.

"Mr. Price," Tyler said with a smile.

"How are you, Tyler?"

"I'm fine, sir. You gonna be our guest counselor today?"

Alex smiled. "No, I'm afraid not. You have time to talk before you have to go in, don't you?" When Tyler nodded, Alex signaled him over to a bench a few feet away from the gym door. "Come sit down."

"All right. I'm not looking for a job right now. Mama says I'm not old enough."

His son obviously saw him as some kind of hero. And knowing that tugged at Alex's heart. "She's right, you're not, but in a few years you will be, and then we'll talk. I didn't come here to talk to you about a job."

"You didn't?"

"No. You and your mother are close, aren't you?"

"Oh, yes, sir, she's the best mom in the whole world."

"I'm glad to hear it. You miss your father a lot, though, don't you?."

"Yeah, I do," he said in a sad voice. "He died last year."

"Yes, I know," Alex said tightly. "Is your mother thinking about marrying again?

"Heck no."

"I know she's been spending time with Howard Atkins."

"She and Mr. Atkins are just friends. Mama says nobody can take Daddy's place." Tyler stood up. "It's time for me to go inside now, Mr. Price. It was cool talkin' to you."

Alex sat for long moments, taking in what his son had told him. Since Valerie wasn't serious about Howard Atkins, that made what he had in mind a lot easier, although he didn't think Valerie would necessarily agree.

Alex went to his office to do some work he'd left undone before leaving Quinneth Falls. Then later he headed out to the lake to see how the construction on his house was progressing. He'd hired an extra crew to work on it. He wanted it completed as soon as humanly possible.

"Mr. Price, you're back," Ralph Spriewell greeted Alex when he drove up.

"Yes, I'm back, Ralph. You been overseeing things while I've been gone?"

"I sure have. With all these extra men working on the house, it should be finished in two months, or maybe less. Stan says you want it finished yesterday." He laughed.

"Stan is right. I'll give bonuses to any who want overtime. They'll get an extra bonus if the house is finished in six weeks."

"Yes sir, Mr. Price. I'll be sure to tell all the guys."

"You do that, Ralph." Alex inspected the grounds before leaving. As he drove around the lake, he stopped when he came to the spot where he and Valerie had made love a week ago. He'd never thought he'd ever want to touch her again, let alone make love to her. But he'd been hurting so badly that he couldn't resist the temptation to find succor in her lovely body. It was more than that. The old chemistry was still working. He'd tried to deny it, but he couldn't any longer. He wanted her as much as he ever did. Knowing they had a son made him desire her even more. That sounded crazy, but it was true nevertheless.

She had power over him. Even after what she'd done he still wanted her. He intended to exert control over that renegade desire if it killed him. He wouldn't allow her to make a fool of him again. If she didn't agree to what he had in mind, there would be hell to pay.

Valerie was surprised, no, dumbfounded was a better word, to describe how she felt when she got home from work and Tyler told her he'd talked with Alex that morning at camp. What was he up to? Why had he approached Tyler there instead of at home? She and Alex needed to talk. When was he planning on discussing their son with her?

"I like Mr. Price, Mama. He's helping so many people."

"Yes, he is."

"He said when I was old enough we'd talk about a job for me.

"I thought you wanted to be a scientist and work at Resource Chemical."

"Well, I do, but…"

"It's all right. You've got plenty of time to decide what you want to do."

Valerie, Kelly and Tyler had just finished eating dinner when the phone rang. Valerie had a feeling about who would be on the other end.

"Valerie, this Alex. I think it's time we talked. Can you come to my office in, say, a half an hour?"

"Alex, I—I'll be there." A feeling of trepidation inundated her as she hung up the phone.

"Is anything wrong?" Kelly asked.

"Alex wants to talk."

"That's a good sign, don't you think?"

"Where Alex is concerned, who knows?"

Kelly put her arms around her niece's shoulders and squeezed. "You've got to think positive. I'm sure he wants what's best for his son and you, too. Trashing you wouldn't accomplish that. In the long run it would only hurt Tyler."

"You saw the look on his face when he realized Tyler was his son."

"The man was in shock. I'm sure that getting away to think has made him see things in a whole new light."

"Always the eternal optimist, aren't you, Aunt Kelly? Well, I'd better be heading over to Alex's office."

Alex saw Valerie's car drive up and opened the door and waited for her to come inside. His secretary had gone home an hour before. He saw the apprehension in Valerie's eyes as they met his.

"Right on time. How is Tyler?" He waved for her to precede him into his office.

"He was fine when I left. He mentioned seeing you this morning."

"Please, sit down."

Valerie remained standing. "Alex, what have you decided about our son?"

"Do you want anything to drink?"

"No. What I want is some answers."

"All right. You agree that Tyler is the important one in all this."

"Yes."

"Good, then what I have to say shouldn't shock you. Our son deserves to know his real father. When I talked to him this morning, I saw how much he misses George Bishop, the only father he's ever known. He needs me, and I intend to be there for him."

"I wasn't going to keep him from you. You can see Tyler whenever you want to."

"That's not good enough."

Valerie frowned. "Not good enough? What do you mean.

"I've lost seven years of my son's life, and I don't intend to lose any more."

Valerie hunched her shoulders. "I don't understand what you're trying to say."

"I want to make a home for my son, and I want him to one day know that I am his real father."

"Make a home for him? He already has a home with me. You can't mean to try and take him away from me," she said, her voice incredulous.

Rage blazed to life in his eyes. "What kind of man do you think I am? I'd never take my son away from his mother. You're the only security he has. When I was his age, my mother died and all I had was my father, so I understand only too well how he feels. And so should you, you were raised by your aunt. What I want to do is reinforce his feelings of security by giving him two parents. I'll never be able to take George Bishop's place in his heart. All I can hope to do is carve a place of my own."

"I still don't understand the point you're trying to make." Valerie's brows arched in puzzlement.

"I want you to marry me."

"What?"

"That way we can share our son, raise him together."

"You can't mean that. You hate me, I've seen it in your eyes. We can't bring Tyler up in a tension-filled atmosphere like that."

"You're wrong, I don't hate you. I may hate what you did, but I don't hate you. I admit that when I first came here all I wanted was revenge, retribution for what you put me through. But now finding out I have a son changes everything.

"After what happened between us by the lake, I know you're not indifferent to me. What you did for me showed compassion. You gave of yourself in a way you never had when we were—in Detroit. I feel that you're truly sorry for hurting me. Now is your chance to make up for it by giving our son his real father and the security of two loving parents. Make no mistake, I've already come to love that little boy. And I'll do anything in my power to see him happy."

"I know he needs all you've mentioned, but to get married… We don't love each other anymore, Alex."

His jaw tensed. "Are you saying no?"

"I have to." It would kill her to be with him knowing that he didn't love her. But she'd lied about not loving him;

she loved this man more than ever. "What about your fiancée?"

"I've broken my engagement to Althea. Are you serious about Howard Atkins?"

"No. He's just a friend."

"So you see there is nothing or no one standing in the way."

Her mind conjured up a mental picture of Michael Price. "I just can't do it."

"You leave me no choice."

Valerie's eyes widened. "No choice?"

"You will marry me, Valerie, because if you don't I'll close down Resource Chemical. You remember the papers you signed?"

"You can't just take over my life like this."

"Oh, I can, and I'll do more than that if you don't agree to marry me. You're still attracted to me. My touch doesn't exactly revolt you, does it?"

"If sex is all you want—"

"It's not. Don't you understand? What I want is to share our son with you, to help raise him to be a good man. To insure that happening I've got to be here. You owe me, Valerie. You owe me big-time."

"Then it is about revenge after all."

"If you want to believe that, but I think you know better. I want my son under my roof and you in my bed. We can make a success of our marriage if you're willing to give it a chance."

Valerie knew she had no choice. It was shades of Michael Price all over again. He'd known the right button to push to make her do what he wanted. And now Alex had found another. The man she used to know no longer existed. She'd evidently hurt Alex beyond redemption, and he intended to make her pay for it. He could couch it in concern for his son, but he still wanted revenge and had no qualms about exacting it in whatever way he could. She should hate him, but she didn't, she couldn't.

"When do you want to get married?" Her voice sounded dull and resigned when she answered.

Alex grimaced, he didn't like hearing the resignation in her voice. He didn't want it this way, but she'd left him no choice. She was going to be his wife; it wasn't negotiable. This wouldn't be a marriage of convenience and certainly wouldn't be one in name only. She would be his wife in every conceivable way.

"My house won't be habitable for at least eight weeks. While we wait for it to be ready, it'll give us time to know one another. And it will give me a chance to get to know my son and pave a road into his affection so that when we marry it won't be a shock to him and he'll accept it."

"You have it all figured out, don't you? What about my feelings? I suppose they don't matter."

"Don't make this a war, Valerie. It doesn't have to be like that between us."

"You're practically frog-marching me to the altar and expect there not to be a war?"

Alex decided to use another avenue of persuasion. "We didn't use protection. You could be pregnant. Unless you're on the pill."

Her breath sucked in. She wasn't on the pill, and she hadn't thought about protection. She mentally calculated and had to admit that she could very well be pregnant. Her periods had never been regular. Oh God, what had she done? By showing Alex compassion she could have created another life to bind them together even tighter. In different circumstances having his baby would have made her the happiest woman in the world. If he only loved her half as much as she loved him. But he didn't. Valerie's shoulders slumped.

Alex drew her into his arms. "I don't intend to make your life hell. Not only will we have our son," he kissed her lips and caressed her breasts, we'll have this. Val, I can give you as much pleasure as you can give me." He kissed her again more arousingly this time. He felt a slight tremor of resistance at first, then she let out a little moan and gave in to desire. He lifted her onto his desk. Pushing her skirt up around her hips, he parted her thighs and stepped between them. Then he slid his hand across the front of her panties, teasing the bud between the crevices of her thighs through the filmy cloth until it was wet with her essence. He quickly eased aside the crotch and delved two fingers inside the damp folds of her womanly core while caressing the now pulsing bud of her desire with his thumb.

Valerie cried out as he moved frenzied fingers against her, in her, building the friction and the pleasure. Seconds later she climaxed into those clever, knowing fingers and collapsed against his chest.

Valerie realized what he said was true. He'd just proven his point. Loving him as she did was going to be both heaven and hell. How was his father going to take the news of their coming marriage? In the past he'd done everything in his power to keep them apart. What about his threat against her aunt? What would he do now? When Alex stepped back, Valerie expected to see triumph, but what she saw was raw, hungry passion. Glancing down, she saw the evidence of his desire ridging his pants. When she lifted her head and looked into his eyes, she could tell how much he wanted to make love to her, yet he was denying himself release.

"I don't have any protection with me; it's in my room." Invitation glowed in his eyes. She knew he wouldn't beg her to share his bed. He left it up to her. If she went to his bed now she'd lose a part of herself she wasn't prepared to lose just yet. He'd already taken a piece of her soul a few moments ago.

"I think I'd better go home." She moved off the desk. Her legs felt the consistency of jelly when she stood up.

"Are you sure that's what you want to do?"

She knew he wanted more, but all he said was, "I'll call you tomorrow."

Alex watched Valerie's car pull away. He moved gingerly because his manly endowments were extremely sensitive. It would take him a while to get back to normal, considering he was suffering from a monumental hard-on. He'd wanted her so badly he thought he'd die from it, but he'd controlled himself. Barely.

He brought his fingers to his nostrils; the scent of her still lingered to torment him further. What he needed was a cold shower, though water, whether hot or cold, could never wash away the memory of stroking her slick, intimate woman's flesh. Nothing could erase how soft her skin felt, the sweet taste of her lips, the jasmine scent in her hair.

He had to keep reminding himself about what she'd done. But knowing that hadn't stopped him from wanting her. What was this hold she had on him? She'd never tried to use their son, so that couldn't be it. She hadn't tried to use feminine wiles on him either. She had him totally confused. Money did strange things to people, but it hadn't changed her in the ways he would have expected. She hadn't used it for herself, at least not directly. Nothing added up and that intrigued him. Valerie intrigued him. But whatever, he was still going to marry her. Maybe he'd find out where her head had been when she'd taken the money from his father.

Alex smiled thinking about Tyler. He thanked God and fate for sending him here. He'd not only found out he had a son, he'd fallen in love with Quinneth Falls. As for his relationship with Valerie, he didn't know what direction that was headed. He desired her and wanted her for his wife. And she was, after all, the mother of his son.

It's more than that, man, and you know it.

CHAPTER SEVENTEEN

Valerie drove out to the house Alex was building. Men were busy working on it even at this late hour. Alex was serious about having it finished in record time. She and her son would be coming here to live after their marriage. Marriage. She'd wanted that with Alex eight years ago. But Michael Price had destroyed her dreams, turning her life into a nightmare.

Valerie had made a success of her professional life, but she was sure that wouldn't count for anything with Michael Price. She wasn't a high society woman with an impeccable background like Alex's ex-fiancée, Althea. Would knowing he had a grandson make a difference? She had her doubts about that.

She remembered Alex showing her the blueprints for the house and how excited he'd been. He'd asked her what she thought, pressing her for her opinion and preferences, little knowing how handy it would become. Since finding out he had a son, Alex was now a man with a purpose.

Tyler was his number one priority.

Valerie got out of the car and walked over to the perimeter of the property, examining the progress. She could see that Alex had taken her advice and hired the Sanderses to do the landscaping. She saw evidence of their expertise all around her. This was one of her favorite spots. Valerie remembered how worried she and the preservation committee had been that Price Industries would ruin it.

They would have never imagined that Valerie would one day become its guardian.

Alex was right. This was the perfect place to build a house and raise a family. She glided her hand across her flat stomach. Could she be carrying his child? If not this time, would she have other children with him? Did a marriage between them really stand a chance of working even without the threat of Michael Price? Only time would give her the answer to her questions.

Alex found Justin in his office staring out the window.

"Here you are. We have a meeting with the Quinneth Falls Planning Commission in fifteen minutes. I expected to see you in my office for a last-minute briefing. It's not like you to forget something like that. What's wrong?"

"It's Mary Ellen. She won't even talk to me."

"She's angry with you because of the Resource Chemical agreement?"

"You got it in one. She thinks I was in collusion with you to take over Valerie's company."

"You want me to talk to her?"

"You're the last person she'd listen to. No, I'll have to deal with her on my own."

"Valerie and I are going to be married. That should soothe her delicate sensibilities. It'll all be in the family."

"Married? How did you pull off that particular miracle? I thought you—never mind. When's the big day?"

"We haven't set a date yet. Judging from the speed in which the construction of the house is progressing, we should be able to move in in a matter of weeks. The master suite and Tyler's bedroom and bathroom, and the kitchen, are a priority. We'll get married when those rooms are finished because I absolutely refuse to move into a house George Bishop lived in with my wife and son."

"You sure you know what you're doing?"

"No, but it'll come to me."

"Let's hope you don't screw things up."

"Not a chance."

"I'm so happy for you," Kelly chirped to Valerie that morning after she clued her in about her coming marriage plans. "This time I'll get to make your wedding dress. I didn't your first time around because you and George flew to Reno on the spur of the moment. Are you and Alex planning to go on a honeymoon?"

"I don't know. We haven't discussed any of the details yet. It's still pretty new."

"You love him, don't you?"

"I guess I never stopped."

"You don't seem as happy as I would have expected. There's something more to this story, isn't there?" Kelly probed. "It's tied up with why you left Alex, isn't it?"

"Don't, Aunt Kelly. I can't talk about it."

"Or won't. You'll have to unburden yourself eventually. If not to me, then to Alex."

Her aunt just didn't know how much she wanted to confide in her, but until she'd dealt with Michael Price she couldn't do it.

"I'm going to go and get my designer wedding gown book. I know the perfect style for you."

"This is a second marriage, Aunt Kelly. You don't have to go to all that trouble."

"It may be a second, but in your heart it's your first. Can you deny it's the way you feel?"

Valerie didn't answer.

"I thought not. Have the two of you decided when and how you're going to present these changes to Tyler?"

"Alex wants to eventually tell him he's his real father. I'm not sure how Tyler will take it. Alex suggested that we spend time together and let his son come to know him and let Tyler know how much Alex really cares about him."

"Sounds like a plan to me. The Labor Day picnic is coming up. This is Tyler's last week at summer camp. You could go on outings. Lansing has some great museums."

"We could go to Sleeping Bear Dunes or even Holland." Valerie was beginning to feel better about things already, thanks to her aunt. She loved her so much and told her so.

"You know how much I love you and Tyler." Tears came to Kelly's eyes. "There's nothing I wouldn't do for you both."

Valerie hugged her aunt. "I know that."

"Wasn't that Justin you were speaking to?" Valerie asked Mary Ellen the next afternoon in the lab.

"Yes, it was."

"Didn't I just hear you call off your date with him?"

"You did."

"I thought you and he were—close. That man is crazy in love with you. A blind person could see that, so why did you do it?"

Her grey eyes flashed angrily. "I have a hard time accepting his part in Alexander Price's takeover of Resource Chemical."

"It's not exactly a takeover, Mary Ellen. I think you should know that Alex and I plan to get married very soon, so it'll all be in the family. Why don't you call Justin back?"

"You're marrying Alexander Price! Since when? I thought you didn't trust him."

"We've resolved our differences."

"Apparently. I can't believe this. Even so, it still doesn't change what Justin did."

"He was acting on Alex's orders."

"It's more than that. And don't tell me you haven't noticed that he doesn't like you and doesn't bother to hide it. I can't for the life of me understand why he feels that way."

"Have you asked him?"

"He won't discuss it."

"I'm sure he has his reasons. His attitude doesn't bother me. I don't want you disrupting your love life because of me."

"You're not telling me everything, are you?"

Valerie picked up the receiver and handed it to Mary Ellen. "Call Justin."

She smiled. "Oh, all right."

"Was that your lady?" Alex asked Justin when he'd hung up the phone.

"Yes." Justin's blue eyes sparkled. "Our date is on for tonight. She said Mrs. Bishop told her about your marriage plans."

"Does that mean she forgives you?"

"I hope so. I can't stand it when she's angry with me."

Alex grinned. "You've got it bad, Justin."

"I won't deny it. I've known a lot of women, but none like Mary Ellen. I've been waiting all my adult life for a girl like her."

"I'm happy for you, man." Alex wished he could be that happy for himself. He wasn't sure how Valerie felt about him. She might want him, but she certainly didn't love him. Considering what he was insisting that she do, she might never come to feel that way about him. And for some reason that really bothered him.

Valerie had just enough time to change before Alex came over for dinner. She'd made sure Tyler had washed up and then changed into clean jeans and a shirt. As he sat on the couch next to her, she observed just how much he looked like his father and felt a lump form in her throat

"Mr. Price really gonna have dinner with us?" Tyler asked.

"Yes, he is."

"That's so cool. I can't wait to tell Danny."

"You like Alex, I mean, Mr. Price, don't you?"

"Oh, yes."

Valerie could see admiration in his eyes. Alex had scored points through his benevolence. How would Tyler feel after he found out they were getting married? He had loved George so much. Would he feel that she was being disloyal to his memory? It had only been a little over a year since his death.

Tyler glanced out the window, then suddenly his eyes widened with excitement. "Mr. Price just drove up."

Valerie swallowed past the catch in her throat. Alex was here. What now?

"I'll go let him in," Tyler said, scrambling off the couch.

Kelly came into the living room as Tyler was ushering Alex through the front door.

Alex smiled at Kelly. "Ms. Harper."

"Please, call me Kelly. May I call you Alex?"

"By all means, please do." He glanced at Valerie, who seemed frozen in a sitting position on the couch. He smiled in sympathy when he saw how nervous she was. He was too.

Valerie finally rose from the couch and advanced to the trio congregated in the middle of the living room.

"I'm glad you could come, Alex. Aunt Kelly has cooked her famous fried chicken for dinner."

"And her jammin' peach cobbler for dessert," Tyler added. "It's one of my favorites."

"Mine too," Alex answered.

Valerie noticed as they ate dinner how Alex kept watching Tyler. His eyes seemed hungry to see everything the boy did, his ears eager to hear anything he uttered. It made her feel guilty for depriving him of his son. How could she ever make it up to him?

"What do you like to do?" Alex asked Tyler as they ate their dessert.

"Ride my scooter and go exploring. I know where some neat caves and stuff are near the falls. Did you know that the great Chief Pontiac and his people once made their home there?"

"No, I sure didn't, but I can understand why. The falls are awesome, aren't they?"

"They sure are. Chief Pontiac was an ancestor of one of my teachers. He told us all kinds of stories about him."

"You know an awful lot about history. At your age I used to be just as curious. What grade are you in?"

"Fourth grade, I got skipped up a grade."

Alex was impressed and so proud. Tyler had inherited his parents' brains, all right. Valerie had graduated top of her class in science, and Alex himself had excelled in history and science, graduating two years ahead of schedule.

He smiled at his son. "Maybe we can go exploring together sometime."

A glint of wonder shone in Tyler's eyes. "You really mean it? Can Danny Cranson come too?"

"If you want him to."

"Now, Tyler, Alex may not have time to—" Valerie began.

"It's all right, Val. I'll make time to take him and his friend exploring."

Minutes later Valerie and Kelly went into the kitchen to clean up and wash the dishes while Alex played video Monopoly with Tyler. When they were done in the kitchen, Kelly excused herself and went to her room. Valerie joined Alex and Tyler in the living room. Alex insisted that she play with them. It struck her that they were already starting to bond as a family. George had put in so much time at Resource, it was a rare occasion when they'd spent quality time together during the week He did devote time to them on weekends, though. After a while Tyler started yawning.

Alex looked fondly at his son. "I think it's time for me to go."

"Aw, can't you stay a little longer," Tyler murmured between yawns.

"You're about to fall asleep where you sir, young man," Valerie chided.

"Are you going to come back, Mr. Price?"

"I sure hope so, Tyler. It's been a long time since I've had such stimulating company and good home-cooked food."

"Can he come to dinner on Sunday, Mama?" Tyler pleaded.

Valerie looked to Alex. "We eat at five. Will you be free?"

"I'll make sure I am," Alex said, easing toward the door. "Good night, Tyler."

"Good night, Mr. Price."

Valerie saw that sad look in Alex's eyes at Tyler's words and she felt like crying. She knew how much Alex wanted to hear his son call· him daddy. At moments like this she hated Michael Price for what he'd forced her to do. But she hated herself even more for her cowardice in nor telling Alex he had a son.

The following Sunday Valerie sat on the porch steps watching Alex pitch a few balls to Tyler in the front yard. Alex was dressed in jeans, a shirt and tenths shoes. She sighed. They looked like the perfect little family.

"It'll happen, Valerie," Kelly said as she stepped out on the porch.

"You know me so well."

"Don't you think I should after all these years?"

"I'm concerned about Tyler's reaction to our wedding."

"He'll take it just fine. He loves you and adores Alex."

"Yes, I've noticed. I sure hope that adoration doesn't turn into something else."

"You mean like resentment? I doubt it will."

"Tyler is not only like Alex in looks, but also in temperament. He can be every bit as stubborn as his father when things don't go as he wants or expects them to."

"I believe Alex will know how to deal with that."

"You have a lot of confidence in him."

"I guess I do. He's that kind of man."

Valerie called Alex and Tyler in for dinner. And afterward they talked while enjoying their dessert.

"Mr. Price wants to take me exploring tomorrow afternoon. If it's okay I'm going to ask Danny to come with us.

Is it okay?" Tyler asked Valerie between mouthfuls of pineapple cake.

"You'll need to ask his mother if it's all right."

"Oh it will be," he said matter-of-factly. "She said she'd do just about anything to get him out from under her feet."

Valerie, Alex and Kelly looked at each other and smiled.

"Where are you guys planning on going to explore?" Kelly asked Alex.

"I thought near Indian Woods. That way Tyler and his friend can watch the construction of the new Price Industry plant."

"That's going to be so cool," Tyler said in an awed voice.

After Tyler had gone to bed, Valerie and Alex went outside and sat in the porch swing.

"You've done a great job raising Tyler."

"Thanks, that's very generous of you, considering."

"I'm sure you had your reasons for not telling me about him."

"But whatever they were, they weren't good enough."

"I didn't say that. Look, I don't want to fight with you, okay? Now is what's important. In a few weeks we'll be together as we should have been eight years ago."

"And you can accept that?"

"If we're to find any degree of happiness together, I think I'll have to."

"But if you still—"

"I no longer want revenge, I told you that. What I want is to be with my son and his mother." He drew her into his arms and placed a tender kiss on her lips.

"Oh, Alex," Valerie murmured softly and slipped her arms around his neck

Alex groaned. "I can't wait to be married to you, woman. I warn you I intend to be a very devoted husband."

"Demanding too, I expect?"

"I expect you to be every bit as demanding." He let her go. "I'd better be going. In a few weeks I won't have to do that. I'll have both you and Tyler in our new home waiting to welcome me every night."

It sounded almost too good to be true, Valerie thought as she watched Alex climb into the Durango and drive off.

She still had to deal with Michael Price. She had a feeling she'd be seeing him sooner than she wanted to. But then seeing him at all, no matter the rime, would be too soon.

CHAPTER EIGHTEEN

"Alex loves your fried chicken, Aunt Kelly. I'm glad you packed some for our picnic lunch." Valerie was excited about their little excursion to Sleeping Bear Dunes National Lakeshore. This time of year it was warm. Sleeping Bear Dunes was a thirty-four mile stretch of beach in northwestern Michigan. She'd gone there once to do a soil and water study for the state, but it was later in the year. She recalled how cold it had been.

Kelly smiled. "You're just as excited about this trip as Tyler."

"I confess, I am. We'll be gone for the entire weekend." She glanced out the kitchen window. "Alex should be here any minute."

"It warms my heart to see you like this, honey."

"It's like a dream I don't dare believe will really come true."

"Well, believe it. I think Alex cares deeply for you."

"I hope you're right."

Kelly frowned. "Hasn't he shown you the depth of his devotion?"

"I guess."

"You guess?"

"I really hurt him, Aunt Kelly. I can't help wondering if he's really forgiven me. Sometimes he looks at me as if—I can't explain it. It's like he's holding something against me and I should know what it is, but I don't. Maybe I'm just being paranoid. He seems truly committed and eager for the marriage, but…"

"You're probably suffering from pre-bridal nerves."

Valerie shrugged her shoulders. "Probably."

Tyler burst into the room. "When is Mr. Price going to get here, Mama?"

"Any minute. Have you packed everything? Your toothbrush and extra underwear?"

"Aw, Mama, I'm not a baby."

"No, you sure aren't. Breakfast is ready."

"I want to wait for Mr. Price."

They had to decide what Tyler was going to call Alex, Valerie thought. He couldn't continue to call him Mr. Price. Alex winced every time he did that. What else could he call him? It was a given that Tyler wouldn't want to call him Daddy. Maybe later he could call him Pops or some other fatherly endearment. Would Tyler ever accept Alex as his father? she wondered. She could only hope.

They heard and then saw the Durango as it pulled up alongside the windowed kitchen door.

"He's here!" Tyler shouted, flinging the door open.

Valerie looked with appreciation as Alex strode into the kitchen. He was wearing jeans that hugged his lean hips and shaped his muscular thighs and calves magnificently. And the T-shirt outlined impressive pecs and a six-pack stomach. And those biceps… Have mercy. As her femininity clinched and dampened, her throat suddenly went dry. It was almost a sin for a man to look this good. His sherry eyes darkened to deep, honey brown as he acknowledged her appreciative look

Valerie cleared her throat. "I'm glad you're here. Tyler is about to drive me and Aunt Kelly crazy."

Tyler grinned. "We been waiting for you to get here so we could all eat breakfast together."

"Those eggs and bacon sure smell good." Alex smiled. "I can't wait to dig in."

"Want me to add a couple of pancakes?" Kelly asked.

"You don't have to go to all that trouble, Kelly."

"It's no trouble at all." She literally beamed.

"I'll get the orange juice," Valerie added, stepping over to the refrigerator.

Alex observed every nuance of Valerie's appearance as she had his. Today she had on a denim shorts-skirt and a red sleeveless top that tied just below her breasts, leaving bare a delicious expanse of her silky, milk chocolate midriff. The woman was pure dynamite to his senses. He was glad to be sitting at the table. Fortunately for him the sides of the red gingham tablecloth hid his stare of arousal. He could feel his jeans tighten and abraid the sensitive area across his lap.

Alex was beginning to regret booking separate rooms at the lodge in Glen Haven. But then he'd had no choice since their son would be with them. God, he was getting carried away and he wanted desperately to have the upper hand on his emotions. But he realized he could exert just so much control over himself when it came to Valerie. As it was, he had to keep reminding himself of what she was capable of, and that he couldn't afford to weaken in his resolve.

Valerie felt Alex's eyes on her and it made her aware of his incredible maleness. God, how she loved this man. She prayed that in the future he would in turn come to love her. At the moment he desired her and wanted her in his life because of their son. Maybe he would one day come to want her for herself. How she longed for that day.

Seeing Valerie like this, she seemed so honest, innocent even. Alex couldn't imagine her raking money from his father and giving it to another man, and then leaving him the way she had, but it was exactly what she'd done. He wanted so much to trust in what he saw, but he was still leery of her. This weekend was about family and sharing, and he wasn't going to let anything spoil it.

It took three hours to drive from Quinneth Falls to Sleeping Bear Dunes. The scenery was some of the most beautiful in Michigan. Alex could see why the Indians had fought so hard to keep it. Tyler kept up an endless stream of chatter all the way there. It amazed Alex how much his son knew about the state's history. He'd mentioned wanting to be a scientist, but Alex wondered if being an archaeologist or maybe an historian would be a better choice. Well, he would wait and see what field his son chose, then be supportive of whatever profession he chose.

On Saturday Alex, Valerie and Tyler spent time exploring the hardwood forest and the arresting sights where glacial lakes had formed. That evening when the tired trio returned to the lodge, they all but fell into their beds fully clothed.

Sunday, they went to the beach, then on to Sleeping Bear. The impressive giant dune stood 450 feet high.

Valerie had her camera and started snapping pictures. "Tyler, stand over there by—" Valerie almost blurted out your father, but caught herself "—Alex."

Alex picked up on the slip and glanced at Tyler to see if he had noticed. He breathed a sigh of relief when he realized he hadn't. He wanted his son to know he was his father, but not yet. He needed more time to prepare him for that revelation.

Alex, Valerie and Tyler concluded the day by eating a whitefish platter, the special of The Leaning Anchor restaurant in the marina at Glen Haven. As Alex began the long drive back to Quinneth Falls, Tyler fell asleep.

"We had a wonderful time, Alex," Valerie said, stuffing a yawn.

"I think it went well."

"You suggested that Tyler call you Alex. That doesn't bother you?"

"It does. I'd much prefer he called me Dad, but I can't expect him to do that. What I hate is hearing him call me Mr. Price like I was some..." He couldn't finish the sentence.

"I know and I'm sorry. Maybe when he knows the truth—"

"Don't count on it. I'm not. Just having him in my life means the world to me. If he calls me anything remotely endearing I'll be content."

"I understand. I wish—never mind."

"What do you wish?" he insisted.

"It doesn't do any good to rehash the past. It's just that, the past."

"But can we completely forget it? God knows I'm trying."

Valerie put her hand on his arm. "I know you are."

Alex put his hand on her thigh and slung her a quick, desire-filled glance and said, "You're so beautiful, Val."

Valerie waited, hoping to hear that he also loved her,

but when he didn't say the words, disappointment streaked through her and she moved her hand away.

Alex saw her expression and wanted to take it away, but he didn't trust her. And he didn't know if time would ever change that.

Over the next two weeks Alex spent as much time as he could with Tyler and Valerie, taking them out to dinner, going exploring with his son and having intimate picnics near their future home. Sometimes they just sat in front of the TV playing games and eating popcorn. Alex constructed a tire swing in the old tree on the side of the house. Although he'd done it for his son, he himself spent more time on it than Tyler.

One evening when Tyler was spending the night at Danny Cranson's, Alex invited Valerie and her aunt out for the evening. Alex had to smile, because Althea had said there weren't any enjoyable perks in a town the size of Quinneth Falls. She'd been wrong. Most people went to a club called The Night Spot when they wanted to let it all hang out.

Alex enjoyed the casual ambiance. They had special rooms: one for the younger set who enjoyed rock, hip-hop

and rap; one for the people who preferred a more serene
type of music; and also one for the people who liked
country. All the rooms were huge and soundproof so that
one type of music didn't infringe on or overpower the other.
Alex chose the serene room. The music was mellow,
contemporary R & B. As they sat at their table, Alex
watched Valerie's aunt. Kelly appeared to be enjoying
herself. Valerie had told him she rarely went out. He
wondered why she didn't have a male friend. The woman
was certainly attractive enough. Looking at her was like
seeing an older version of Valerie.

"Why don't the two of you dance?" Kelly suggested.

Alex stood up and held his hand our to Valerie. She
smiled, then rose from her chair.

"Your aunt. seems to be enjoying the evening," Alex
commented as they danced.

"Yes, she does. I wish she had someone special in her
life." When Valerie saw Jackson and Eugenia Crawford enter
the room, Valerie fell out of step.

"What's wrong?" Alex asked.

"Nothing." She glanced at her aunt

Alex's eyes narrowed, and he followed her line of vision
from the Crawfords to her aunt. He studied the uncomfortable, almost panicky look on Kelly Harper's face. He
wondered what was between her and the Crawfords. From
the expression on her face Valerie knew what it was. The
music ended and he and Valerie returned to the table.

Valerie kneaded her bottom lip. Of all nights, why did
the Crawfords choose tonight to come here? She saw the
pain in her aunt's eyes. In the past Kelly had made sure not

to go anywhere near the Crawfords. Valerie groaned when she saw the objects of her aunt's despair head in their direction.

"Alex and Valerie. I'd heard that you two were seeing each other. I think it's wonderful." Eugenia looked at Kelly and asked. "How have you been, Kelly?"

"Just fine, Eugenia." She shifted her gaze to the man beside her. "How have you been, Jackson?"

The older man gave her a small smile and answered, "Great, Kelly. It's good to see you, Valerie and Alex." He cleared his throat and said to his wife, "I believe our table is ready, dear."

Alex watched the byplay between the Crawfords and Kelly. He'd picked up on the tension between Jackson and Kelly and wondered if they'd ever been involved.

"Dance with me, Kelly," he said.

As Alex danced with her aunt, Valerie wondered what he'd been thinking. She'd seen that curious assessing look he'd given her aunt. Had he guessed the relationship between Kelly and Jackson Crawford? Just then Howard walked in with Gina Amos, Alex's secretary. They saw her and came to the table.

"Valerie, are best wishes in order?" Howard asked.

"How did you find out about me and Alex? Don't tell me, I think I already know. Jake Spriewell. Right?"

Howard smiled. "You guessed it. His son Ralph mentioned to him seeing you and Price and Tyler picnicking near the house. And that you looked cozy. You know Jake. He's driven by your house and seen the Durango parked there several times. He also saw the three of you heading out of town. And of course he noted that you were gone for several days." Amusement flickered in Howard's eyes.

Valerie shook her head. Nothing surprised her about Jake Spriewell. "Gina, how are you doing? I didn't know you and Howard were seeing each other."

"We have been for a while now," Gina answered with a blushing smile.

"I've known Gina for years." Howard gave Gina an adoring look. "But just recently I realized that I wanted to get to know her better."

"I'm glad. And yes, best wishes are in order Alex and I are getting married very soon."

Kelly and Alex returned to the table.

Valerie saw the wary expression on Alex's face when he saw Howard, and she tensed. But a few minutes later she relaxed when she saw the look on Alex's face ease into a relieved smile upon learning that Howard and Gina were a couple. Had that been jealousy glittering in Alex's eyes? It had to mean that he loved her just a little, didn't it?

Alex invited Howard and Gina to share their table. Howard asked Valerie to dance and Alex asked Gina. Jackson walked over to the table and requested that Kelly dance with him. She hesitated, but then agreed and followed him out on the dance floor.

"You love Alexander Price, don't you, Valerie?" Howard inquired as they swayed to the music.

"What about Tyler? Have you told him Price is his father?"

"Nor yet, but we plan to when the time is right."

"Tyler loved George. I hope he doesn't resent your marrying again. And think Alex is trying to take George's place."

"I hope not too. But we'll deal with it."

"I wish you all the best, Valerie."

"Thanks. You've been a real friend to me. Is it serious between you and Gina?"

Howard grinned. "You're not jealous, are you?"

"Extremely." She laughed.

"The answer to your question is yes, it is. Gina is a wonderful girl."

"I'm glad for you. I'll bet Hattie is over the moon; she's wanted you to find someone for a long time."

"You're right, she has. She is happy, although she would have preferred it to be you."

Valerie watched her aunt as she danced with Jackson Crawford and wondered what they were talking so intensely about. She shifted her attention to Eugenia, who was talking to someone and seemed not at all concerned. Valerie realized she wasn't the only one who'd noticed; Alex was also watching her aunt and Jackson.

Following her dance with Jackson, Kelly was reserved, even withdrawn, and suggested cutting the evening short. Within minutes the trio left.

After Kelly had gone into the house, Valerie remained outside and talked to Alex.

"Is Kelly all right?" he asked.

"I think so, but she does seem disturbed."

"What could Jackson Crawford have said to her? They have a past, don't they?"

"Yes. They were in love a long time ago. It's a complicated story, and not mine to tell."

"I won't pry. Kelly is a warm, giving person. Too bad my father never found anybody like that after my mother died."

Valerie winced inwardly at his words. She knew she would have to make herself tolerate Michael Price for Tyler's sake. Although he was her son's grandfather, and she was about to marry Alex, Valerie didn't think her intense hatred of Michael would ever change.

Alex noticed Valerie's obvious revulsion at the mention of his father. Taking into consideration the history between his father and Valerie, he foresaw unpleasantness between them. They would both have to resolve it because he wouldn't allow either of them to hurt Tyler. He had been putting off telling his father about the wedding, but knew he couldn't for much longer.

Alex drew Valerie into his arms and kissed her. He groaned. He didn't know how long he could stand not making love to her. His senses went on overload every time he was near her. With a frustrated sigh, he reluctantly let her go.

"You're a dangerous woman, Valerie Bishop."

"What do you mean?"

"You know damn well what I mean. I feel like laying you down on the grass and having my way with you, woman."

"Really?"

His kiss was a promise and a demand, all at the same time. "Yes, really."

Valerie felt him tremble and knew he was exerting superhuman control over himself She knew how he felt; it was just as hard for her She smiled when he made to take a step away from her and he swayed slightly.

"I feel like sweeping you up in my arms and tossing you in the Durango and driving to my place, and then making love to you all night, but I'm not going to do it. The next time we make love it'll be on our wedding night." He gave her one last kiss and climbed into the Durango and drove away.

Valerie stood watching until his taillights disappeared as the car turned the corner. She waited for her senses to calm down before going inside the house. She needed to talk to her aunt. Valerie knocked on Kelly's door.

"I really don't feel like company, Valerie."

"I think it is exactly what you need. Can I come in?"

"All right."

Kelly was standing in front of her window looking out. When she turned, Valerie saw tears glistening in her eyes. "Oh, Aunt Kelly," she said, walking over to her and taking in her arms.

"It's all right. I'm all right. Jackson and I had a healing talk. I found out tonight that I still love him, but am no longer in love with him. He's totally and irrevocably committed to Eugenia."

"I wish you had someone special in your life."

"I do, I have you and Tyler."

"Are you going to come and live with us?"

"Oh, no, dear. This house belonged to my sister and I intend to keep living here."

"But you'll be all alone."

"You and Tyler will be only a few miles away. I can come visit and you can visit me."

"But still—"

"I'll be all right. I do have my work So you don't have to worry about me."

"I'll always worry because I love you."

"And I love you."

A few days later Alex, Valerie, Tyler and Kelly went to Holland, Michigan. Alex had insisted that Kelly come along. It warmed Valerie's heart when he told her he wanted to include her aunt, that she was a member of his family.

"You don't have to invite me along," Kelly countered.

"I won't take no for an answer."

"Please come, Aunt Kelly," Tyler pleaded.

Valerie added her own plea. "We want you to, Aunt Kelly."

"All right, it looks like I'm outnumbered," Kelly finally agreed.

Sounding like a young tour guide, Tyler told them that Holland, Michigan, which was established by religious dissenters from the Netherlands in 1847, reflected its Dutch heritage. They drove on to Windmill Island and toured Little Netherlands, a town recreated to resemble a Dutch village.

"The windmills are awesome, aren't they?" Tyler commented.

Alex was amazed by his son's knowledge of the area and answered, "Yes, they sure are." At his young age, Tyler was turning into a history buff.

"The tulips are beautiful, don't you agree, Aunt Kelly?" Valerie asked.

"I do indeed. The only time I've ever been here was when your mother and I were Tyler's age. We came in the month of May when the Tulip Time Festival was going on."

"I think we should go to the Netherlands Museum," Tyler suggested.

Alex glanced at the points of interest map they'd been given on the island and they laid out their route. Valerie and Kelly bought clogs at the Wooden Shoe Factory. From there they went to the Baker Furniture Museum. Tyler thoroughly enjoyed the Dutch Village theme park

At the end of an activity-filled day, they stayed in an original Dutch inn that night and the next morning, following a big breakfast of pecan pancakes, ham and eggs, drove back to Quinneth Falls.

CHAPTER NINETEEN

As Alex sat behind his desk in the temporary Quinneth Falls branch office of Price Industries, he replayed the last few weeks. Although he now felt he was on more solid ground with his son, Alex couldn't help wondering how Tyler would react to their revelation. True, he and his son got along like a house afire, but they'd never crossed over that boundary of friendship, onto more familial ground. He and Valerie agreed that it was time they broached the subject of their coming marriage to Tyler; test the waters so to speak.

"Alex?"

"Justin."

"You certainly were deep in thought. Didn't you hear me knock?"

"No. Did we have a meeting this afternoon?"

Justin laughed. "None that I'm aware of. You talk about me having it bad. Look at you. I'd say I'm not the only one in love."

"Just because I'm marrying Valerie doesn't mean—"

"I think it does. You've got the besotted look of love about you, my friend, my boss."

"Give it a rest, Justin."

"Your father called when you were out at the site. Didn't you pick up your messages when you came back?"

"No. I didn't." He buzzed Gina and she brought the messages in. He checked through them. His father had left several. He knew he would have to talk to him sooner or later, so he might as well get it over with. He picked up the receiver and punched in his father's number.

"Dad."

"I was wondering when you'd get back to me. We need to talk, Alexander."

"I agree, we do. I'll be busy helping iron out problems at the site all this week. Can you come here this Friday?"

"I'll be there."

"Dad—Dad?" He heard the dial tone. Alex glanced at Justin. "He sounded strange. I wonder if he's feeling all right," Alex said thoughtfully. He grimaced. "In any case I'm not looking forward to seeing him. Dad's not going to be happy about my plans to marry Valerie. But that's his problem."

"I'd say you both have a problem," Justin pointed out, his tone insightful.

Michael mopped the sweat from his forehead with his handkerchief after his phone conversation with his son. How was he going to tell Alexander the truth? Michael had never been a coward when it came to facing up to things he'd done, but this was different. He had so much more to lose. He couldn't help wondering about his grandson. According to Alexander, he strongly resembled him. Which meant that he also probably favored Michael.

He'd had plenty of time to think things over the last few weeks. Maybe he should consider approaching Valerie Bishop first. But after all the dire threats to expose her aunt, she probably wouldn't let him within a hundred feet of her. And he couldn't blame her. If Alexander hadn't mentioned the money to her, she had no idea of the extent of Michael's interference in her life.

He hadn't always been such a bastard. Only in business had he been ruthless, until his marriage to Irene. He had to admit in hindsight that his experience with her had left him deeply scarred. But there was no excuse for what he'd done. All women weren't like her. Alexander's mother, Arlene, had been nothing like Irene, and neither had his sister-in-law, Joyce.

He didn't know what kind of person Kelly Harper was, either. Even if he did, who was he to judge her? Or anybody else. His own character was far from sterling. His judgmental attitude was sure to have tragic repercussions once Alexander found out the extent of his perfidy.

Michael hated to think about what he had to face when that happened.

❦

Valerie had stopped in the middle of checking a list of supplies to order for Resource. Her thoughts drifted to Alex. So far he'd been so patient and understanding where she was concerned. Valerie didn't know if she would have been if their situations were reversed. Alex wouldn't be having to go through this if not for his father.

"I hope there are no serpents lurking in your paradise," Mary Ellen quipped.

"Mary Ellen, when did you come in?"

"About five minutes ago. It goes to show how much attention you pay me."

"I'm sorry. I've had a lot on my mind." Valerie recalled her assistant's joke about a serpent. There was certainly one lurking in her paradise, and his initials were Michael Price. And like that snake, he lay in wait, ready to sink his fangs into her.

"I'd say that Alexander Price was quite a lot for any woman to have on her mind."

"How are things between you and Justin?"

"Ah, changing the subject."

"Mary Ellen," she warned.

"All right, I'll play. You haven't even noticed the ring on my finger?" Valerie saw that Mary Ellen's face literally glowed and her grey eyes sparkled as she held out her left hand.

Valerie gasped. "It's beautiful." Tears stung her eyes. Alex hadn't given her one. She wondered if he planned to. "I'm so happy for you and Justin."

Mary Ellen shot her a concerned look "Is everything all right between you and Alex?"

"Yes." She nodded. "I'm just a little anxious. We're going to talk to Tyler about our marriage plans this evening."

"From what I've seen of the two together, you shouldn't have a problem there. Tyler hero worships Alex. And I know you're crazy in love with the man."

"Is it that obvious?"

"Only to me because I'm afflicted with the exact same condition. Don't worry, things'll work out for you guys."

Valerie hoped Mary Ellen was right.

When she got home, Valerie searched through her closet for something to wear. The experiment she'd been running that afternoon had taken longer to finish than she had expected, leaving her no time to go shopping. She couldn't understand her agitation. The purpose of the evening was to sound Tyler out on the subject of her and Alex's relationship and get his reaction to the subject of marriage.

Come on, be honest. You want to look good for your man. And, too it might lend you confidence for what lies ahead.

Valerie found a red sundress with straps that criss-crossed in back. The slender skirt reached just above her knees. Red was a good color on her. She decided to wear her hair down. She pulled out a drawer in her jewelry box and reverently lifted out the heart-shaped, diamond pendant Alex had given her years ago and fastened it around her neck. She remembered how he loved giving her presents—back when he loved her. She scrutinized her reflection in the mirror and was reminded of how she had looked and felt eight years ago. She was older now, and hopefully a lot wiser and stronger.

Once dressed and downstairs, Valerie kept glancing out the window every few minutes, pacing impatiently as she waited for Alex to arrive.

"If you don't stop pacing, you're going to wear a hole in the carpet," Kelly remarked.

Valerie stopped. "I'm so anxious about this evening, Aunt Kelly."

"I know you are, honey, but working yourself up like this isn't going to help. I made sure Tyler changed his clothes. He's curious to know why, since it was only Alex that was coming over. I told him to wait and find out. Needless to say, he wasn't satisfied with that answer."

"It'll all be over soon. Thank goodness." But would it really? Valerie wondered. Or would it only be the beginning? She still had Michael Price to deal with.

"Your young man just drove up. I'll keep Tyler in the kitchen with me for a while. It'll give you and Alex some time alone to talk."

"Thanks, Aunt Kelly." Valerie heard the bell and letting out a nervous breath, moved to answer its summons.

As Alex stepped inside, he slid an appreciative eye over Valerie. His eyes caught on the pendant around her neck reached our to touch it. "I wondered if you still had me."

"You needn't have wondered. It was very special."

Alex cleared this throat. "You look lovely tonight, Val." He glanced past her and not seeing Tyler, he let out a relieved breath. "Can we go out on the porch and talk first before we face Tyler?"

"All right."

His lips curved with faint amusement. "You look as nervous as I feel."

She gave him a commiserating smile and preceded him out the door.

"Have you said anything to him about us?" Alex asked once they were on the porch.

"Not really. He still misses George a great deal. But he mentioned that he was glad he had you to do father and son things with."

"Well, I guess that's a start in the right direction. The question is, will he still feel that way after he knows our plans?"

"He's very fond of you, Alex."

"As I am of him, but will he accept me as a substitute for the man he thinks of as his father. Damn it, I hate this. He's my son."

"I'm so sorry for putting you through this," she said, tears trickling down her cheeks.

"I didn't mean to make you feel bad, Val." He gathered her in his arms and just held her close for a few minutes.

Valerie pulled away and wiped the tears away with the heels of her hands. "I think we'd better go inside and get on with it."

They'd come back inside and were sitting on the couch when Tyler entered the living room.

"Aunt Kelly said you wanted to talk to me?" Tyler looked anxiously at his mother, and then at Alex.

"Yes, we do. Come sit down." Alex indicated a place on the couch between him and Valerie. "You know how fond I am of you and your mother, don't you?"

"Yes." Tyler frowned. "You're not going to go away too?"

"Away too?"

"Like my daddy did."

"No, I'm never going to go away, Tyler. I've asked your mother to marry me. Would you mind having me for a stepfather?"

Tyler looked to his mother, then back to Alex. "You'd be coming here to live with us?"

"Well, not exactly. You know about the house by the lake?"

He nodded.

"We'll be moving in there after the wedding. What do you think about that? Would you mind living by the falls?"

"Heck no. I think that's tight. I can't wait to tell Danny."

"You don't object to my marrying your mother?"

"Heck no. We'll be able to do things together all the time, like a real family." He suddenly shot Valerie an anxious look. "You don't think my daddy'll mind, do you, Mama?"

Tears welled in Valerie's eyes. "I'm sure he won't mind, baby."

"'Cause you're marrying Alex doesn't mean you won't still love my daddy, does it?"

"No. He'll always have a special place in my heart as he will in yours."

"Can I call Danny now?"

Alex let out a relieved sigh.

Valerie smiled. "Don't you want to know when Alex and I are going to get married?"

"Yes. But can't we do it later?" he asked, glancing impatiently at the phone.

"Make your call." Valerie made to stand, but Alex put a hand on hers, then pulled a small, black velvet box from his jacket pocket.

"I want to make our engagement official." He opened the box and lifted out a diamond-cut, three-karat aquamarine ring.

Valerie lifted her left hand and rubbed her thumb across her wedding band, then took it off and laid it on the coffee table. When she raised her eyes, her look told Alex the emotion she was feeling.

He slipped the engagement ring on her finger and said in a low husky voice, "Will you marry me, Val?"

This must be the day for tears, Valerie thought, because they rolled down her cheeks for the second time that day. "Yes, I'll marry you." She wanted to add that she also loved him, but decided against it.

As Tyler talked to his friend, Alex stood up, pulled Valerie to her feet, then drew her into his arms and kissed her.

Valerie lay awake that night thinking about everything. Tyler didn't seem to have any objections to the marriage, but then he hadn't taken time to consider the changes it would bring into his life. There would have to be adjustments. She wondered if he was really ready for that. But if problems did arise, they'd face them together as a family.

Valerie turned the light on and sat up in bed and examined her ring. It was unusual. Most men went in for diamonds, sapphires or emeralds, some even rubies. The stone Alex had chosen was her birthstone. He was as unpredictable in his actions as he was spontaneous in their lovemaking. She couldn't help wondering what life with Alex was going to be like.

She loved him so much. Was it asking too much that he return her love? They'd never really talked about what happened eight years ago because she'd skirted the issue.

Did she dare tell him what his father had threatened to do if she'd stayed in Detroit? And about his attempt to bribe her?

Surely after all this time, and considering their present relationship, Michael Price wouldn't do as he had threatened, but she needed to make sure. Her aunt had finally come to terms with her feelings for Jackson Crawford. What she didn't need was a scandal in her life.

Alex sat in the Durango watching the falls. It was as though a weight had been lifted from his soul. Tyler had not objected to his marrying Valerie and to his becoming a father-figure in his life. Hallelujah, his mind rejoiced. He'd be making a home for his son. In time, when Tyler was mature enough to accept it, he would tell him the truth: that he was his real father.

The look in Valerie's eyes said he could trust her, but could he really? That bitter empty feeling that had taken up residency inside him after she'd left him hadn't completely gone away. He wondered if it ever would. He still had doubts about her degree of commitment. Oh, he was sure she was deeply committed to their son. And as Alex had given her no choice about the role he intended to play in Tyler's life, she'd included him in that commitment. Only

God knew how much he wanted to trust her. He desired her, but could he trust her?

Alex drove around the lake to his house. They'd be able to move in in another four to six weeks from the look of things. It was time that he and Valerie proceeded with the details for the wedding. First, he had to talk to his father. He didn't want him mentioning the money to Valerie. He never wanted Tyler to find our what his mother had done. He would allow no one, not his father or Valerie, to hurt their son.

CHAPTER TWENTY

When Gina showed his father into his office, Alex rose from the chair behind his desk.

"Dad, I'm glad you could—"

"Is there no chance of you coming back to Detroit and mending fences with Althea?"

"Dad, I told you that I intended to make Quinneth Falls my home. I haven't changed my mind. As for Althea, it's all over between us. I've made other plans."

"Other plans?"

"Valerie and my son are what I want to talk to you about. I've already told you I wanted to make a home for my son. What I didn't tell you is that I plan to marry Valerie so we can be a family."

"What?"

"Accept it, Dad, because it's going to happen."

Michael was quiet so long Alex didn't think he would answer. Finally he said, "It looks like I'll have to."

Alex frowned. The last thing he'd expected was for his father to give in without a fight. "Are you feeling all right, Dad?"

"I'm fine."

Alex's eyes narrowed. He had his doubts about that. This wasn't at all like his father Something wasn't right. "Does this mean that you're willing to accept my marriage and be a part of your grandson's life?"

"I'd like to see the boy."

"To judge for yourself that he's a Price? I don't think so. I won't risk you hurting him, Dad."

"I wasn't planning on hurting him, Alexander."

Alex didn't know if he should trust his father's sudden about-face, especially knowing his feelings toward Valerie. Was this another one of his manipulative tricks to get his way? "When I'm sure you've truly come to accept my marriage, then and only then will I allow you to see Tyler."

Michael knew he would have to prove himself to his son. He also knew that he would have to confess everything he'd done. He wasn't sure if he approved of Alexander marrying Valerie Bishop, but if he wanted any kind of relationship with his son and grandson, he would have to accept Valerie and this marriage.

"I'll be returning to Detroit. I have some important business to take care of later today," Michael said quietly.

Alex felt as though he'd been flung into the Twilight Zone. "All right, Dad. Why don't you—"

The phone buzzed and Alex picked up the receiver.

"Yes, Gina? Can't Justin handle it? Oh, he is? All right. Tell them I'm on my way. Look, Dad, I have to take care of an urgent problem at the site."

"You go ahead."

Alex moved to leave the office. He studied his father for a moment and then, shaking his head, exited the room.

Michael seated himself in his son's chair. The business he had to take care of lived in Quinneth Falls. And he definitely wasn't looking forward to it.

Valerie was busy doing paperwork in her office at Resource Chemical when her new receptionist informed her that Mr. Price was there to see her. She smiled and stood, straightening her skirt. Her smile died when Michael Price was ushered into her office. It was shades of *déjà vu*. That last awful time in the executive suite at Price Industries eight years ago came to mind, chilling her to the bone.

"What are you doing here? More to the point, why are you here?

"I've come to pay a visit to my future daughter-in-law."

"I see Alex has told you about our plans and you've come here to convince me to change them."

"Actually I've come to..."

The door suddenly opened and in walked Kelly Harper.

"Valerie, your receptionist was away from her desk so I decided to just walk in. Oh, I didn't know you—"

"It's all right, Aunt Kelly." Valerie cleared her throat. "This is Michael Price, Alex's father and Tyler's grandfather. Michael Price, my aunt, Kelly Harper."

Michael stood for a few seconds as if in a trance, glancing first at Kelly, then Valerie, surprised by the striking resemblance between aunt and niece.

"Ms. Harper."

"So you're the man who has made my niece's life hell." Kelly glanced at Valerie and then Michael. "You have a nerve coming here to harass her like this. What kind of man does what you did to a young girl? Maybe the title of monster instead of human being fits you better."

"Now wait just a—"

"No, you wait." Kelly said, walking up to him and poking her finger into his chest. "You're not dealing with a young, vulnerable girl anymore. If you do anything else to hurt Valerie, you're gonna have me to deal with. Do I make myself clear?"

"As crystal." With that he walked out of the office.

"So that's Michael Price. It's like looking at an older version of Alex. And Tyler will no doubt look like that, too. Michael Price is a very attractive man. It's hard to believe he could do what he did to you."

"I'm sure he came here to convince me to break my engagement to Alex. Knowing how Alex is once he's made up his mind about something, I'm surprised he would bother coming here."

Kelly crossed her arms over her chest and glanced thoughtfully at the door Michael had just walked through. "Something in his manner disturbs me. I sense a kind of desperation about him. People are oftentimes their most dangerous when desperate." Kelly quirked her lips. "But he somehow didn't seem all that dangerous today. If I didn't know better, I'd say he looked fearful."

"Fearful? Michael Price? Believe me, Aunt Kelly, that man isn't fearful of anything or anybody, not even God."

"I wouldn't be too sure about that. Everybody fears something." Kelly frowned in exasperation. "I wish you'd tell me what he's holding over your head."

"I can't, Aunt Kelly."

"Or won't." After a few seconds her expression brightened. "Are you ready to go to lunch?"

"More than ready." Valerie glanced at her watch. "We'd better hurry. I have an experiment to document later this afternoon."

"One of the Cranson twins will be bringing Tyler home at two. And I need to get back to add the finishing touches to Candace Maynard's wedding gown."

That evening when he came to Valerie's house for dinner, Alex noticed that she was preoccupied. After they'd all eaten and Kelly had gone to her room, he, Valerie and Tyler went into the living room. Alex wondered why Valerie kept staring at her ring, and then at Tyler who was sprawled on the floor watching TV. Was she having second thoughts? No, that couldn't be it. He was sure that she knew by now he wouldn't do anything to hurt her company. Didn't she?

"It's getting late, Tyler. I think you should go take your bath, then go to bed."

"Aw, Mama, I want to stay up a little while longer."

"Do as your mother said," Alex said firmly.

Valerie saw surprise, then momentary defiance flash in her son's eyes before she heard him answer.

"Oh, all right." He shot Alex a mutinous look before marching out of the room.

"I do believe the lull before the storm is here," Alex quipped.

"It's just dawned on Tyler that he won't always have everything his own way."

"I hate to come off as the bad guy, but he has to learn that disobedience will not be tolerated." Alex saw the troubled look was back in Valerie's eyes. "What's wrong, Val? You still intend to marry me, don't you?"

"Maybe we should…"

Alex shot her a narrowed glinting stare. "Should what?"

"Maybe we should wait." "What should we be waiting for?"

"Your father—maybe we should give him more time to, ah, get used to the idea."

Alex's brows beetled into a curious frown. "He didn't happen to pay you a visit today, by any chance?"

Valerie didn't answer.

"I want to know exactly what he said to you." Alex demanded.

"He didn't actually get to say anything because Aunt Kelly walked in."

"Don't let him upset you. When I told him we were getting married and making a home for Tyler, he reluctantly accepted that it indeed was going to happen. I want you to plan the wedding for six weeks from Sunday."

"But your father—"

"I'm not going to allow him to run our lives. The time for us to be together as a family is way overdue."

"Not another word." Alex stopped the flow with a kiss. "I won't put off our wedding a moment longer than necessary. I can't keep my hands off you as it is. Every time I'm near you I want to lay you down and make hot passionate love to you."

"We can go to your place."

"I know, but hard as it is to resist temptation, I'm going to wait until you are Mrs. Alexander Price."

"You sure you can hold out that long?" she teased seductively.

"Don't play with me, woman." He kissed her one last time before leaving.

"Come with us, Kelly," Alex said just before he, Valerie and Tyler were ready to leave on their trip to Lansing.

"It was your idea, Aunt Kelly," Valerie reminded her. Kelly smiled. "I know, but I want to finish your wedding dress. There are only three weeks left before the big day."

Valerie was curious about the dress. Her aunt hadn't even let her see it, opting to wait for the final fitting. Valerie couldn't help the excitement vibrating through her. She was going to marry the only man she'd ever truly loved. And she was more than a little afraid it wouldn't happen. Though Michael's threat still hovered, she didn't let it stifle her joy. She wasn't that same easily-intimidated girl she used to be. She'd deal with Michael when she had to. But today she, Alex and their son were going to enjoy themselves.

"You ready to go, Mama?" Tyler trilled impatiently.

"Yes."

Alex smiled at his woman and his son. They would be happy, because he would settle for nothing less.

Michael sat in his car, parked down the street from the house Valerie shared with her son and her aunt. He'd seen Valerie, Alexander and Tyler wave good-bye to Kelly Harper and drive away an hour ago. He was still trying to work up the courage to walk up to the front door.

He'd decided it would be best if he approached Valerie's aunt first. When he'd met her a few weeks ago, he'd quickly sized up her character. Kelly Harper was the first woman since Arlene to stand up to him and give him hell. Oh, Irene had berated him and even cursed him, but never really stood up to him. Michael felt that if he could get the aunt to... What? He didn't know. The only way he'd find out was to talk to her

Michael got out of the car and walked up to the front door and knocked.

"Who is it?" Kelly called out.

"Michael Price. I'd like to talk to you, Ms. Harper."

Kelly flung the door open. "If you've come here to—"

"I came here to talk. And that's all. No threats."

Kelly frowned suspiciously, but said, "All right." She moved aside and let Michael in.

"What do you want to talk about that I'll want to hear?"

"You have every right to hate me for what I put your niece through."

"You're right, I do."

"I believed I was doing the best thing for my son by protecting him from being taken advantage of."

"Valerie would never do something like that."

"I've come to realize that, but I've done some pretty despicable things."

"Like what? I know you've told Valerie you thought she wasn't good enough for Alex. But I know there must be more to the story than that."

"Yes, there is. Much more."

"I'm all ears."

⚬⚬⚬

As they approached the capital city of Lansing, Tyler remarked, "See the Red Cedar and Grand Rivers? I read that the Grand River supplies all the city's water and power." Then he was off on another subject. "Did you know that Ransome E. Olds built and named the Oldsmobile? Can we visit his museum?"

"I often wondered where the name for that car originated," Alex commented. "I'd like to go there too. How about you, Val?"

"Count me in," Valerie said with a smile, surmising that Alex knew those facts about the Oldsmobile, but had allowed their son to believe he was enlightening him. As Tyler went on to tell them other historical facts she began to realize how interested her son really was in history. Alex was right when he said their son might not get into scientific research, but historic endeavors.

They next visited the state capital building, then on to the Michigan Historical Museum. When Tyler wanted to visit the Impression 5 Science Museum, Valerie wondered if aerospace science fascinated him more. There was no reason he couldn't major in both history and some form of science. She had to laugh. Her son was only seven and here she was attempting to map out his future professional aspirations.

After a tour of the Potter Park and Zoo, they were so exhausted no one, not even Tyler, complained about a bath and turning in early when they arrived at the hotel.

Just before dawn Alex awoke and went to look in on Tyler as he slept. He was still awed by the knowledge that this wonderful child was his. He would be the one to insure the continuation of the Price line, but he didn't carry the Price name. Alex couldn't help resenting that fact. He wanted so badly to do something about it. But when? He'd noticed Tyler's negative reaction when Alex had absently called him son. He didn't say anything, but Alex had got the feeling Tyler thought he was trying to usurp George Bishop's position as his father

How should he handle this? He was Tyler's real father, damn it. Frustration sliced through him like a jagged edged knife cutting into vulnerable skin. That closeness he and Tyler had shared from day one was no longer as close, or as warm, and Alex didn't know what to do to bring it back

"He is beautiful, isn't he?" Valerie said softly, her voice filled with motherly love and pride as she walked up behind Alex.

"Yes, he is." Alex stiffened and walked past her out of Tyler's room.

"What's wrong, Alex?" Valerie asked, closing the door and following him into the suite living room.

"Nothing." He walked over to the windows and looked out at the early rising sun.

Valerie wondered why he looked so sad. "There has to be something."

Alex turned to face her. "I really don't want to get into it. Telling you won't change anything."

"What things?" Valerie wrapped her arms around his waist. "What do you mean? Please, tell me."

"We can't alter the last eight years."

Valerie sighed. "No, we can't. I wish we could."

"Why did you leave me, Val? I have to know. That note clarified nothing."

She let her arms drop. "I thought it was for the best at the time."

"You married another man within weeks of leaving Detroit."

"You're right, and you know why I did. It doesn't matter now what my reasons were, does it? George is dead. We have a chance to be a family. We're going to be married in a matter of weeks."

True, it wouldn't affect the here and now, Alex thought. If she would only admit that money had motivated her, maybe he would—what? Come to completely trust her? No, it wouldn't make him...what? Understand? Maybe. If there was only some way he could be sure of her feelings for him. But there wasn't. He loved her and he knew that love didn't come with a guarantee that she would one day return his feelings.

Alex held her close. "You're right, Val, it doesn't matter."

Despite what he said, Valerie knew it did. She was now sure that he was keeping something from her. Whatever it was, it had to do with her leaving him eight years ago. What could it be? Did it involve his father in some way? Could Michael have said something? But what could he possibly have said? She had turned down his offer of money to leave Alex.

Valerie caressed Alex's cheek "I'm going to make up for all the pain I've caused you. This I promise you, Alex." She pulled his head down and kissed his lips.

Alex groaned. "I want you so much, Val." Eager hands removed her robe. And equally eager fingers found and caressed her breasts, teasing the nipples into hardened peaks. He quickly lowered his mouth to a nipple and suckled it through the thin material of her nightgown. The whimpering sound she made turned him hard as granite. To hell with waiting. He had lifted her in his arms and started for his bedroom when he heard a doorknob rattle.

He immediately lowered Valerie to her feet and grabbed her robe and helped her into it. Seconds later Tyler walked into the room rubbing his eyes.

Alex looked at Valerie and saw the frustrated desire in her eyes that he knew mirrored his own. He could see the still hardened peaks of her nipples through her robe. The ache in his groin attested to his own degree of arousal. They had only a few more weeks remaining before their wedding. Then they both could give free rein to their passion.

CHAPTER TWENTY-ONE

The wedding was now only three days away and Valerie hadn't heard anything from Michael Price. She didn't know whether to feel relieved or anxious. Had he really accepted things? Or was he waiting to destroy her happiness yet again?

Your guess is as good as anybody else's, a little voice inside her head admonished.

From her position on the bed, Valerie glanced at her wedding gown hanging on the closet door. It had to be the most beautiful dress she'd ever seen. It was made up in a butter yellow satin material. The sleeveless bodice had a sweetheart neckline embroidered with gold thread in a buttercup pattern. Lattice-laced, wide yellow, satin ribbons cleverly closed the back of the gown. Valerie's skin heated at the thought of Alex pulling the bow loose and splaying his fingers across her bare back The long, full satin skirt had a scalloped border train also embroidered with the same gold thread in the buttercup pattern. This dress was her idea of the perfect wedding gown.

"Valerie, you're going to stare a hole right through that dress," Kelly teased from the open doorway. "Can I come in?"

"Of course, Aunt Kelly. I can't help admiring this beautiful creation. You really outdid yourself."

"I agree. And why shouldn't I? You're my favorite person in the whole world."

Valerie rose from the bed and walked over to her aunt and hugged her. "I love you so much, Aunt Kelly."

"As I love you."

Valerie noticed that her aunt had a flat box in her hand.

"I want you to wear this." Kelly opened the box and lifted out a gold chain with a pearl pendant attached to it. "Your mother gave this to me. She wanted me to start a tradition with my daughter when I had one. Then have her daughter pass it on to her daughter."

Tears came to Valerie's eyes because she knew her aunt would never have a daughter of her own. And for a moment she was speechless, then said in a voice quivering with emotion, "Oh, Aunt Kelly, it's exquisite and I'll treasure it always."

"You are the daughter of my heart," she said softly.

Valerie kissed her aunt's cheek. "If I'm blessed with a daughter of my own, I'll give this to her on her wedding day."

Alex took Tyler out to the new house. He'd had most of their personal things moved in a few days earlier and had the furniture for the bedrooms and kitchen delivered just the day before. Alex smiled, thinking about the look of pride he'd seen on Ralph Spriewell's face when he'd informed Alex that the house was ready for them to move into. Alex gave him a well-deserved bonus and offered him a permanent position at the new plant as maintenance engineer.

"How do you like your room, Tyler?" Alex asked when they reached it.

"It's all right, I guess. Why can't we live in our old house?

"I thought you understood why when we discussed it. You told me you loved this house."

"I know and I do, but..." His voice trailed away. Tyler walked over to the corner desk set and sat in the chair behind it, tracing his fingers over the woodwork on top.

"But what, son?"

"I'm not your son, and you'll never take my daddy's place."

Pain knifed into Alex at Tyler's words. "I know I can never take his place. And I wouldn't even try."

Tyler gave him a distressed look. "Why did he have to die, Alex?"

Alex's heart went out to his son. He walked over to him and hunkered down in front of him and brushed the tears from his cheeks. "I can't tell you that, but I do know what you're feeling."

"How can you, when your father is still living?"

"Yes, he is, but I lost my mother when I was about your age. She died from breast cancer. I remember how much I missed her. I can still hear her laugh, remember her coming to my room when I woke up afraid and crying from a nightmare."

"I used to have nightmares sometimes when I watched scary movies or read scary stories. Daddy used to come in and make me feel safe. Now..."

"I want to be there for you, Tyler." He drew him into his arms and closed his eyes. "I want you to feel safe with me."

Tyler pulled away and sniffed. "I won't ever forget him."

"I know you won't. I don't expect you to. If we can just be friends." In that moment Alex despaired of their relationship going beyond friendship.

"Danny said you and Mama are going to have babies and won't care about me anymore."

"We may have other children, Tyler, but you'll always be very special to us."

"I will?"

Alex drew his son back into his arms. "You always will, I promise." Alex's outlook brightened. He and Tyler had a ways to go, but he felt they had made progress. He wanted his son to trust and confide in him, but knew it would take time, and Alex intended to give him as much time as he needed. "I have a surprise for you."

Tyler moved out of Alex's embrace and looked him in the eye and said, "You do? Where is it?"

Alex smiled. "I'll show you. Just follow me."

Tyler followed Alex out to the backyard and over to an old oak tree.

"A tree house!" Tyler burst out. "My very own tree house!"

"Do you like it?" "It's tight."

Alex took the comment to mean he loved it. "You want to go inside and look around?" He wanted to see the expression on his face. Alex had had Stan and another carpenter build the tree house. He recalled always wanting one at his age. Alex had it built as much for himself as for Tyler. With supporting braces, it was sturdy enough to take the weight of five two hundred pound men or at least seven or eight hefty-sized kids comfortably. Beneath it was a sturdy ladder.

"My birthday is next week. Is this my present?"

Alex's insides shrank at Tyler's question because he hadn't known the date of his son's birth. "I couldn't wait until then to show it to you." Alex coughed to clear the emotion catching in his throat, and batted his eyes furiously to cool the heat in his burning eyelids.

It was the evening of Alex's and Valerie's wedding rehearsal at the entertainment hall. The Crawfords had given a dinner party in their honor. Afterward as Alex listened to Tyler talk a mile a minute about his tree house, he caught Valerie watching him intensely. He was sure that she sensed all was not as it should be with him. At times she seemed to know him better than he knew himself. When Tyler wound down, he and Danny scurried over to the table which was laden with the chocolate brownies her aunt had baked for the kids. Valerie joined Alex.

"You don't seem like yourself this evening. Surely you're not having second thoughts," she teased. When he didn't smile, she frowned. "What is it?"

"When I showed Tyler the tree house, he asked me if it was for his birthday. Hell, I couldn't tell him because I didn't even know the date he was born."

"Oh, Alex. I'm sorry, I didn't think. It's next Friday. I planned to have a sleepover party for him and his friends. I should have told you, it's just that I'm used to—"

"Doing things without me."

Valerie heard the anguish in his voice and it broke her heart. She'd never meant this to happen. She had so much to make up to him. Alex needed to be close to her and his son. They were his family now and she vowed never to let anyone destroy it. She would have to tell her aunt about Michael's threat, something she now wished in hindsight that she had all those years ago. She had wanted to protect her aunt, but she could not continue to do so at the price of Alex and Tyler's future happiness.

Valerie took Alex's hand in hers. "I can only imagine how much it must have hurt you."

Her words soothed him somewhat, but didn't erase the feeling that he would never attain that special closeness he sought with his son and the woman he loved. It hurt knowing how easy it had been for Valerie to exclude him. He wondered if anything could ever make him feel secure?

Valerie saw the uncertainty in Alex's eyes and a feeling of despair edged into her mind. She knew in that moment he would probably never come to completely trust her. She couldn't really blame him. He didn't know the real reason why she'd left. And until she talked to her aunt, she couldn't tell him.

As it turned out, Valerie didn't get a chance to talk to her aunt. There was a message from Candace Maynard on the answering machine when they got home that evening. She tearfully complained that her wedding dress didn't fit. Her Aunt Kelly had to go over to the Maynards for a refitting of the dress. Candace was going to be married the Sunday after Valerie's wedding and she was almost hysterical. By the time her aunt got home it was late and Valerie decided to wait until morning to talk to her. But as luck would have it, the next morning was hectic and the opportunity to talk was lost in the chaos.

CHAPTER TWENTY-TWO

The moment Valerie had always dreamed of since she'd met and fallen in love with Alex was almost here: her wedding to him. She frowned as the memory of her wedding to George came to mind. They had flown to Reno and had been married in one of those commercial wedding chapels. The preacher was an Elvis Presley wannabe who looked and dressed the part and wore the slicked-back hairstyle to perfection. The chapel had had oodles of phony flowers, flashing neon lights and loud recorded '60s rock-and-roll music.

Mrs. Crawford had really gone all out in decorating the entertainment hall for Valerie's wedding to Alex. The smell of fresh flowers filled the room and dulcet organ music floated on the air. Valerie peeped outside the dressing room door at the altar Ralph and Stan had constructed and Gina and Mary Ellen had decorated with flower garlands and ribbons.

"You look beautiful, Valerie," Kelly sniffed.

Valerie closed the door and walked over to her aunt. "It's the wedding gown."

"No, it's more than that. You're positively glowing."

"I agree," Mary Ellen chimed in. "I love the bridesmaid dress you made for me, Kelly," she remarked patting it here and smoothing it there.

"The butter yellow color is a perfect foil for your red hair. Justin's eyes will literally pop out of his head when he sees you. He may even insist on making it a double ceremony."

"He'd better not. I want my parents to be at my wedding."

"How do you feel, Valerie? Are you nervous?" Gina asked.

"No, I'm only paralyzed, that's all."

"From what I've heard it's a normal reaction," Mary Ellen added.

Eugenia Crawford swept into the room. "You look positively radiant, Valerie. How ever did you get a hunk like Alexander Price to propose? From what I understand, he already had a fiancée when he arrived in Quinneth Falls. You must have made quite an impression on the man."

"I guess I did."

"Is everything ready?" Kelly asked.

"In about twenty minutes Judge Farrell's wife, Clarissa, will come in and let us know when they're ready to begin."

"If you all wouldn't mind, I'd like to be alone for a while," Valerie said with a smile. As they all filed out of the room, Valerie let out a nervous breath. She'd be Mrs. Alexander Price in a matter of minutes. Also in those same few minutes she, Alex and Tyler would become a family. She had to pinch herself to make sure this was all real. Considering what had happened eight years ago, she never dreamed they'd ever be together like this.

What surprised her most was that Michael Price seemed to have accepted their marriage and hadn't tried to put a stop to it. But it could all be just an act. He could have plans to do something later.

She heard another knock at the door. It was Mrs. Farrell this time. Valerie took one last look in the mirror. It was nervous time.

As Alex stood at the altar awaiting his bride, Justin asked, "How are you holding up?"

"Just barely. Did you make sure Tyler has the rings?"

"Oh, no. I forgot."

"You what?" Alex blew out a relieved breath when he saw his friend's lips twitch.

Justin grinned. "Gotcha!"

"Wait until it's your turn."

When the music to the wedding march began to play, the room quieted. Tyler, dressed in a tux similar to Alex's, came marching up to the altar, carrying a yellow satin pillow bearing the wedding rings. He took his place beside Alex. Next came Mary Ellen, smiling and holding a bouquet of flowers. Justin smiled as she took her place to the left of the altar.

Alex's breath caught in his throat as Valerie marched up to the altar. To him she'd never looked more beautiful. This was the woman he loved, the mother of his child. They had a chance to be happy together and he wasn't going to let anything or anyone destroy it, he vowed.

Valerie wondered if what she saw in Alex's eyes when she reached his side was something more than desire. Could it be love? She prayed that it was. She knew he wanted to make a home for his son. But could he ever come to love her as much as she loved him?

Judge Farrell cleared his throat. "Valerie and Alexander stand before you all, ready to make a life-long pledge of love and commitment to each other."

As the judge proceeded with the ceremony, Valerie gazed into Alex's eyes, hoping to recapture the love they'd once shared and build a new life together with their son.

At the appropriate time Tyler lifted the pillow and Alex took the smaller ring and placed it on Valerie's finger.

"With this ring, I promise to love and cherish you for the rest of my life and give you all I have within my power to give."

Tyler stepped over to his mother and she took the remaining ring from the pillow and then eased it onto Alex's finger.

"With this ring, I promise to love and respect you in all things and share every aspect of my life with you."

The judge cleared his throat. "If anyone can show just cause why they should not marry, let him speak now or forever hold his peace." He waited the obligatory seconds to see if there were any objections.

Valerie glanced in Michael Price's direction. But all he did was silently stand beside her aunt. She returned her full attention to the judge.

"I now pronounce you husband and wife, and let no man interfere or try to destroy the union that God has approved and man has witnessed."

Judge Farrell said to Alex, "You may now kiss your bride."

Alex lowered his lips to Valerie's and placed a long, lingering kiss on them. As Alex and Valerie marched down the aisle as husband and wife, the photographer flashed pictures. And continued to do so for the next fifteen minutes. Then people gathered around offering congratulations and best wishes. Valerie tossed her bouquet and Mary Ellen and Gina both caught it. After that the reception commenced. First came the cutting of the huge, elaborate butter yellow three-tiered wedding cake with two spiraling candy staircases. Valerie and Alex led off the first dance.

The children headed for a place set up out back for them to play.

Valerie and Alex carried cups of punch over to the couch and sat, glancing out the window at their son as he played with his friends.

"Tyler looks happy, don't you think?" Valerie remarked.

"Yes, he appears to be. I hope he stays that way."

"Why wouldn't he?"

"Don't mind me. Whatever adjustment we may have to make, we'll make."

They both heard voices coming from behind a rubber plant a few feet away.

"That boy sure looks a lot like Alexander Price, doesn't he, Jessie? When the man first came to town I said to myself he sure looks familiar."

Valerie's brows arched when she recognized the voice: it belonged to Stella Mason.

"Me too. I wonder if poor George knew that Tyler wasn't his son," Jessie Mason speculated.

"I'll bet you anything he did and that's why Valerie rushed him off to Reno to get married in such an all-fired hurry."

"It hardly matters now. George is dead."

Alex and Valerie heard the two sisters move away.

"I guess everyone in town will soon know or suspect that I'm Tyler's real father. I wonder how long it'll be before Tyler hears it?" Alex asked.

It was a problem they would have to address sooner than they wanted to. Alex probably blamed her, Valerie thought, not that he didn't have every right to. If she had only told him she was pregnant when she found out. If only, the two most futile words in the universe, she thought sadly.

Valerie wished she could cement the Mason sisters' mouths shut. She'd learned how cruel their careless tongues could be when she had overheard them gossiping about her aunt at the annual picnic at the lake.

❧

Valerie and Alex left the reception and slipped away to the dressing room to change. Once inside Alex locked the door, then came up behind Valerie.

"The moment I've been waiting for ever since I saw the back of this dress. You look like a beautifully-wrapped present."

"And you want to unwrap me. Right?"

Alex turned her around and pulled the bow enclosing the dress, then began unlacing the ribbons.

Valerie gasped when she felt his cool fingers splay across her bare skin.

Alex eased the dress off her shoulders and watched it slide down her body, then pool at her feet.

Valerie stepped out of it. She smiled when she saw the desire in his eyes and heard him groan. His eyes darkened with desire as they lingered on her garter belt and the elastic suspenders holding up her pale yellow stockings.

Alex caressed her thighs and buttocks. "Oh, Val." He lowered the strapless bra and suckled a nipple.

"Alex," she moaned. "We have to change now or we'll be late getting to the airport."

"You're right." He hated to stop, but reluctantly moved away and let Valerie change into a peach summer suit. Justin had delivered Alex's sport coat and slacks to the room earlier. They were taking only a few days for a honeymoon, but planned on taking more time later after everything had settled down and the plant was finished.

Valerie felt less nervous now that the ceremony was over and they were preparing to leave the hall. Alex had aroused her in the dressing room, making her eager to be alone with him and experience his lovemaking.

Desire streaked through Alex when he saw that look. All he could think about was how sexy she had looked moments before when she had stepped out of her wedding gown. He could still smell the sweet scent of her skin and feel its rose petal softness. His mind conjured up the feel of her hot-slick opening as it completely encompassed his hardened male flesh. The near-to-bursting tightening in his groin made him groan in pain.

When Valerie heard the low sensual sound, she felt a tingling in her breasts and a burning sensation curl deep inside her.

"I think we'd better be on our way. I can't wait to be inside you, sweetheart," Alex said in a soft husky voice only she could hear.

"It's exactly where I want you to be. Yes, I think we should hurry up and go." As it was, her legs were threatening to collapse.

Tyler walked up to them with a slightly lost look on his face.

Valerie hugged him. "We'll only be gone a few days,

"Your mother is right. We'll be back in time for your sleepover party on Friday. While we're gone, you and Danny can outfit your tree house."

"With anything I want?" His voice brightened.

Alex laughed. "Yes, within reason. I talked to Stan and he'll be around to help you."

"And I can make you some curtains," Kelly added.

"Oh, Aunt Kelly, that's girl stuff."

"I'll let you pick the material. How does that sound?"

"Okay, I guess." He smiled his charming Alex smile.

"See, you won't even have time to miss us, Tyler," Valerie reassured him.

Michael, who had elected to hang back, stood watching his grandson. He was filled with remorse for what he'd done. He glanced at Kelly. He truly admired her. Even after all he had revealed to her, she had treated him more kindly than he deserved. He had expected her to pour out her wrath, by the bucketful, over his head. She'd told him that if he didn't tell Alex and Valerie the truth, she would. She had suggested that he approach Valerie first. If she could forgive him, then maybe Alex eventually would too. They had both agreed it would be criminal to spoil the pair's honeymoon. His revelation could wait until they got back.

Alex shot a quick look at his father, not sure how to take his silent acquiescence. He wondered if he would ever understand him. Alex turned his attention to his wife and said, "Val, we really should be getting to the airport."

"All right." Valerie eased her lips into an affectionate smile and said to her son, "We'll bring you something back to put in your tree house."

"Promise?"

"I promise."

Taking one last look at Tyler, Valerie and Alex hurried down the walk to the waiting limousine amidst a shower of rice, merriment and boisterous farewells. The limousine took them to the airport where they'd chartered a plane to fly them to Mackinac City. From there they would catch a ferry to Mackinac Island.

"Do you think Tyler is all right with us leaving?" Valerie asked Alex as they relaxed in the plane while waiting for take-off.

"He seemed to be."

"Your father was awfully quiet."

"I noticed."

Valerie cleared her throat and sought a different subject. "I've never been to Mackinac Island before. Have you?"

"Once when I was little and my mother was still alive. I'll never forget how fascinated I was when I first saw Fort

Mackinac. I could picture how it must have looked during the wars. I could almost hear the rifle shots buffeting back and forth between the French and British. Tyler would be interested in that. When we come back we'll have to bring him with us."

"Oh, are we coming back?"

Alex leaned over and kissed Valerie. "Yes, because I don't think we'll be getting that much sightseeing done this time around."

"Why would you say that?"

"Because I intend to keep you occupied with other more important pursuits."

"Such as?"

"I can hardly wait to get you alone, Mrs. Price. I may not let you out of the suite the entire time we're there."

"And deprive me of seeing all that beautiful scenery?"

"You're the best scenery there is."

"Naked or clothed?"

"Oh, woman, you just wait." He kissed her again.

CHAPTER TWENTY-THREE

"I've never been on a ferry before," Valerie trilled excitedly as they neared the island. "I feel like a little kid again."

"From what I can see you're all woman, Valerie Price."

"Oh, behave. You're supposed be looking at the scenery."

"I already told you the only scenery I'm interested in."

Valerie glanced through the brochure they'd been given just before the ferry cast off. "It says that no automobiles are allowed on the island and that walking, bicycles and horse-drawn carriage are the only modes of transportation."

"It's because the island is only three miles long and two miles wide. Although it is the perfect size for a resort, it's certainly not big enough to accommodate a lot of cars. Look, you can see the Grand Hotel from here."

"Look at all the birds," Valerie enthused. "And those rocks and the lush green woods. It looks like a giant wilderness park."

"That about says it all. I have to tell you that I'm a wilderness buff. I like roughing it. I go camping whenever I get the chance. I usually go to the Superior Uplands, but there are plenty of wilderness parks and campsites all over the state."

"Maybe I can go with you sometime."

"You really think you'd like it?"

"As long as I was with you I wouldn't mind where we were."

They rode in a horse-drawn carriage to the hotel.

"I'm surprised you didn't rent a bicycle," Valerie quipped.

"I couldn't very well fit all of our luggage on it."

"I often wondered how you keep so fit. Bicycle riding, right?"

"Occasionally. I also run and lift weights. You like the way I look?"

Valerie gave him a long appreciative once-over. "Oh, yes."

Minutes later they were shown into their suite. Before Valerie could put her purse down, Alex pulled her into his arms and kissed her, stealing her breath, and she dropped it.

"It seems like I've been waiting forever to get you alone, woman."

"Now that you have, what are you planning to do with me?" she asked sultrily.

He didn't answer with words, just started undressing her. As eager as he, she helped him do it. When she stood naked before him, she heard his breath catch in his throat.

"You have the most beautiful breasts I've ever seen." He lowered his mouth to a nipple and sucked.

A moan of pleasure left her lips as he paid homage to her other breast. He suckled her until she went limp and nearly slid to the floor. He lifted her into his arms and carried her over to the bed. With his eyes he worshipped her body as he knelt down beside the bed and starting from her feet, trailed light caressing kisses upward along her calf and knee, then up her thigh to the black curly juncture between her thighs.

"Oh, baby, you sexy thing you. I can hardly wait to come inside you. You'll probably scorch me on contact."

"But what a lovely way to burn."

"And you definitely give me fever But first, before I let you do that, I want to give you pleasure."

Alex bypassed her femininity and kissed her stomach and strowed more kisses along her midriff, zeroing in on her sensitive nipples again.

Valerie thought she would melt when she felt his fingers find her while he sucked at her breasts. The double assault on her senses nearly drove her over the edge.

Alex left her breasts and kissed a path to her lips, still working the bud between the moist crevice of her silky woman's flesh. He felt her jerk and raise her hips up and down as he worked her faster and faster, exciting every nerve ending.

Valerie cried out as pleasure surged through her inner core.

Alex smiled. She was ready. He quickly shed his clothes and moved over her. Parting her thighs, he slid into her hot damp heat. His tumescent flesh swelled and thickened within her. He began to employ powerful thrusts, delving deep into the heart of her.

Valerie's mind drifted in a haze of pleasure. Alex had never loved her this intensely before. His mouth was on hers hot and firm, devastating in its impact on her senses. She now understood the term *mind-blowing* for he was doing just that. He withdrew, then tunneled in slowly, the soft drag of his withdrawal was an exquisite torture only partially soothed when he filled her. She felt him move flesh into flesh, heat into heat, sliding and probing, making her gasp and writhe and cry out her pleasure.

When Alex felt her enveloping heat pulse around him, he moved more frantically within her, extending her climax into yet another until her body shuddered. And as it did so, his own release exploded, sending his seed deep inside her. As he felt the last flutters of her climax quiver around his semi-hard flesh, he closed his eyes and rejoiced in the rapture as the remaining essence of his release ebbed from his body into hers.

"What did you just do to me?" Valerie asked in a dazed voice when he moved onto his back

"Loved you out of your mind. You aren't complaining, are you?"

"Uh, uh." She dragged the last syllable out. "If you keep making love to me like that I won't want to leave this bed."

"Maybe I'd better cool it because you won't last the rest of our stay here."

"Is that a challenge?"

"Do you intend making it one?" He grinned, arching his brows wickedly.

"I'm thinking about it." Without further ado she slid her body over his, sheathing his hard male flesh to the hilt inside her. She moaned at the delicious sensations jetting through her. She began to move against him. When she heard a groan of pleasure vibrate in Alex's throat, she undulated over him, exulting in the feel of him.

"Oh, woman, what are you doing to me?"

"Blowing your mind the way you blew mine."

He drew a nipple into his mouth and sucked, laying his tongue across the sensitive tip. A whimper of delight eased from her lips. When Alex thrust upward, she cried out in bliss, collapsing over him like a rag doll. As her moans of completion filled the air, Alex reversed their positions and repeatedly stroked her velvet interior, reviving her ecstasy. He drew almost all of the way out only to thrust back in more sensuously, burying himself in the deepest heart of her.

Valerie felt herself moving toward an exhilarating climax yet again, feeling the sensations build faster as he moved in a wildly erotic dance within her. She was on fire, threatening to burn to cinders. White-hot pleasure burst through her with his next thrust. As her body began to quake in titillating culmination, he lifted her hips for deeper penetration. He rolled back and forth inside her until she felt him shudder, then splinter apart in an explosive release.

His breath jerking in and out, Alex muttered, "You meant what you said, didn't you?"

"What I said?" Valerie answered, equally breathless.

"About blowing my mind."

"Oh, that." She dazzled him with a smile. "Then I succeeded?"

"You know you did. Do you need a lift to the bathroom, woman?"

"I believe I do."

Alex carried Valerie into the luxurious bathroom, complete with a sunken tub big enough for two. He lowered her to her feet, then bent to turn on the Jacuzzi jets.

Valerie couldn't resist pinching his firm, lean buttocks. She laughed when he yelped in surprise.

"Sexual harassment!"

"Do you believe you can prove your allegation?"

"Yes, and when I do I expect to be compensated."

"How do you want payment?"

"Any way I can get it."

"When do you want compensation to start?"

"Immediately, you wench."

"Oh, so now I'm a wench, huh?"

"Come here, woman." And he pulled her into his arms, then stepped into the tub and sat down, letting the warm water sluice over them.

Valerie reached for the bubble bath and splashed some in before he could stop her Within seconds a mountain of foam rose from the tub.

"You're crazy, do you know that? It's a good thing that bubble bath is unscented. I'd be embarrassed to go in to dinner smelling like flowers or worse."

"Who's to say I was going to allow you out of here?"

"You want to order room service, then?"

"I'm already getting that."

Alex laughed. "You really are crazy."

"Yes, about you," she said, pulling his head down and ravishing his mouth.

Later, much later they got around to calling room service.

Valerie awoke to the feel of wave after wave of pleasurable sensations throbbing through her womanhood. As she felt a finger glide over her pearl of passion, she closed her thighs and began to move against the instrument giving her pleasure. She cried out in ecstasy as a sudden climax took her.

"Ooh, I love your interpretation of a wake-up call," she gasped, then kissed Alex. "You evidently didn't need one this morning."

"I wouldn't say that." He positioned himself between her thighs and delved into her, tipping her hips up so she could feel the long, masterful slide, deeper, deeper, until her slippery flesh began to shudder and she groaned. As he continued to move within her, he heard harsh breathing noises and realized they were coming from him. As he thrust over and over again, he could feel her inner contractions squeeze him and stroke him, propelling him closer and closer to oblivion. When the contractions turned into spasming waves riding his shaft, he cried out in release, dashing his essence against her womb.

"God, woman, if we don't take a breather neither one of us will be worth a quarter."

"Well, you did start it."

Alex eased off the bed, pulling Valerie with him to the bathroom.

As Valerie and Alex ate a late breakfast in the dining hall, they looked out the window at Fort Mackinac.

"They've done a lot to it since I was here last. It looks even more authentic now. You want to take a walk along the beach?"

"After that big breakfast, I think I'd better." Valerie laughed.

They walked down the path leading to the fort. "The rock formations the fort is built on are spectacular. It must have been a formidable fortress in its day, hard to breech, I would imagine."

"Oh, it was, but the British found a way."

"Aren't we supposed to go on a cruise around the Island?"

Alex glanced at his watch. "We've got a few minutes."

"How few? Surely you don't mean to..."

"I want you so bad I'm hurting, Val."

"So soon?"

"Indulge me, sweetheart."

She grinned wickedly. "Oh, I intend to."

"The salt smell of the lake is so invigorating," Valerie said, taking a deep breath of the air as the boat moved over the water.

Alex wrapped his arms around her waist. "I can think of things even more invigorating."

"I'll bet you can."

When the boat docked, Alex took Valerie on a tour of the woods and park, then they ate dinner in the dining room and from there moved on to the lounge where they had drinks and danced until one. By the time they reached their suite Valerie was more than ready for Alex to make love to her.

As they lay still entwined afterward, Alex held Valerie close, savoring the contact.

"I enjoy making love to you, Val, but I enjoy holding you like this even more. I can hardly believe you are finally my wife."

"Believe it. We have a second chance at happiness."

Alex kissed her. "And I intend to take advantage of every moment."

"Oh, in what way?"

"In every conceivable way possible. I love you, Valerie Price. You are everything that is precious to me. I love our son, but I love you more."

Valerie was surprised by this admission. When he'd first come to Quinneth Falls, revenge was his sole purpose. Then later she'd thought it was Tyler. But now to find out he truly did love her for herself made her heart swell with joy and overflow with love.

"I meant every word of our wedding vows." He took her face in his hands and kissed her mouth.

"So did I." She kissed him back "I love you, Alex."

They made slow, sweet, tender love. Alex smiled when he heard Valerie's even breathing moments afterward. He'd completely tired her out with his demands. He trailed a finger down her cheek, longing to hear her reason for having left him. He sensed that it would probably surprise him. Her taking the money somehow didn't wash. She'd given him her virginity, and he had been sure that she had loved him.

He'd seen the cancelled check and had believed she had betrayed him for money until he'd come to really know her. He'd seen for himself that Valerie was not a selfish, gold-digging bitch like his stepmother. Yet she'd sunk money into a business that was on a precarious footing for a man she couldn't possibly have loved. At least not the way she'd loved him. But, he reminded himself, what humans did was rarely ever logical where love was concerned.

Alex eased out of bed and walked over to the window and looked out over the lake. He thought about just coming out and demanding an answer, but he didn't want to ruin what they had by mentioning the painful past. At that moment he felt soft warm arms encircle his waist.

Valerie kissed his back and then moved her fingers around to his manhood. She smiled when she felt him harden.

"I think you're going to get into trouble doing that."

"What kind of trouble? Will consequences follow?"

Alex brought her around in front of him and lifted her to place her legs up around his waist. And as she wrapped them around him, he sank the hardened column of his flesh deep within her.

Valerie moaned, wriggling her hips, seating him to the hilt. As he walked the few steps to the bed the massaging movements of his sex nearly pitched her over the edge.

Alex eased onto the bed, keeping her connected to him.

"Ride me, Val," he commanded huskily.

"It would be my pleasure." And pleasure him she did until midnight met the dawn.

It was Thursday, their last day on the island.

"We'll definitely have to come back and really enjoy the scenery next time," Valerie commented as the ferry left the shore, headed for Mackinac City.

"I enjoyed the scenery tremendously."

"I meant of the island, lover man."

"Me too." He grinned.

"No, you didn't."

"I was enjoying my honeymoon. You can't tell me you didn't enjoy what we shared and how often we shared it."

"No, I definitely can't."

"Are you happy, Val?"

"Very happy." Valerie thought about their son. Earlier she and Alex had gone shopping for a present for Tyler. They had decided on an exact replica of Fort Mackinac, complete with soldiers, Indians and a cannon. It also came with a carrying case to store them in. Valerie could picture Tyler and his friends playing with the set on the tree house floor.

CHAPTER TWENTY-FOUR

The first person Alex and Valerie encountered when they arrived in Quinneth Falls was Jake Spriewell. Alex laughed because he knew their arrival would be public knowledge in a matter of minutes.

Alex couldn't help feeling apprehensive about picking up their son. Would Tyler be ready to move into the new house with him and Valerie? Alex knew how attached Tyler was to his parent house. It was only natural he'd want to stay there and hold on to the memories he associated with the man he thought was his father.

Valerie studied Alex as he drove and saw the trepidation in the set of his jaw. Hopefully there wouldn't be any trouble with Tyler. Naturally they would all have to go through a transition period. She'd decided to extend her time off from Resource to help make it smoother.

Valerie put a hand on Alex's arm and smiled. "Everything will work out. You'll see."

"I hope you're right."

"I know I am."

Alex wished he had her confidence. When he saw his father's Rolls-Royce parked in the drive, Alex was curious to know why he was there. Could his father be taking a genuine interest in his grandson? Alex hoped he was.

Valerie saw her aunt and Michael Price sitting on the front porch swing talking. Surely he hadn't mentioned anything to her about the past. Valerie wanted to be the one to tell her. Then and only then could she be completely honest with Alex.

When Alex pulled in behind his father's car, Tyler jumped off the tire swing and ran over to greet his parents.

"I'm so glad you're home, Mama." He launched himself into her arms seconds after she'd climbed out of the Durango.

"What about me?" Alex asked. "Aren't you glad to see me too?"

Tyler didn't answer, just shrugged his shoulders.

Valerie saw the hurt look in Alex's eyes. She couldn't understand her son's sudden nonchalance toward his father. He and Alex had gotten along so well before—before she and Alex had gotten married. Did Tyler feel threatened by their relationship? Did he resent Alex for marrying his mother? Did he think Alex was trying to take his father's place? Was that the crux of the problem? If so, what could she do to help?

"We have a present for you, Tyler," Alex said, walking around the side of the Durango to unlock the trunk.

Tyler followed him. "You have? What did you get me?"

Alex lifted out the fort case. "An authentic replica of Fort Mackinac."

"We read about the fort in history last year. I can't believe I have my very own model."

"What do you say, young man?" Kelly admonished.

"Thank you."

"You're welcome, Tyler. Your mother and I chose it for you. Since you love history I thought you'd appreciate it better than a simple souvenir."

"I do." Tyler went over to Alex and hugged him.

Valerie noticed the over bright gleam in Alex's eyes. If it was the last thing she did, she would bring her son and his father closer together. When she saw Michael standing on the periphery, Valerie thought about what Alex had told her about Michael's former wife and how bitter it had made him. She realized how lonely his life must be. She was beginning to understand why he was so hard. Maybe one day he would make an effort to understand her.

Valerie smiled as she watched her son and his friends lug their sleeping bags, flashlights, and other paraphernalia out to the tree house. She took a huge picnic basket packed full of Aunt Kelly's fried chicken, potato salad, rolls and brownies. Valerie had made a gallon of lemonade, and Alex had contributed a radio and plenty of batteries.

Alex and Valerie walked back to the house, leaving Tyler and his friends to their sleepover.

Valerie loved the house and was excited about her first night in it. She and Alex had chosen the furniture and carpet together, but Alex had pretty much left the color scheme and the choice of appliances to Valerie.

Valerie's heartbeat quickened when they neared the master bedroom suite. The bathroom door stood open, revealing the dynamic black and gold color scheme. The lavish black, gold-veined marble tub was like a mini swimming pool.

"I'll bet you can't wait to try it out," Alex said in a low husky voice. "I sure as hell can't." He started undressing her.

"What if the boys should—"

"I had Stan install a monitor and instruct Tyler on how to use it. If they need anything they'll let us know."

"You seem to have thought of everything."

"No more subterfuge, woman. I want you naked."

"You do, do you?"

Alex finished undressing Valerie and then just stood mouth agape taking in the beauty of her slender yet voluptuous body. He felt the tightening sensation in his groin intensify to the point of pain.

She took a step back "Now, you. I want to drink my fill of you."

Alex undressed slowly, taking his time discarding each piece. When he saw Valerie's nipples peak and her breathing turn ragged, he grinned. She was just as ready as he was. He cupped her breasts, caressing her nipples with his thumbs.

Valerie cried out her pleasure and then took him in her hands and stroked the length of him.

"If you're not careful I won't be able to stand up."

"I wonder what it would feel like to have you on your knees before me."

Alex moved her hands and went down on his knees, then bringing her down on hers, he drew Valerie into his arms and moved his mouth over hers, devouring its sweetness.

"With my lips I drink from the fountain of your lips. With my arms I embrace your beautiful body. And with my man's body I will worship yours." He eased her back onto the soft bathroom rug and parting her legs, slid deep inside her.

"Oh, Alex," she moaned, curling her legs around his waist.

Alex grasped her hips and began to move more urgently against her, each thrust carrying him deeper. He caressed her swollen bud of desire with his fingers until she cried out in a bliss-filled release.

"Keep your legs laced around me, baby, while I run the bath water."

With every movement of his hips, the friction built the fire hotter and hotter. As they waited for the tub to fill with water, Alex sat on the ledge surrounding it and moved Valerie's hips against him.

"Alex, I can't stand it!"

"Then don't hold back. I want to see your face when you come."

Seconds later she wailed as a wondrous climax rocked her body.

The tub was now full.

As the spasms of release ebbed inside Valerie, Alex could feel her sensitive flesh kneading his sex. He began to thrust until the kneading got stronger and her womanhood began to tighten around his passion-swollen flesh. He closed his eyes.

"No, open them. I want to see you splinter into a million pieces."

Alex opened his eyes and began to move faster and faster. And when she started to shatter around him again, he shouted in male triumph as he felt his release geyser like an artesian well, seltzering his seed against her womb.

Gasping, Alex said in hoarse voice, "I don't know if I have the strength to climb into the tub now."

Valerie stepped into the tub and held out her arms to Alex. Mindless with desire he followed, easing onto his back, laying his head against the black terry cloth head rest.

Valerie turned the Jacuzzi jets on. A moan of pleasure escaped his lips! Valerie lowered herself on top of him, embedding him to the max.

"I'll be your strength, lover man." She moved her hips in a circular motion.

"More like my weakness. Ah, yes, oh yes," Alex cried out in quick chanting-like groans as the rapture continued to build.

Valerie felt herself racing toward oblivion with every titillating movement against her husband. When she heard his rapid catches of breath as his pleasure escalated to the explosion point, she rode him faster and faster. Moments later they were catapulting into ecstasy together.

"My God, woman, what did you do to me?"

"I just made love to my tired husband."

"I'm definitely not tired now."

"Prove it."

And he did. It was much later before they made it to the bed. And later still when he proceeded to further emphasize his point.

Alex awoke to the feel of a small warm hand moving up and then down the length of his manhood, then back up again. His heart began to pound and an ache palpitated through his groin.

"Haven't you had enough yet?"

"Are you complaining?"

Alex flipped Valerie onto her stomach and arching her buttocks, slowly sank his shaft between the hot giving folds of her womanhood. As he moved against her damp heat, the friction singed his flesh and he groaned. When he felt Valerie's climax shudder through her seconds later, his own release launched him into oblivion right after her.

Strong sunlight streamed through the window onto the bed.

"We really christened this bed right, didn't we?"

Alex brushed back strands of Valerie's hair from her face. "We certainly did." He kissed her eyelids, her nose and her mouth.

"You aren't still tired, are you?"

Before he could answer the monitor came on.

"What are you gonna fix us for breakfast, Mama?" Tyler asked. "Danny and Mike and Jordan want pancakes. I want some too."

"All right, pancakes it is," she said, switching off the monitor. Then she glanced at Alex. "What do you want? Don't answer that."

CHAPTER TWENTY-FIVE

Pride in his son flowed through Alex as he sat across the breakfast table from Tyler. What he wouldn't give to hear the word "Daddy" come from Tyler's lips, addressed to him. He realized that Tyler closely resembled pictures of himself taken at that age. Those two town busybodies had certainly noticed the resemblance. Other people were bound to also. He and Valerie had to decide when to tell Tyler the truth. But how could they do it without hurting him?

Valerie watched the play of emotions on her husband's face and had a pretty good idea what he was thinking. Tyler was so like Alex it clutched at her heart. And he was also just as stubborn and sensitive. As soon as they settled in as a family, then they would tell Tyler the truth.

"These pancakes are the bomb, Mrs. Bishop—I mean Price," Danny blurted, anxiously glancing from Valerie to Alex to Tyler.

Valerie smiled. "I'm glad you like them, Danny. You want some more?"

"Yes, ma'am."

Alex noticed the strained look that came over Tyler's face at Danny's slip of the lip. He wondered when Tyler would come to accept that his mother's last name was no longer Bishop. Once he knew the truth, Alex wondered if Tyler would one day want to embrace the Price name.

After the boys had gone back out to the tree house, Alex got up from his chair and started helping Valerie clear the table.

"You don't have to do that," Valerie said.

"I want to help."

"Far be it from me to turn down free labor." She laughed.

"I'm going to make you pay for insulting me."

"When? I can hardly wait to receive retribution."

"You're something else, Val."

"And don't you forget it."

"Never." As he started to help her put the dishes into the dishwasher, the phone rang.

Valerie answered it, then signaled for him to go on into the living room. She would join him when she got off the phone.

Minutes later Valerie was snuggled close to Alex on the couch.

"With a house full of kids, what can a newly married man do?"

"Since it's Saturday, he could always mow the lawn."

"Considering the size of this estate, you've got to be joking. It's the reason we hired landscaping people.

"It was only a suggestion. Now that we've ruled that out, you could wash the car or do maintenance on it. What do you think?"

"I'd much rather wash and do maintenance on you."

"You would? Where would you want to start?"

"Anywhere you want me to. But unfortunately with the kids underfoot, I'll have to wait until they are asleep tonight."

"No, you won't. That was Aunt Kelly on the phone. She called to tell me she'll be taking the boys off our hands for a few hours this afternoon."

"What time will she be picking the boys up? More to the point, when will she be bringing them back?"

'You're as eager as I am to be alone together, aren't you?"

"I confess. Your lovemaking is addictive."

"That being the case, I can hardly wait to feel you OD on me."

Valerie was so busy whipping the house into shape, taking care of Tyler and being a wife to Alex, she put off talking to her aunt. The plant was nearing completion. Before the end of the year, Alex expected it to be at least partially operational. Alex and Tyler seemed to be getting closer. Surely there was no reason to upset her aunt by telling her what Michael had done.

You can convince yourself of just about anything if you try hard enough.

Valerie let out a soul-weary breath. She'd never considered herself a procrastinator until now. Michael had been at the root of all her heartache. Would she ever be able to forgive him?

Valerie stared contemplatively at the phone, but before she could pick up the receiver it rang. It was her aunt.

"Valerie, I need to talk to you, but I have one last alteration to do on an evening gown for Gina, then I'll come over."

School had started on Monday and Tyler wouldn't be home.

Valerie frowned several hours later because Kelly hadn't arrived. When she saw her aunt's car swing into the driveway, she let out a sigh of relief until she saw that she wasn't alone: Michael was with her.

"I'm sorry I'm late. The alterations took longer than I expected."

"Aunt Kelly—"

"Mr. Price has something he wants to say to you." Kelly looked at Michael as though giving him courage.

"Valerie, I've done you a grave disservice. What I did was unforgivable. I was a judgmental fool. I thought you weren't good enough for Alexander. I assumed you were a gold-digger like my ex-wife, Irene. And because of your aunt's past—well, you know what I threatened to do and why."

Valerie was stunned speechless.

"I know you have every reason not to ever have anything to do with me. And I can't blame you."

Valerie didn't know what to say. This man had wrecked her life and forced her to leave the man she loved. He'd deprived her son of knowing his father. Deprived Alex of raising his child. He'd threatened to expose the aunt that she loved to public ridicule. And now he expected her to forgive him just like that.

"I know this is a shock, honey," Kelly said, "It was a shock to me too. After he told me what he'd done, I felt like committing murder. To say he's sorry doesn't begin to absolve him from blame, but—"

"Please, listen to me, Valerie." Michael looked imploringly at her "To my warped way of thinking, the majority of women were grasping greedy bitches like my ex-wife, Irene.

What I failed to realize is that you can't judge one person by the actions of another. I knew how wrong I'd been when I found out you'd given birth to Alexander's child, my grandchild."

They heard a strangled gasp and then a door slamming.

"Oh, my God, no!" Valerie cried, looking at the clock over the mantle. "I forgot about Tyler. He must have heard everything." She ran from the room and headed out to the kitchen, calling her son's name. When she reached the back door, she didn't see any sign of Tyler. She hurried outside and searched the yard. She noticed that the back gate was standing open.

"This is all my fault," Michael said, "If I hadn't—I'll help you find him."

Valerie glared at Michael. "You've already done enough."

"Don't be like that," Kelly chided. "I know Michael hurt you, but he wouldn't deliberately hurt Tyler. He's grown to love his grandson."

"He loved Alex too and look what he did to him."

"I think finding Tyler is what's important right now. Don't you?"

Valerie bit her lip. "I know you're right. You two can check outside the back gate while I—I've got to call Alex and let him know what's happened."

"When are you and Mary Ellen going to tie the knot?" Alex asked Justin as they shared a late lunch of sandwiches and coffee they'd ordered in from the cafe down the street.

"With all the work we have to do in the next few months probably not until after the first of the year. Mary Ellen has her heart set on a June wedding." Alex smiled. "Sure you can hold out that long?"

"I guess I'll have to, won't I? How are things working out between you and Valerie?"

"That's a hard question to answer. Sometimes I think great, perfect, and then others…"

"Have you and she discussed—you know—the money and her reasons for taking it and walking out on you?"

"It's a subject I'd rather not bring up right now. Besides, it was in the past. I don't want to cause any waves."

"But, Alex, you two need to talk, get everything out in the open."

"I know, but I don't want to risk it just yet. Maybe after we've been married a while and had time to adjust."

"Are you sure that time is the cure-all?"

"No, but—"

The phone buzzed. Alex picked it up. "Yes, Gina? Put her on. Val, I—"

"You've got to come home, Alex."

"What's wrong?"

"Tyler has run away."

"What? Why?"

"He overheard a conversation between me and Michael. He knows you're his real father."

"Oh, God. I'm leaving the office right now."

"What is it, Alex?" Justin asked, his voice concerned.

"Tyler has run away. I've got to go."

"I'll wrap things up here. I hope you find him."

"Me, too. If anything has happened to him…"

"Kids run away all the time. They usually come back within a few hours. After they've given everybody a scare. I remember doing that a time or two when I was his age."

"That may very well be true, but most kids don't have the reason he does for running away. He's learned that I'm his real father."

The worried, frightened look on Valerie's face wrenched Alex's guts. "Has anyone seen him?" he asked.

"No. I've got Michael, Aunt Kelly and the gardener and his helper combing the grounds. I've been on the phone calling all his friends. And so far nothing. If anything happens to him… Oh, Alex," she cried.

Alex drew her into his arms. "I'm sure nothing will. We'll find him, I promise you."

Michael and Kelly returned.

"We haven't seen a sign of him anywhere," Kelly said worriedly.

"We've looked everywhere: the tree house, the land surrounding the estate. This is all my fault," Michael said, his voice a study in misery.

"Placing blame is not going to help us find Tyler, Dad."

"It's getting late, Alex," Valerie sobbed, her voice fraught with fear. "We've got to find my baby!"

Alex grimaced. Tyler hadn't taken anything with him and already the weather was turning cool. Where could he have run to? And was he all right, given his present frame of mind?

Alex called the police and an officer came out and talked to them. The search had officially started.

It was morning and no one had called to say they'd seen Tyler. Valerie was a basket case. She hadn't rested for one moment since Tyler had left, and Alex was worried about her. She didn't touch her breakfast, just sat at the table staring at it. Dark shadows ringed her eyes. Every time the phone rang she jumped. Alex was grateful that Kelly had stayed the night. He was even grateful for his father's presence.

Alex had gone over to Danny Cranson's, but the little boy hadn't seen his best friend. When he found out he was missing he started crying. Alex talked to his other friends. They hadn't seen him either. When he got back to the house, Alex saw the hope in Valerie's eyes die when he was forced to tell her that none of Tyler's friends had seen him.

"If anything happens…" She burst into tears and collapsed on the couch.

Alex was by her side, gently drawing her into his arms. She was trembling. No matter what he did, he couldn't seem to calm her. Kelly walked into the room.

"What's wrong?" she asked, switching her gaze from Valerie to Alex. "Nothing has happened to Tyler, has it?"

"No, we haven't heard anything. But I think you'd better call the doctor."

Alex took Valerie up to their room and held her until Dr. Jeffries came. After much protest, Alex convinced her to let the doctor give her a mild sedative.

An hour later Alex came back downstairs. Kelly made coffee and brought it into the living room, then she excused herself, saying she wanted to go upstairs and be with Valerie in case she woke up.

"We've searched the grounds surrounding the falls and every place I could think of." Alex sipped his coffee.

"We have to think the way an eight-year-old would think," Michael remarked. "He didn't take anything with him. He has to be hungry by now."

"I'm sure he is." Alex glared at his father. "What I want to know is how the conversation about Tyler's parentage came up."

"All I wanted to do was apologize to Valerie for what I did. The three of you would have been a family if I hadn't interfered."

"What you did? You only offered her money. She didn't have to accept it. How were you to know she was pregnant? Dad, is there something you're not telling me? I don't understand your sudden about-face."

"I've grown to love that little boy. If anything happens to Tyler…"

"It won't, so don't even think like that."

"There is—"

"I've just thought of something," Alex interrupted. "I might know where Tyler is. If Valerie wakes up before I get back, Dad, don't tell her anything. I don't want to raise her hopes in case I'm wrong."

"I hope your hunch is right, Alexander."

"I'm going to find my son." Alex took his keys out of his pocket, then rushed out the back door.

CHAPTER TWENTY-SIX

Alex searched the many caves near the falls and found candy bars. He recalled the times they'd gone exploring and how Tyler had insisted they leave candy bars, blankets and bottles of water in several of the caves in case someone needed them. Alex had laughed at the time, but he'd humored him.

It was late afternoon when Alex entered yet another cave. There he found a rumpled blanket and several candy wrappers. He'd bet his life Tyler had been here. What he wanted to know was where Tyler was now. It would be getting dark in a couple of hours.

Alex drove to the falls, parked the Durango, got out and started looking around.

"Tyler," he called to his son. "Are you here? Can you hear me?"

Silence.

"If you can, please listen, okay? I know what you heard has confused and upset you."

The silence continued.

Alex searched around the rocks on the south side of the falls, talking to Tyler the whole time. He saw movement near the runoff on the left side of the falls and stealthily made his way there.

"Tyler, I know you hear me. I want to talk to you, son." Alex heard soft crying at the word son, and pain wrenched his heart.

"Tyler, I know you overheard your grandfather say you were my son. It's true."

"You didn't want me and Mama," Tyler sobbed.

"You're wrong. I didn't know about you until I moved to Quinneth Falls. It's hard to explain. Please, come out so we can talk."

Alex moved closer. His heart leaped into his throat when he found Tyler behind some bushes, shivering and balled in a fetal position on a precarious rock precipice near the edge of the falls. Tears stung Alex eyes and he started toward him.

"I love you, Tyler. Ever since I heard you were my son I've wanted to be the kind of father you needed. I know you thought George Bishop was your father and you loved him. He did a wonderful job raising you. I'm grateful to him for that."

"You are?" Tyler asked, uncertainty trembling in his voice.

"Yes, I am. I know how much he really cared about you."

"Why didn't Mama tell me who you were before you came to town?"

Alex inched closer. "You'll have to ask her. I'm coming to get you."

As Tyler unfolded from his position, the giant piece of rock crumbled, tumbling Tyler over the falls into the lake below. Alex dived into the water after him. He came up sputtering, looking this way and that, frantically searching for his son. He finally spotted Tyler's small arms flailing wildly above the surface of the water, a ways away from the rushing water. Alex swam over to him and grabbed hold of Tyler before he went under for the second time.

It was all Alex could do to keep from panicking. He had to keep a clear head if he wanted to save Tyler's life.

"I've got you, son. You're going to be all right."

Alex towed Tyler over to the bank and pulled him onto the grass. Gasping for breath himself, Alex flipped Tyler onto his stomach and began kneading the water out of his lungs over and over again until he heard Tyler cough and saw water trickle from his mouth. At the precious sight and sound, relief like nothing Alex had ever felt before eased his worried mind. A frown replaced the relief when he saw blood oozing from a gash on the side of Tyler's head.

Alex carried Tyler to the Durango and gently lowered him onto the seat. He drove as fast as he dared to the Quinneth Falls hospital.

While he waited for the doctor to come out of the emergency room to tell him about Tyler's condition, Alex called Valerie.

Fifteen minutes later Valerie, Kelly and Michael arrived at the hospital. When Valerie saw Alex sitting in a chair just outside of the emergency room, wrapped in a blanket, she ran into his outstretched arms.

"Has the doctor come out to tell you anything?" she asked anxiously.

"Only that Tyler is unconscious and they are running tests."

"Tests? What kind of tests?" Valerie cried. "You said he tumbled over the falls."

"How badly was he injured?" Kelly asked.

"He has a head injury. Falling pieces of rock rained down on him as he fell. And he slipped into unconsciousness on the way to the hospital."

"Oh, my God," Valerie said, closing her eyes and hugging Alex tighter.

"Are you all right, Alexander?" Michael asked, his face fraught with concern.

"I'm fine. It's Tyler—"

The door to the emergency room opened and a doctor walked over to them.

"Are you Tyler Bishop's parents?"

"Yes. How is he?" Valerie asked, leaving Alex's arms, rushing over to the doctor.

"He has a concussion and swallowed quite a bit of water, but he isn't critical; at least not yet. What we're concerned about is that the congestion in his lungs doesn't turn into pneumonia."

"When will you know?"

"The next eight hours should tell us something."

"Is he conscious?" Alex asked.

"Not yet. With a head injury like his, it may be a while before he comes around. For now all we can do is wait. I'm having him moved to intensive care just as a precaution. I don't expect any complications, but to be on the safe side I prefer him to be there so he can get more personalized care."

"My baby," Valerie sobbed.

Alex drew her back into his arms.

The next morning found Valerie sitting beside Tyler's bed. Tears rolled down her cheeks. The doctor had ordered a mist tent to help Tyler breathe easier. Valerie kept hoping against hope his condition wouldn't turn into pneumonia and so far it hadn't. And for that she thanked God. She took her son's hand in hers and looked into his still face and asked Alex who was standing beside her, "Do you think he looks better?"

"He sounds better."

"Oh, Alex, he's so precious."

"He is. I love him with all my heart."

"I know you do. What happened when you found him?"

"We talked a little. He wanted answers to questions only you can provide."

"I hate that he learned the truth the way he did."

"Me too. He didn't seem to hate me for turning his world inside out, though. He was just hurt and confused."

"It's probably me he hates for not telling him the truth."

Alex glanced down at his son and smiled. Although the resemblance between him and Tyler was arresting, as he lay unconscious Alex could see some of his mother's features in the boy's face. His brows were shaped like hers, and when he arched them when confused or curious, he reminded Alex of Valerie.

"The doctor doesn't expect him to wake up until later today or maybe even this evening," Alex said. "You're wiped out, Val. Why don't you let me drive you home so you can get some sleep."

"I can't leave until I know for sure Tyler's going to be all right."

"You won't be any help to him if you make yourself sick. I'll see if they can get you a bed."

"It won't be necessary. I wouldn't be able to sleep in it anyway."

When they had to leave so the nurse and doctor could check Tyler, Alex walked Valerie over to the couch in the waiting room and sat holding her until they allowed them back inside.

Michael and Kelly returned with a change of clothes for Alex and Valerie and some sandwiches that Kelly had made.

Alex frowned when Valerie refused to eat hers. He didn't voice his concern because he didn't have much of an appetite himself.

Finally the doctor came out. He had a smile on his face. "Tyler is improving. We're going to take the mist tent off later this afternoon. Then I'm going to have him transferred to a private room on the pediatric floor."

"Thank God," Valerie uttered before fainting in Alex's arms. He carried her over to the couch. The doctor went to the nurse's station and returned to wave smelling salts under Valerie's nose.

"Are you all right, Val?" Alex asked when she came around.

"I am now. I can't tell you how relieved I feel."

"You don't have to. He's my son too."

Tyler was awake when Valerie walked into his room that evening.

"How do you feel, baby?" she asked, going over to the bed and hugging him.

"My head hurts a little. Mama, why didn't you tell me that Daddy wasn't my real father?"

"Before you were born Alex and I were separated, and I thought I would never see him again. I didn't find out I was going to have you until after I had come back to Quinneth Falls. George had always cared about me so when he asked me to marry him I agreed."

"But you could have told me that. Just before I fell in the lake, Alex—my father said he loved me."

"You can believe him. He really does, Tyler. Once he saw you and knew you were his son, he wanted us to be a family."

Alex walked in on the end of the conversation. "Your mother is right. You're my family."

"Was Grandfather Michael the reason you and Mama didn't get married before I was born?"

"Your mother and my father had a misunderstanding, but it's all straightened out now." Alex pulled up a chair beside the bed. "I don't ever want you to worry that you're not loved." He drew Tyler into his arms and hugged him tight. When he didn't pull away, Alex closed his eyes and thanked God for allowing him this chance to know his son. He looked into Valerie's eyes. And to be with his son's mother.

That night when they got home Alex carried Valerie upstairs to their bedroom and reverently undressed her.

"I need and want you so, Val. Knowing our son is going to be all right has made me cherish all the more the life we have together."

"I know what you mean. I feel the same way. We came so close to losing Tyler. I never want to go through something like that again. Make love to me, Alex. I want to feel the joy of life in every pore."

"I want to glory in the warmth of your body and celebrate the precious gift of our son's life with you."

Valerie helped him out of his clothes and stared in awe at his huge erection. The womanly cavern between her thighs moistened at the sight of him and an arousing heat sizzled to life inside her. And seconds later a desire for him to submerge his hardened hot flesh inside her was something she craved with all her being.

Alex lifted Valerie in his arms and strode over to the bed and lowered her down on it, then climbed in beside her. He kissed her lips and stroked her breasts until her nipples peaked and he felt desire quiver through her When she parted her thighs, he slipped between them and sank his throbbing, erect flesh inside her to the hilt. Her moan of pleasure nearly drove him crazy. He pulled almost all the way out only to slide in again with urgent, demanding thrusts.

Valerie moved her head from side to side, reveling in the ecstasy he was giving her She clasped her legs around his hips, snuggly encasing him within her, employing a smooth rocking motion.

"I won't last five minutes if you keep that up."

"At this moment that's the last thing I want to happen."

The rhythm they set propelled them into heavenly bliss seconds later and afterward they fell into an exhausted sleep.

Alex was the first to awaken that next morning. For a few minutes all he did was study his wife's contented face as she slept. She was everything to him. If she would only— no, he'd promised himself he wouldn't go there. Maybe in time she'd come to trust him enough to tell him the truth about why she'd left him. If she would just get it out in the open, they could both put it completely behind them. If...

CHAPTER TWENTY-SEVEN

Tyler was finally released from the hospital. He sported a bandage on his forehead. Valerie smiled when she passed by his room and heard him proudly bragging to Danny about how his father had rescued him. Boys would be boys, she guessed.

Things began to settle into a routine over the next few weeks. Alex spent as much time as he could with Valerie and with Tyler, but Valerie sensed a subtle distancing in his manner toward her Something was bothering him, but he wouldn't come out and tell her what it was. It was as though he wanted to say something, but for some reason couldn't bring himself to do it.

One night Valerie walked into the study and saw Alex sitting behind his desk, staring intently out the window.

"A penny for your thoughts," she said softly.

Alex smiled. "You couldn't wait for me to come upstairs and make love to you, right?"

"I did find it difficult, but it's not the reason I came looking for you."

Alex rose from his chair, circled his desk, pulled her into his arms and kissed her lips again and again until he heard her gasp. "Why don't we lock the door so I can have my wicked way with you?"

"Tyler is asleep, but—"

Alex didn't give her a chance to finish her sentence before deftly and quickly removing her panties. He unzipped his pants and maneuvered his aching distended flesh out of his briefs. Then he brought Valerie's legs up around his waist and thrust his shaft hard and deep inside her, bringing them both instant gratification.

"You're a dangerous man, Alexander Price, but I must say you know how to please."

"It's being near you when my true colors shine through."

As she and Alex adjusted their clothes, she said. "Alex, I want—I need to talk to you."

Now he would finally hear the truth, he thought. "What do you want to talk about?"

"Something has been bothering you and I have to know what it is. Is it anything I've done?"

He wondered why she—"You never really explained why you did it."

"You mean why I left you eight years ago? Your father threatened to expose some hurtful information about someone very dear to me, and I couldn't let him do it so I did as he said and left Detroit."

Alex's jaw tightened. It was clear to him that she had no intention of mentioning the money she'd taken from his father, and it made him angry. "You're leaving out a very important fact, aren't you?"

"Aunt Kelly is the person he threatened."

"I didn't mean that, and you know it. What you did went beyond protecting your aunt's reputation or sparing her feelings."

"I don't know what you're talking about. Aunt Kelly was the reason I left. The only reason. When your father found out you were going to build a factory in Quinneth Falls, he initially wanted me to change your mind about building here. He threatened to reveal what he knew about my aunt if I didn't at least convince you to leave all dealings having to do with the plant to Justin. But I knew once you'd made up your mind you wouldn't change it."

"I don't want to hear all that. The money, Valerie. What about the million dollars you took from my father and gave to another man, namely your husband George Bishop?"

"A million dollars? I never took any money from your father. I refused to accept anything from him."

"You can stop lying, Valerie. I know you took it. I believed you really cared for me until I found out the price you put on your affection."

"I never did anything of the kind."

"I saw proof, damn it," he roared. "I saw the cancelled check."

"I don't know what you saw, but I never accepted a check from your father."

Alex hadn't expected her to lie once it was all out in the open.

"You don't believe me, do you?" she accused.

"I know what I saw. If you would just admit doing it I would forgive you and we could put the whole thing behind us."

Valerie was dazed. "You would forgive me? The only thing I need forgiveness for is keeping you from knowing about Tyler."

"If you can't face the truth…What's the use." He stormed out of the room and a few seconds later Valerie heard the front door slam.

Valerie glanced out the window and saw the Durango tearing down the drive. Alex actually believed she had taken money from his father. It explained his anger and that remote look she'd oftentimes seen in his eyes. All this time he thought she was capable of. Every time they'd made love he must have believed it was in atonement for her sins. What a low opinion he must have of her. And she thought that— All this time she was waiting for him to come to trust her. He had said that he loved her when they were on Mackinac Island, but he couldn't have meant it if this was how he really felt. He'd evidently married her to be near his son and he would say or do anything to that end.

Tears slipped down her face. Oh Alex, I loved you so much.

Loved? You still love the man despite what he thinks about you.

What good did it do? He was never going to trust her. She had wanted to know what was bothering him and now she did. The pain was more than she could bear. If no trust existed between them, what did they have? And where did they go from here?

❧

Alex couldn't believe that Valerie had denied taking the money. As he paced back and forth in the dark office, he heard the door open. Justin turned on the light and came in dressed for bed, rubbing his eyes.

"Alex, what's wrong? What are you doing here this time of night?"

"I'm sorry if I woke you up, man."

"Never mind that. I want to know why you're here."

"I found out something that threw me for a loop. Valerie denies ever having taken the money."

Justin scratched his head. "She did, huh? Didn't you tell her that you saw the cancelled check?"

"Yes, I confronted her with it, but you know what, she still denies doing it. I don't know what to think or do right now. I will always love her no matter what, but can I live with her?"

"Is it possible what she did was so repugnant she's blocked it out of her memory?"

"I don't think that's it. She's adamant that the reason she left was because my father was blackmailing her."

"That quite possibly might be true. Did you ask what Michael had held over her head?"

"No, she volunteered the information. Something about damaging evidence against her aunt."

"We all know how she feels about her aunt. Naturally she would be protective of her."

"I know that, but why deny taking the money?"

"Maybe she's too ashamed to admit it even to herself, or maybe there's another explanation. Have you talked to your father?"

"When I tried to call him, I got his voice mail and he'd left a message for me. He said my Uncle Steve has been taken sick and he'd be staying with him for a week or maybe longer."

"You need to get him and Valerie together and make them tell you what really happened. Why don't you go home?"

"I'm so damned mad, I could spit."

"You could stay here in your old suite until your father gets back, but won't that seem strange to Tyler? He has to still be feeling a little unsure of you and your role as his father If you leave now…"

"I get your point. I'll go home, but I don't know what's going to happen between me and Valerie."

"Love will find a way."

Valerie lay awake thinking about what had happened. It had been hours since Alex had stormed out. She hoped he was all right. Surely she'd have heard if he wasn't. It hurt her to her very soul that Alex believed what he did about her. She'd have thought he knew her better than that. Evidently not.

How could Michael have done such a thing? What was this cancelled check he had shown Alex? Were there no limits to his treachery? When he came to her the day Tyler ran away Valerie thought that he had changed. He hadn't mentioned anything about a check. Maybe he would have if Tyler—if Tyler hadn't run away.

Valerie heard the Durango drive up. She tensed, wondering what Alex would do. Would he come to their bedroom or sleep in one of the guest rooms?

Alex opened their bedroom door and stood staring at his wife for a few seconds before going into the bathroom.

Valerie heard the shower, then ten minutes later Alex came to bed. He climbed in and presented his back to her and didn't say anything.

"Alex, you've got to believe me. I never took that money from your father."

"I don't want to talk about this. My father is away, but when he gets back we're going to have it out. Until then, I don't think we should get into it."

"You don't think? Are we going to walk around like strangers and pretend nothing is wrong?"

"We can't, because something is wrong. What I'm saying is that for Tyler's sake our relationship must appear to be normal. He's gone through enough."

"So you're going to tolerate me, is that it?"

"Valerie, I—"

"I'll go along with it. But I think you should spend most of your time with our son so we won't have to walk on eggshells around each other."

"If you would only—never mind."

"I've told you the truth."

"I wish I could believe you. Just go to sleep, Val."

Even knowing that he didn't trust her, Valerie still loved him. Could her love weather his distrust? Would their relationship be able to survive the truth?

The next morning Valerie watched Alex leave for the office and Tyler for school. She'd tried to be cheerful so Tyler wouldn't suspect that anything was wrong. She had to hand it to Alex; he'd tried to act like his usual self. Valerie let out a sigh of relief when she finally had the house to herself.

She recalled as she cleared the table how George had miraculously come up with the money to save Resource Chemical. Was it mere coincidence that he'd gotten that loan in just the nick of time? And that the amount of money happened to be a million dollars? Was it possible he had— no, he couldn't, no, he wouldn't have taken...

But what if he had?

She had to know for sure. A lot of George's old papers and files were in Aunt Kelly's basement. At the time he'd gotten the loan she was so relieved she hadn't asked the name of the company that had given it to him. Now she wished she had. Could it have been a person, not a company? And could that person have been Michael Price? If it were true, they must have had some kind of agreement between them. Had George kept the paperwork? George was never a person to leave things to chance if he could help it. If this agreement existed, where could it be? She would start her search in the basement, and if she didn't find it there she would try the storage room at Resource Chemical.

"Valerie, you didn't tell me you were coming over for a visit. I didn't expect you would for a while. You and Alex are newlyweds and probably still on your honeymoon." Kelly's eyes twinkled with mischief.

"Aunt Kelly!"

"I'm not so old I don't remember what it's like to be in love."

"I never thought you were. The reason I came over is I need to look for some important papers in the basement."

"What important papers? Concerning what?"

"I need to update my files at Resource. George signed some papers that I need to unearth."

"Is there a problem?" Kelly frowned.

"There could be."

Kelly went down to the basement with Valerie.

"I can help you if I know what to look for."

"That won't be necessary, Aunt Kelly. I know you're busy with Della Watson's wedding dress."

"I am, but if you—"

Valerie smiled. "I'll be fine."

"If you're sure."

Valerie waited until her aunt had gone up the stairs and closed the door before walking over to the dusty file cabinet in the corner. It took three hours to go through everything, and to her dismay she could find neither a loan document nor an agreement between George and Michael. That left Resource Chemical. She'd had George's old office furniture and files taken to the storage room in the attic at Resource.

She glanced at her watch. She had a meeting with the preservation committee that afternoon, so she would have to resume her search tomorrow. One thing was sure; she wouldn't give up. She would prove to Alex that he was mistaken about her and that Michael Price had lied.

CHAPTER TWENTY-EIGHT

It was several days before Valerie got the chance to go to Resource Chemical and search through the storage room because Tyler came down with a cold. Considering his experience at the falls, she didn't want to risk it turning into something more serious so she watched over him like a mother hen over her only chick. Finally he was well enough to go back to school. Alex had been concerned and had helped her take care of their son, but he all but ignored Valerie. Each night he waited until he was sure she was asleep before coming to bed.

Valerie drove to Resource one morning after Alex and Tyler had left the house.

"Valerie, I didn't think you were ready to come back to work so soon!" Mary Ellen exclaimed in a surprised voice when she saw her walk through the lab door

Valerie smiled. "Don't worry, I'm not ready to come back to work yet. I just need to look for something in the storage room."

"Anything I can help you with?"

"No, I'll find it."

"Is something wrong?"

"Why do you ask?"

"I don't know, but for some reason you don't seem like yourself."

"I'm fine. So stop worrying, okay? I only stopped in to say hi. Look, I'd better head on up to the storage room."

Layers of dust covered the canvases draped over the office furniture as Valerie walked in. She spotted two file cabinets in the corner and headed for them. After several hours, she hadn't come up with anything, and decided to call off the search until the following day because she wanted to be home when Tyler got there. Something, a document of some sort, had to be among the papers.

What if it wasn't? What will you do then?

She'd worry about that if she had to.

Alex noticed how on edge Valerie was and commented on it after Tyler had gone to his room to do his homework.

"Val, are you all right?"

"I'm fine. Everything is fine, my life is only floating in limbo, that's all. And all because of one man's—forget it."

"Go ahead, finish what you were going to say."

"I don't want to fight with you, Alex."

"If you would only admit what you've done."

"I haven't done anything," she said, gritting her teeth.

"My father will be here tomorrow evening. And we're going to discuss exactly what did or did not happen eight years ago."

"I've already told you the truth, but you refuse to believe me."

He sighed impatiently. "I'm going into the study."

Valerie watched her husband stride out of the kitchen. Once he knew the truth, then what?

Valerie resumed her search the next morning. It was nearly two when she finished. A moan of disappointment and defeat left her lips. She sank down on an old office chair behind the desk. She glanced at the desk. She hadn't gone through it yet. When Valerie tried the middle drawer, she found it was stuck. After one hard jerk, the drawer opened. A file folder was partially hanging down. It had evidently been taped to the bottom of the drawer.

Valerie's heart started racing. Could this be what she was looking for? She prayed that it was. She slowly opened the folder.

That evening Kelly and Michael arrived at Alex and Valerie's house. After sending Tyler to bed, they all congregated in the study. Michael and Kelly sat on the couch. Valerie sat in a chair near the desk. Alex chose to stand.

"I got your message, Alexander. I was going to come here as soon as I could. There is something I didn't get the chance to tell you and Valerie because of what happened with Tyler." Michael paused. "I'm not proud of what I did."

"What exactly did you do, Dad?" Alex asked.

"I'll get to that in a moment." Michael cleared his throat. "The day Tyler ran away, I had just asked for Valerie's forgiveness."

"Forgiveness? For what?"

"For the wrong I'd done her."

"What wrong? We've been all through that. Valerie and I discussed the money, Dad. Would you please get to the point," Alex said, his voice laced with frustration and impatience.

"I forced Valerie to leave you eight years ago. You see, I thought she was like Irene and I wanted to protect you—"

"Protect me? I didn't need protection from the woman I loved. What Valerie said about you blackmailing her is all true, isn't it?"

"Yes, it is. I threatened to expose something in her aunt's past if she didn't agree to leave Detroit."

"Dad, how could you?" Alex glanced at Valerie, then back to his father, observing his anxious expression. "What about the check? You showed me a cancelled check that Valerie had cashed. She says she never accepted a check from you. Do you still have it?"

"She never signed or cashed that check. She did, however, sign a paper to get her severance pay…" Michael's voice trailed away.

"What you're telling me is that you forged her name on that check!" Alex reeled with shock, hurt and finally anger. He stalked over to his father. "You lied to me. All this time I thought—I thought the woman I loved had betrayed me, didn't love me," Alex said, his voice incredulous. "I can't believe you did that. I poured my heart out to you that day. And you knew all along that she hadn't done what you accused her of." Alex focused pain-filled eyes on Valerie. "Val, I…"

Valerie turned away.

Kelly shot Alex a sympathetic look.

Michael reached his hand out to touch his son, then dropped it to his side when he saw the look of contempt in Alex's eyes. "I admit that I was wrong about Valerie. And what I did wasn't right, but—you don't understand."

"You're damn right, I don't understand. How could you do it, Dad? I loved her. I told you I wanted to marry her. I even showed you the ring I'd bought for her. Nothing I said thawed that cold heart of yours. I almost went out of my mind when Valerie left me. And you watched me suffer and never said the words you knew would alleviate my misery. And what makes it so killing, you drove her into the arms of another man. You're responsible for that same man raising my son, your grandson."

"I didn't know she was pregnant."

"Would it have made any difference? I doubt it."

"It would have, believe me. I never told you this, but I found out Irene was pregnant."

"I don't see how that has anything to—"

"It does. When I told her I was divorcing her, she told me she was pregnant and that if I wanted custody of the baby, I'd have to pay for it."

"Oh, my God," Alex whispered. "What happened to the child?"

"Two weeks after the divorce was final, she had an abortion."

"That bitch."

"Exactly. That's exactly what she was and still is. The point is, I let her actions color my perception of other women. I began to believe all women to be lying, deceitful bitches. When you told me Valerie's son was your son…"

"You realized she wasn't like Irene. If she had wanted to she could have taken the money and aborted my child." Alex recalled his father's strange behavior after Alex's revelation. "You also realized that you might be wrong about Valerie herself. And it bothered what shred of conscience you still possess."

"That's not all, is it, Michael?" Valerie said pointedly.

"What else is left?" Alex asked.

"The money from the check for one million dollars I was supposed to have cashed. The same amount of money that miraculously saved Resource Chemical from going under."

Michael directed his attention to his son. "You see, I didn't trust Valerie to stay away from you, Alexander. I wasn't sure the threat to expose her aunt would be enough, so I had my investigator keep tabs on her. He informed me when George and Valerie flew to Reno to get married. The investigator discovered that George Bishop was in desperate need of money. If I provided the money to save his business, I figured he would ensure that Valerie would be happy to never come back to Detroit."

Valerie held up the folder. "I have in this the agreement between Michael and George. I found it when I went through George's papers."

"So that's what you were looking for in the basement," Kelly said. "If I'd only known—Michael had already told me everything. But what with all that happened to Tyler, and Michael being called away to be with his brother, he hadn't yet had the chance to tell you."

"Even so it doesn't excuse what you did to Valerie and to me, Dad."

"Can you both find in your hearts to forgive me? I know it's asking a lot."

"It damn sure is," Alex ground out, his voice crackling with anger.

Kelly put her band on Alex 's arm. "If I can forgive Michael for what he did, surely you can consider doing so, Alex."

Could he forgive his father? Had this entire experience taught him anything? He'd seen what hatred and holding grudges had done to his father, turning him into a hard, bitter disillusioned man. And what it had almost done to him. His quest for revenge had nearly destroyed his and Valerie's and Tyler's lives. Not to mention the pain he'd caused Althea.

The room turned deathly silent for what seemed like endless moments.

"Since we're all being honest and baring our souls, I have something to tell you, Valerie," Kelly said, rising from the couch and walking over to her. "You know I was in love and had an affair with Jackson Crawford, and that it would have ruined not only my life, but wrecked Jackson and Eugenia's marriage had it been made known. But what you, Alex and Michael don't know is that there's more to the story."

"More? What are you talking about, Aunt Kelly?"

"The scandal Michael uncovered was only, as they say, the tip of the iceberg. It was almost *thirty years* ago that I had the affair with Jackson Crawford. When he broke it off and went back to Eugenia, I was devastated and went to Chicago.

"My sister came to take care of me when I became sick. Brian, her husband, came to pick Lydia up a few weeks later. They were in a horrible accident."

"And my parents were killed. I know all that, Aunt Kelly. Why are you bringing this up now?"

"I'm coming to that. I'll connect it; just be patient with me." Kelly walked over to the fireplace. "The reason Lydia came to care for me was because I was pregnant and threatening to lose the baby. I had developed toxemia and nearly died."

"I don't understand. Are you saying that you arid my mother were pregnant at the same time? And you lost yours? I'm so sorry Aunt Kelly. I can only imagine what having to take care of me did to you."

"Valerie, I—"

"You don't have to tell me any more."

'Yes, I do. Lydia was the one who lost her baby in the accident that killed her and her husband. You see the accident caused her to go into premature labor. She was only five months along in her pregnancy. You're not my niece—you are my child, Valerie. Mine and Jackson's."

"What?" Valerie, feeling as though she'd been punched in the stomach, stumbled over to the couch.

"The one thing Jackson always wanted, I couldn't reveal that I'd given him: a child. Will you ever be able to forgive me for keeping this from you all these years?"

"Does Eugenia know?" Valerie asked. "Does Jackson?"

"Eugenia doesn't. But I think Jackson suspects. Luckily you favored me and not him. If Eugenia had known, it would have killed her because she wasn't able to give Jackson a child."

"I don't know what to say. How to feel." Valerie headed for the door.

"Val."

"I can't cope with any of this right now, Alex." Valerie stared at her aunt—no, her mother. She now truly knew how her son had felt when he found out Alex was his father. She all but ran from the room.

"Valerie, wait," Kelly called to her.

Alex followed Valerie. "Val—"

"I can't stay here," Valerie answered, pulling her coat out of the hail closet and hurrying out of the house.

Alex aught up with her just as she was about to open the car door and climb inside. He put himself in front of it.

"Get out of my way, Alex."

"I can't let you go like this."

"Don't try to stop me."

Alex saw all the pain, uncertainty and hurt in her eyes. And when he stepped back from the car, Valerie got in and drove off.

Kelly met Alex on the front steps. "Is she going to be all right, Alex?"

"I hope so. I owe her a king-sized apology, among other things. I accused her of being a liar and a cheat. I wouldn't blame her if she couldn't forgive me. I'm having a hard time with that myself."

"Alexander, I'm sorry for what I did to you and Valerie. I deeply regret causing you and Valerie so much heartache. I don't expect her or you to believe me, but it's true."

"I believe you, Dad. As for forgiving you, that might take a while. Look, I don't want to talk about this right now. I think I know where my wife might have gone and I'm going to go there now. She shouldn't be alone at a time like this."

"You'll need somebody to stay with Tyler," Kelly said. "Michael and I will stay until one of you gets back. And if it's very late we can spend the night. You have plenty of guest rooms."

"You go and find your wife and the two of you make up," Michael said with feeling. "You have so much going for you."

Alex realized what a change had come over his father since learning he had a grandson and meeting a strong, straightforward woman like Kelly. His thoughts shifted to Valerie. She was probably feeling angry and betrayed. He knew the emotions well. He had some serious foot kissing to do when he found his wife. Hopefully she wouldn't kick him in the teeth, not that he didn't deserve it.

CHAPTER TWENTY-NINE

Valerie drove around aimlessly for several hours before ending up at the falls. The night was crisp, and a partial moon shone on the water as it flowed over the rocks into the lake below. This had always been her sanctuary. Now no place gave her that feeling anymore. She knew she had to find the strength within herself to get over this confusing time in her life.

She felt like a shell-shocked soldier. She remembered feeling this way when Alex stormed back into her life. Only this time—oh, God, what was she going to do? The world as she knew it no longer existed. The foundation of her life had been snatched out from under her.

Valerie took a blanket out of the trunk of the car and walked over to the flat rock she considered her meditation spot and spread it out. She had so much to think about, to sort through.

First off, her aunt wasn't her aunt, but her mother! The thought completely blew her mind. She'd always had a close relationship with her aunt. In a way she had thought of her in the role of mother all her life. They had done mother/daughter things together like baking cookies, making doll dresses, going shopping whenever their right budget allowed them to. Her aunt had taken care of her when she was sick and bandaged her knees when she fell. And most of all, she'd loved her.

Valerie wasn't exactly angry about finding out Kelly was her mother. She recalled the few times they'd run into Jackson Crawford when she was growing up. And every time she'd looked into his eyes they were sad, Valerie believed he knew she was his daughter. She remembered thinking that she would have liked for him to be her father and for Kelly to be her mother. The saying, "You should be careful what you wish for," came to mind.

Now that she knew Kelly was her mother, what now? Should she call her "Mother?" If she did that… What about Tyler? How would she explain this to him? He was having a rough enough time adjusting to the reality that Alex was his father. She knew now how confused and vulnerable he must have felt when he found out the truth.

"Share the load," Alex said, coming out from behind a crop of trees near the rocks.

"Alex. I thought you understood that I needed time alone."

"I've waited hours for you. Of all the places you might have gone, I knew you would eventually come here. I come here myself when I want to think. The peace and serenity it gives one is therapeutic."

"Look, I don't—"

"I can only imagine what you've been going through after my father's confession and Kelly's revelation."

"As for your father—I'll think about how to deal with him later. But as for my aunt—mother—I've always loved her. She didn't put me up for adoption. She cared for me and loved me with all her heart. No mother could have loved her child more. It was like I knew she was my mother all along! Does that sound crazy?"

"Not at all. You're such a loving person yourself, Val. You could never hurt anyone the way I've hurt you. I should have known you'd never put a price on what we had. But I was really messed up. I thought I'd lose my mind after you left."

"I don't know if I can handle this right now. Before we were married I thought, believed, that you'd come to love me as I loved you. You said you had, but had you really? And to find out you thought I could…"

"I do love you, Val."

Valerie rose from her place on the rock. "How can you love someone you don't trust?"

"It didn't matter what I'd thought you'd done because I loved you. I was willing to put that knowledge aside and make a life with you and our son. At least I thought I could. I guess the idea of you giving money to George Bishop bothered me more than anything else. It told me how little you had really cared about me."

"I would never have married George if I had thought we could have a life together. I was so confused and hurt back then. Your father's threats against aunt—my mother—made logical thought impossible. I was so young, not so much in age as experience. I wanted to protect the one person who had taken care of me and loved me all my life.".

"If you'd only come to me?

"Don't you see? I couldn't. I was afraid of Michael and his threats. I couldn't take the chance that he would do as he said, regardless."

"Val, give me another chance. Give us another chance. I know I've caused you a lot of pain, but can't we put this behind us and start over? We need each other, girl. I know you have every reason not to forgive me, but please, don't toss me out of your life, I love you so much."

"I love you too, but... You have no idea what your refusal to believe me did to me."

"I know, baby, and I'm sorry, so sorry for hurting you like that. I promise to make it up to you, if you'll let me."

"I don't know, Alex."

Alex walked over to her and drew her into his arms and closed his eyes. All that was important to him he held close to his heart. He bent his head and kissed her tenderly on the lips, then trailed kisses down her throat.

"I want you so much, Val."

Valerie's breaths came in short, jerky gasps as Alex stroked her breasts. Her nipples hardened into eager, aroused peaks.

"Make love to me, Alex. I need you, I want you with my entire being."

"Are you sure?" he rasped. His breathing sounded as labored as hers.

"I love you. I have no choice but to forgive you. You owe me and I want you to start paying up immediately."

"It will be a labor of love."

Alex undressed her and then himself, then laid Valerie on the blanket. Neither of them noticed the coolness of the night air. It was more than simple passion they were about to share. This was a special affirmation of their love.

When Valerie parted her thighs and welcomed Alex into her body, she allowed him back into her heart.

Exaltations of love erupted from Valerie's lips with Alex's first thrust; then moans of pleasure came with each thrust thereafter.

When Alex felt Valerie's feminine muscles flutter around him, his already swollen flesh expanded and the hot tide of his passion burst forth, hurling them both over the edge into rapturous oblivion.

As the cool wind whispered over their damp bodies and their desire waned, Alex pulled the blanket over them.

Alex made love to Valerie again before they left their sanctuary and went home to start again with total honesty between them this time.

EPILOGUE

A lot had happened in a year. Once again Valerie found herself at the annual Quinneth Falls picnic. From her seat on the rocks by the falls, Valerie watched Justin and Mary Ellen as they sat beneath a tree eating their picnic lunch. They'd been married four months and she was already pregnant. Valerie laughed because they had decided that they couldn't wait until June to get married. If Hattie Atkins could have had her way, Gina and Howard would have been the ones to tie the knot in June.

Valerie's interest shifted to the Crawfords. As usual, there was that sad look in Jackson's eyes. She also read the longing in them when he looked at her and Tyler. Valerie didn't know how she felt about him, but she no longer resented him for hurting her mother. And Michael…

Alex came and sat down beside Valerie.

"I see you are enjoying our favorite spot."

"And I was thinking about a few other things as well."

"Like yours truly?"

"Among others."

"You were thinking about my father, weren't you?"

"I didn't think I could bring myself to forgive him, but I have. He is, after all, my son's grandfather. And I do believe he has really changed."

"I think he has too, thanks to Kelly."

"Do you think there could be something going on between them?"

"I don't know. It has taken me a while to forgive him, but Kelly has made me see that life is too short to hold grudges. She believes that everyone—even my father—deserves another chance. She said that if you could forgive him after what he'd done to you, I could do no less."

"My mother is someone special, isn't she?"

"And so is her daughter. I love you with all my heart, Valerie Price. I don't ever want you to doubt it again. And I don't intend to ever give you a reason." And he sealed his vow with a kiss.